EVERY STEP YOU TAKE

EVERY STEP YOU TAKE

KEVIN SCHUMACHER

abbott press®

A DIVISION OF WRITER'S DIGEST

Abbott Press books may be ordered through booksellers or by contacting:

Abbott Press
1663 Liberty Drive
Bloomington, IN 47403
www.abbottpress.com
Phone: 1-866-697-5310

Because of the dynamic nature of the Internet, any web addresses or links contained in this book may have changed since publication and may no longer be valid. The views expressed in this work are solely those of the author and do not necessarily reflect the views of the publisher, and the publisher hereby disclaims any responsibility for them.

Any people depicted in stock imagery provided by Thinkstock are models, and such images are being used for illustrative purposes only.
Certain stock imagery © Thinkstock.

ISBN: 978-1-4582-1376-1 (sc)
ISBN: 978-1-4582-1375-4 (hc)
ISBN: 978-1-4582-1374-7 (e)

Library of Congress Control Number: 2014900933

Printed in the United States of America.

Abbott Press rev. date: 2/13/2014

Photos by Cody Wilson

Preface

Several years ago, in the late nineties, a co-worker told me an intriguing story. I was working at a sawmill, and one day, during the lunch half-hour, a friend asked me if I would like to read an account of a murder that had happened in Oregon. The book was written by a well-known true-crime author, and it looked like a good read, so I said that I would read it.

Before I took it home that day, my friend told me that this murder had occurred in his hometown, that he knew the victim, and the person who was convicted of the crime. This made the story even more intriguing. I read the entire story that evening, and it was every bit as entertaining as I hoped it would be.

The reason the author wrote about this particular murder was because the victim's body had never been found, yet a person was convicted of first-degree murder. The body was never recovered. This was only the second time in Pacific Northwest history that this had happened.

The next day, when I saw my friend, he asked me if I had read the story and if I liked it or not. I told him that I had finished it already, and that I liked it a lot. Then he looked at me in a strange kind of way, and then said something even stranger.

He said to me, "But they got it all wrong."

To which I responded, "What are you talking about? Who got it all wrong, the author?"

"Everybody got it wrong—the author, the jury, everybody!"—and then he said something to me that absolutely floored me—"and I know where the body is."

Needless to say, I was stunned. He then proceeded to tell me a very different version of what had really happened. My friend was the last person to see the victim alive, other than the killer. He hadn't told his version to anyone in over twenty years. Why did he tell me? I'm not sure, but I think the reason was that he had carried it around for so long, and he needed to get it off his chest. He had carried this burden for a lot of years.

Over the years, I thought about it often. I even contacted the author of the book and shared my friend's version of the case. The author was intrigued, too, but said there was nothing that could be done. Still, the story stuck with me.

One day, a couple of years ago now, I sat down at my computer and started writing a story. I never thought that it would become a book, especially a fictional police-procedural murder mystery. But I just kept writing. I asked our adult daughter to read what I had written and to please be honest with me—should I keep writing, or should I quit while I was ahead? She encouraged me to keep writing, so I did. I can't thank her enough. She has been a great encourager for me, and urged me to keep on writing. She also has helped me with editing, although I still take the credit for any mistakes that might be found.

Several others, friends and family, have read the manuscript, given helpful suggestions, editing tips, and encouraged me to keep on writing. Although my wife doesn't like to read very much, she allowed me to take the time to write, even when she had many other things that she would have liked me to do. I thank her for that.

The story that follows is fiction, but it is based on actual events. And if you're as curious as I was, keep reading—fiction may not be fiction at all!

Prologue

Oregon City, the setting for Part 2 of this book, has a unique history, and sometimes a violent one. I include it here for the reader who enjoys a deeper look at the background and setting of a story.

Founded in 1829, and incorporated in 1844, it first became the home of fur traders and missionaries at the end of the Oregon Trail. It was designated the first capital of the Oregon Territory in 1848, an honor it held until 1852, when the capital was moved south to the city of Salem. During its four-year stint as capital, officials from a fast-growing boom town named San Francisco, then part of the Oregon Territory, sent delegates to Oregon City to submit the incorporation plat for that city. One grew, the other, not so much.

Oregon City is also unique in its topography. The business section is in the lower level of the town, along the Willamette River, just downstream from the falls. The residential area is on the upper level, on a high bluff above the city. An elevator was built to provide access for pedestrians to the two levels, one of only two such elevators in the world, the other being in Valparaiso, Chile. Available for use in December of 1915, nearly the entire population of Oregon City turned out for the grand opening. Most of them took the eighty-nine foot trip to the top, with the elevator wheezing and jerking for the entire five-minute ride. Other fascinating pieces of history abound, including stories of haunted houses and tales of ghosts, goblins, and demons.

In 1936, construction began on the Clackamas County Courthouse, which would be located in the downtown business-section. It was completed in January of 1937. Marble floors and ornate ceilings adorned the building, which had been fashioned by artisans of that era, making it both unique and beautiful. Funding for the project came from one of the many federal programs in the New Deal, FDR's response to the Great Depression.

Over the years, countless trials and hearings have been held in the courthouse. A number of them have been murder trials, which have been both brutal and bizarre. One such trial was that of Dayton Leroy Rogers, who, in two separate trials, was convicted of killing eight women.

In the first trial, Rogers pleaded not guilty, but, after weeks of testimony, was found guilty and sentenced to life in prison, thought he succeeded in escaping the death penalty. After his arrest for the first murder, police found evidence that linked Rogers to seven more murder victims—six prostitutes, and an unidentified victim. All of them, who were found nude and in varying stages of decomposition, had been tortured and stabbed to death. Most of the victims' feet had been severed at the ankle while they were still alive. Rogers buried his victims in shallow graves ten miles from Molalla, Oregon, in the hills above the river. They became known as the "Molalla Forest Killings".

The courthouse was also the site for the trial of an Oregon City man named Ward Weaver. He was tried and convicted for the murder of two young girls—Ashley Pond and Miranda Gaddis. Weaver's history, from his early years forward, was filled with abuse, violence, drugs, and alcohol.

This story began with an affair that Weaver had with a woman whom he had met at work, and they eventually moved into his rental house on Beavercreek Road, in Oregon City, right across from the old Fred Meyer store. Four years later, Weaver's twelve-year-old daughter became friends with Ashley Pond and Miranda Gaddis, classmates at Gardiner Junior High School. One of the girls, Ashley, accused Weaver of attempting to rape her, but the police didn't investigate. Five months later, Ashley disappeared on her way to school. Friends and family, including Miranda, began a search for her. Two months later, Miranda vanished. Neither girl was ever seen alive again.

Weaver, with the help of his son, dug a hole in his yard and covered it with concrete. He told his son it was a pad for a hot tub. Five months later, in August, Weaver was arrested for the rape of his son's nineteen-year-old girlfriend. When his son called 9-1-1, he told emergency dispatchers that his father admitted to killing Ashley and Miranda.

Later that same month, FBI agents found the remains of Miranda Gaddis in a microwave box in the storage shed behind the house. The next day, they found the remains of Ashley Pond in a 55-gallon barrel, buried beneath the concrete slab. Interestingly, Weaver's father was convicted of murder some twenty years earlier, burying his victim under a slab of cement in the back yard—like father, like son.

Neither the Roger's case, nor the Weaver case, are related to this story, other than to say that unusual and gruesome crimes are not unfamiliar in the region. Given the history of Oregon City and rural Clackamas County, along with my familiarity with the area, I decided that this would be the perfect setting for the story you are about to read.

Tuesday evening, January 22, 1985

It was that wet and windy kind of cold that cuts clear to the bone. Sandi dropped off the last kid on the activity bus and was on her way back to the garage. It was dark and the roads were wet, but not slick yet—that would come later tonight. She slowed to make the turn onto East Fifth Street that went past the front of the school. A lone soul was sitting on the steps in front of the school. She slowed to see who it was. Nicole. It was the Parker girl. Nice kid. She stopped the big yellow bus in front, offering to give her a ride after she parked the bus, but Nicole said her dad would be there soon. She closed the doors, letting out the clutch at the same time, moving toward the garage. She was feeling pretty good, considering the mess she had gotten herself into. She pulled forward to the door that had to be opened from the inside. Leaving the bus running, Sandi hopped down the three steps onto the gravel driveway and walked around to the left side of the building. She got out the keys to open the door, but it was already open. That wasn't all that unusual. Wes must not have latched it all the way and the wind had blown it open. She flipped the light switch inside the door and the garage lights flickered to life. She walked to the rope and pulled down hard as the door creaked its way up along the metal tracks. When it was open far enough, she hopped back on the bus and drove it into the empty bay. She shut the bus down and set the brake, then skipped down the steps and out the doors that she wouldn't bother to close. She reversed the door opening and closing process and the heavy garage door came down much faster and easier than it had gone up. She turned just in time to see movement to her right. Turns out that would be the last thing she would see. Three reports from the .44 Magnum pierced the frigid night air.

Part 1

Chapter 1

Wednesday morning, January 23, 1985

It never ceases to amaze me. I'm talkin' about how much blood the human body holds, which is about six quarts, I'm told, and how much blood that body spills out when multiple bullets tear it apart. It looks more like six gallons. I've seen it all too many times over my forty-year career. Not here, though. I moved to Molalla, Oregon, from Los Angeles in '83 to get away from it all. All that blood takes a toll on a guy, and all I wanted to do was finish out my career quietly, away from the bloody crime that happens in large metropolitan areas.

Molalla is located about thirty-five miles south of Portland, in the foothills of the Cascade Mountain range. Molalla is one of those Indian names that no one knows how to pronounce unless they grew up there.

"It's *MO-lal-la*," the mayor told me early on, "with the accent on the first syllable and the last two syllables said fast, so they just roll off your tongue. *MO-lal-la*."

My name is Frank Thomas, born to John and Cora Thomas in

1920. I grew up in the Northwest, in a small town called Puyallup, which is pronounced *pew-AL-up*, again said fast, with the accent on the second syllable. Puyallup, another Indian name of course, located up in Washington State. I started my law-enforcement career patrolling the streets of Tacoma, just twenty minutes away from my hometown. That was in January of 1941.

When the Japanese bombed Pearl Harbor later that year, I answered the call of duty for my country and enlisted in the army. I had police experience, a whopping eleven months' worth, so it was decided that I would be an MP—military policeman. I served for four years, a year of it in Germany.

I came home and went back to work for the Tacoma Police Department. After a couple of years, I got restless, wanting something more exciting, adventurous, and that's how I ended up in LA, where I stayed for good. That is, until two years ago. Both of my parents died several years ago. I was an only child, and I never did find the right girl to marry. Most people would consider it a very lonely life, but I never did. I was okay with it. I had friends and was content to keep it that way.

Eventually, I became a homicide detective with the LAPD. My partner of nearly twenty years, Richard "Dickey" Cook, was my closest friend. Dickey was like the brother that I never had. Two years ago, Dickey and I were in the midst of investigating several homicides that were gang related drug wars, turf wars. I hated it and Dickey did too. Back in the day, murder used to be, well, cleaner. It used to be that a jealous husband would kill his wife's lover and maybe his wife too. Or partners in crime would get greedy and want it all for themselves, so one bad guy would whack another bad guy. They were clean murders, good old-fashioned murders, Perry Mason kind of murders—but not anymore.

It seems like they're all gang related now—whites, blacks, Hispanics, Asians, you name it. Punks whack other punks, and sometimes whack the police. That's what happened to Dickey. We were in the wrong place at the wrong time and Dickey paid the price. He didn't die that day, but his career was over. He retired from the department with full honors, and a cane that would be his companion for the rest of his life. That's when I decided to get out. Move somewhere, maybe back to the Northwest where life was much slower and not nearly as bloody.

I started my end-of-career job search and when I saw that the small town of Molalla was looking for a new police chief, I applied and got the job. It was quiet. Not much happened here—a few burglaries, some kids vandalizing the school on a Saturday night—things like that. Nothing too serious. Some of the crimes were even funny.

I hadn't been in town very long when I heard about the White Horse Tavern, a local landmark. It sits right in the middle of town just a hundred feet east of the four-way stop. In front of the building is a big white stallion—not real, of course, but life-size—mounted up high, rearing on its hind legs in the classic western style. One early morning, some graffiti artists decided to paint its underside blue, if you know what I mean. And that's how it came to be called the Blue Ball Tavern. At least by some. That's about as serious as crime got in Molalla.

And homicides? There hadn't been one for years, not since the Miller brothers—Fred and Frank—were drinking and playing quick-draw in the hills above town. Fred shot Frank, went to get help, and then couldn't find his way back to the scene—too much Jack Daniels in the system. By the time he did find Frank, he was already dead. It was declared an accident, but some of the locals thought otherwise. So now I'm here and things are going pretty much as I hoped they would—quiet, uneventful, and boring. Boring is not a bad thing when you get to be my age.

But unfortunately, it didn't stay that way. It all changed in one day.

It was cold that morning. I was just getting ready to go out the door of the one-bedroom house I called home and down to the police station on North Molalla Avenue, just around the corner from the White Horse. The phone rang before I got out the door so I went back to answer it. It was only seven fifteen, kind of early to be getting calls around here. Being the only full-time employee in the police department did have its drawbacks, like being on call 24-7.

I lifted the receiver to my ear.

"This is Chief Thomas."

"Chief Thomas? This is Robert Payne. We have a problem down here at the high school. Could you come down here, like right now?"

Robert was the principal. He'd been here five or six years now.

"Sure, Robert. I was just headin' out the door. What's up?"

"Well, it seems we have a lot of blood in the bus garage, at least I think it's blood. Chief, I've never seen so much blood. It looks like there's six gallons here on the floor!"

"Blood? From what?"

This was farm country with lots of hunters and lots of animals around. It could have been just some kids' idea of a joke.

"I don't know, but if it is blood, whatever it's from isn't alive anymore. There's no carcass or nothing, just a lot of blood."

"All right, I'm on my way. Be there in five minutes."

It didn't take long to get places in Molalla.

Chapter 2

Thirteen hours earlier

Nicole Parker didn't give much thought to the cold, wet, and dark weather in northwest Oregon as she waited on the steps of Molalla High School. It was January, got dark early, around four thirty, and it had been another boring day of school. It wouldn't be long before she graduated with the class of '85. Nicole couldn't think about much else. She wanted to get out of this small logging town in which she had lived all her life, and when she graduated, she intended to do just that: get out!

"Hey Nicole, what ya still doin' around here?"

Sherry, her best friend since elementary school, came out the front door of the ancient redbrick school building built in the early 1900s. Not much changed in Molalla. Sherry had aspirations of being an actress. Like Nicole, she would be graduating come June and couldn't wait to escape the town that used to have more sawmills and taverns than anything else. Some of that had changed in recent years because of the spotted owl. The tree huggers' campaign was successful. The mills were struggling to survive, but the taverns continued to thrive.

"I stayed after today to work on my senior project," Nicole said. "I have to get that done soon if I want to graduate on time. I'm just waiting for Dad to come and pick me up. How's the play coming along?"

Sherry was starring in the last play of her high school career, a murder mystery called *Power Play*.

"It's goin' good. We still have a month before it opens, so it should come together by then."

As Sherry turned to go back to practice, two gunshots sounded from inside the building. Nicole jumped at the sound.

"I hate those immature sophomores. They're always messing around," Sherry grumbled, explaining that during the break from play practice, a few boys had decided it would be fun to play with the prop pistol, with blanks of course. But it still was some good kind of fun for teenage boys.

"Okay. I'll see you in the morning, Sherry."

"Tay. Take care."

Nicole ignored the *tay* that really annoyed her, and continued the watch for her dad who never seemed to be in a hurry to pick her up. She rode the bus most of the time, on the way to school and back home, but on the few occasions that she stayed after, her dad would pick her up. But he would make her wait. He was a good dad though. He loved his little girl who was growing up all too fast. And the fact that Nicole wanted to leave home after graduating made his eyes a little teary when he thought about it.

Nicole watched the street, looking the direction from which he would be coming. Two lone streetlights shone on the black, wet pavement, looking frozen. "I can't wait to get out of this place," she said to herself out loud. Then there were headlights coming around the corner. It was about time!

The vehicle came into view, but it wasn't her dad's '64 Chevy pickup. It was the school's activity bus. The bus had already dropped off its load of jocks—basketball players and wrestlers. The bus slowed and stopped at the front of the school and the folding bus doors opened.

"Hey, Nicole! You need a ride?" Sandi Riggs didn't quite yell it, but almost, in order to be heard over the noisy bus. Nicole walked toward the bus to answer.

"Hi, Sandi. Thanks, but my dad should be here by now. I'm sure he'll be here in a minute or two."

"You sure? It's no problem. I just have to park the bus, get my car and I'll take you home. It's cold out there—don't want ya gettin' sick!"

It was definitely cold, the temperature hovering around freezing. A storm coming in from the Pacific Ocean would provide plenty of moisture, and the cold Canadian air coming down from the Arctic regions would combine for a good snowstorm, the first of the winter.

"No, thanks, but I'm fine. He'll be here. If he got here and I wasn't, he would be pissed."

"Well, I'll see ya tomorrow then, Nicole."

"Okay. See ya, Sandi. And thanks again for offering."

"No problem." The bus doors closed and Sandi drove down the street to park the bus.

Nicole walked back toward the front steps and waited. It was already five forty-five, but it could be six o'clock before he came, maybe six fifteen. She thought about Sandi. She grew up in another small logging town about sixty miles south of Molalla called Mill City. There weren't any mills there anymore and it was hardly a city. Sandi was still young, around twenty-five or so, but she hadn't gotten away from the small-town environment, annoying as it was. *I guess some people like it*, Nicole thought to herself.

Sandi had worked here in Molalla for a few years now. A guy named Steve Carlson was the reason she stayed. He was a Molalla native who hadn't moved away from his hometown. Steve and some buddies decided to go to Seaside one summer day a few years ago. That's the place to go for guys who wanted to pick up girls, and that's where Sandi met him. They hit it off right away. It didn't take long, only a few weeks, before Steve talked Sandi into coming to Molalla to move in with him.

A year or so later Steve got the idea to join the Marines. So off he went, leaving Sandi behind. She decided to stay in Molalla and wait for him to come back home. It was a long four years, but Sandi believed that they had something special, so she waited. And he did come back, six or seven months ago, and their relationship picked up where it had left off. But then something happened. Nicole didn't know what it was, but they weren't living together anymore. *Too bad*, she thought, *they made such a cute couple.*

Six o'clock," she muttered, her teeth chattering as she pulled her sleeve back down over her wristwatch. Three more gunshots sounded, farther away than the previous ones. The boys must be roaming the school. Shivering, Nicole thought she should have at least followed Sherry inside, but who knew her dad would take this long? Now the doors were locked, leaving her out in the cold. The '64 Chevy pickup came around the corner five minutes later.

"Finally!"

Chapter 3

Five days earlier

He looked at his watch with the cracked crystal. There were still three hours before quitting time and the beginning of the weekend. Even though he was late for work, missing the first hour of the five-to-one swing shift, time was passing slowly.

Every week was the same boring, monotonous routine, and every week he waited for the weekend to arrive. Not that anything exciting would happen on the weekend. Not in Molalla. Steve Carlson mindlessly pulled the lumber from the green chain onto the loads of lumber at Brazier Forest Products. There was one good thing about this job—a guy had plenty of time to think. Looking back on the last five or six years, he asked, 'What if?' a lot. Back then, Sandi and he lived together for about a year and a half and things were going good, but he felt like he was going nowhere. He felt trapped. One night, while he and Sandi were watching TV, a commercial came on saying that the U.S. Marine Corps was looking for a few good men. And that moment he decided to enlist. He slept on his decision and the next day, he

went to the recruiting center. That decision changed his life...
and Sandi's.

He was stationed in Beirut, Lebanon, one of twelve hundred
or so Marines whose mission it was to assist in stabilizing the new
Lebanese government and its army. October 23, 1983, would be a
day that Steve would never forget. Two suicide truck bombs struck
separate buildings that housed American and French forces. Two-
hundred twenty Marines died that day, and if Steve hadn't been
on guard duty in another part of the compound, there would have
been 221 casualties. He saw more blood that one day than he ever
wanted to see in a lifetime. Friends died that day. He wanted out.
He was ready to go home.

It was early summer in 1984 when he landed at Portland
International Airport. There was no hero's welcome for him. His
mom and Sandi were the only ones there to greet him. But that
was okay. He was happy to be home and knew he was one of the
fortunate. He dealt with guilt though. There were so many who
didn't come home, but he did, and he wondered why.

"Steeeeve!"

It came out as a shriek when she saw him emerge from the
tunnel that led from the plane to the terminal. Sandi fought her
way through the crowd of off-boarding passengers to reach him.

"O baby, I'm so glad you're home. I missed you so much."

"Me too." It was all he could say as he took her in his arms.

Steve's mother approached after giving the couple a few
moments.

"Anyone remember me?"

"Mom! Mom, I'm so glad to be home!"

Steve took the two women into his big arms as they walked
down to the baggage area. He retrieved his bags from the carousel
and stepped out of the terminal and into the Oregon summer. It

felt so good. Arriving from the hot and humid hell hole called Beirut, he felt like he had just stepped into paradise. It was good to be home.

That was almost eight months ago. He looked at his watch again—still two hours before quitting time. Steve didn't care much for swing shift, but there weren't any openings on days, and he needed the work. And no longer did it feel like paradise. Things hadn't gone as planned, far from it.

The first month had been great. He was back with the woman he felt would one day be his wife. A melancholy smile crossed his face as he thought of the old Neil Sedaka song...

Oo, I hear laughter in the rain
Walking hand in hand with the one I love
Oo how I love the rainy days
And the happy way I feel inside

But it didn't last. He moved back in with Sandi when he got home from Beirut, back in the cozy one-bedroom up on the river. It was their place. But when September rolled around, their relationship soured. Sandi was back driving bus for the school district, transporting kids to school and back home again. She often volunteered to drive the extra runs as well. There were ball games and the after-school activity bus. Occasionally she would drive for longer trips, like last spring when the school's band went to Reno for a jazz competition.

She started driving bus just after Steve became one of the "few good men" and, while he was away stabilizing governments, Sandi became involved in other activities. It wasn't another guy, even though Sandi was very attractive and could have had any guy she wanted. As it turned out, another guy would have been a lot easier to deal with. Steve knew something was going on, but couldn't tell what it was, not right away. He'd talk to her, ask her what was wrong, but she would just shrug it off, or she'd start yelling at him if he pushed her too far.

It was a hot September night when it finally blew up. Steve was back working at the mill, had been for a little over a month. It was a long night and he was ready to go home and crawl in bed. He'd been thinking all night about talking to her again, but not until morning. He crossed the Molalla River at Feyrer Park (pronounced 'fryer'), made the right turn and drove another ten minutes to the house.

"Damn!" Steve slammed the palm of his hand on the steering wheel. Sandi's truck wasn't in the driveway. *Where was she?* He pulled the house key out of his pocket as he walked to the door, unlocked it, and headed straight for the refrigerator. He'd been looking forward to having a nice cold beer when he got home. He walked in the house and went straight to the fridge. He opened the door—no beer.

"Shit!"

He didn't remember drinking the last one. He slammed it shut and walked to the bedroom.

It was two thirty in the morning when Sandi pulled into the driveway. She got out of her truck and walked to the front door. She tried to open the door quietly, but that was impossible with hinges that were in bad need of oil. The screech of the door shook Steve out of a restless sleep. He stood up, moved to the front room, stubbing his toe on the coffee table on the way.

"Ouch! Dammit!"

He forgot about waiting until later in the morning to talk about things; he wanted to talk now.

"Where have you been?"

Sandi, on the other hand, was in no mood to talk.

"Out," was all she said.

"Out where?"

"With some friends—get off my case! I wanna go to bed."

"You're high again." It wasn't a question.

He knew that she had started smoking pot when he was gone, but now she was using other stuff as well, harder stuff. Crack cocaine had made its way from the inner city out to the surrounding countryside. It was cheap, plentiful, and hideously addictive, and its effects were deadly. He tried to get her to stop, but she wasn't interested.

"Not this again! Just leave me alone. I did fine without you, so get the hell off my case!"

He didn't feel it coming and she didn't see it coming. His fist slammed into the side of her face before he realized what he had done. She hit her head on the coffee table on the way down, the same one that Steve had kicked just a few minutes before. She didn't move. He could see blood running down the side of her face from the gash that was hidden by her hair. She was on her back, her left arm pinned underneath her. Her ear filled with blood that seeped onto the orange shag carpet. The other side of her face, the side he hit her on, was a bloody mess. Her eye was swollen, a thin slit in a growing field of purple. She didn't move.

WHACK! He jumped, startled, roused from his thoughts.

"Steve! What'ya doin', man? You're letting all your wood go by."

Benny, one of his buddies on the chain, loved to throw the boards that Steve missed back at him, slamming them down on the wooden catwalk. He liked it best when he hit Steve on his ankle, causing a blue streak to fly out of his mouth.

"Sorry, asshole."

Steve wasn't in the mood to retaliate. He bent over to pick up the twelve-footer and stacked it on the load in front of him. There was still an hour to go before the end of the shift. He thought back again to that September night. He thought he had killed her. She didn't regain consciousness for a good five minutes. He had cradled her in his arms and sobbed.

He took her to the emergency room at Willamette Falls Hospital in Oregon City, about a forty minute drive. She needed twenty stitches from that ugly gash and had a cracked cheekbone and a cracked eye socket on the other side of her face. She could have pressed charges against him, but instead just told him to take her back home and get out of their house and her life.

Benny threw another twelve-footer at his feet, missing his ankles again.

He moved out after that night, back into his mom's house, back into his old room. That's where he was heading as soon as that whistle blew, just five more minutes.

Chapter 4

Wednesday morning, January 23

The Parkers lived out on Wildcat Road, south of Molalla. The old-timers would say they lived up in the sticks. A foot of snow fell overnight, but down in town, there wouldn't be any snow at all. The thousand-foot increase in elevation made a big difference when it came to snow and where it would stick and stay.

Nicole stood at the end of their long gravel driveway that was in much need of repair. She laughed, thinking about the night before, when she and her dad drove up the lane to their house. He cranked the steering wheel one way, then the other. There was no power steering, of course, in a '64 Chevy truck. He tried to miss the potholes that cratered the quarter-mile long driveway. He hit more than he missed, and Nicole started laughing uncontrollably as she was continuously slammed into the passenger-side door.

Pete left for work in Milwaukie—an hour-long drive—where he was employed as a machinist. He gave Nicole a ride out to the road where she waited for the bus. It was a much smoother ride to the end of the driveway this morning, the snow cushioning the way.

The sun still hid behind the mountains, straining to rise above them, just to be hidden all day by the dense cloud cover. It was a frigid twenty-eight degrees on the front porch of the Parkers' home, and the wind was blowing, making it feel closer to eight degrees.

Nicole knew that she might have to wait this morning because of the snow, but it turned out to be only five minutes when the number two school bus came around the corner, making a racket in chains. Nicole stood way back until it had come to a complete stop. It would not be a great start to the day, getting run over by a bus. The doors opened and she hopped up the three steps into bus, getting out of the freezing cold as quickly as she could.

"Mornin', Nicole." Connie Williams, the driver, greeted her.

"Hi, Connie. How are you doing this morning?"

"All right, I guess, so far, anyway," she said with a sly grin.

Nicole was the first customer of the day. On most school days, Connie drove the bus to her home after dropping off the last of the kids on her route. That would save her a trip all the way down to town the next morning to get the bus, and then back up again. It was an arrangement that the bus owners had no problem with. The fact that her father-in-law and his brother were the owners had a lot to do with the agreed-upon arrangement.

Nicole walked down the aisle to a middle seat, the one on the right side of the bus that had the heater vent on the floorboard. There was only one other person on the bus, a little five-year-old who was Connie's daughter. Even though Kayleen wasn't in school yet, she was a frequent rider because there was no one at home to take care of her, so her mom would bring her along on the bus.

She sat in the seat just ahead of Nicole, sound asleep. Usually she was wide awake and very chatty, but not this morning.

Nicole used the sleeve of her coat to wipe off the fog that had formed on the inside of the window and looked at the winter wonderland. She closed her eyes for a while, knowing that her friend, Sherry, would be boarding the bus a couple of stops later. She dozed off to the drone of the diesel engine and the vibration from the tire chains.

It was only ten minutes, but Nicole was sound asleep when Sherry shook her shoulder. "Wake up, sleepy head."

Nicole looked up to see Sherry's smiling and too-wide-awake look on her face.

"Leave me alone. Can't a girl get some sleep around here?"

She groaned and smiled as she said it and scooted closer to the window, giving Sherry room to sit down.

"Looks like you're not the only one that's sleepy this morning," Sherry said, as Kayleen continued in dreamland in the seat ahead of them.

Not much was said for the next few stops, but when the Taylor twins got on the bus, the silence was shattered, which in turn woke up Kayleen. She sat up in her seat and looked behind her.

"Hi, Kayleen."

"Hi, Nicole. Hi, Sherry." She stretched, yawned, and spoke, all in one motion.

"Why are you so sleepy this morning?" Nicole was the one that started the questioning.

"I kept wakin' up last night."

"Really? Why?"

"Cuz Daddy and Uncle Bryce and Uncle Tim were making lotsa noise and I couldn't sleep."

"Why were they making so much noise?"

"They were digging and stuff."

Like most five-year-olds, Kayleen was offering minimal responses to Nicole's questioning.

"What were they digging?"

"Mommy said they were making a driveway."

"A driveway in the middle of the night?"

Kayleen didn't respond. She had gone back to sleep, just like that.

Nicole looked at Sherry and said, "That's weird. Why would anyone be putting in a driveway in the middle of the night, and during a snowstorm even? That's really weird."

Sherry shrugged. "Yeah, it's weird for sure, but don't forget, this is Molalla."

"True. I guess there's no law against putting in a driveway in the middle of the night during a snowstorm. At least not out here. Just weird. It's still half an hour before we get to school, Sherry. Let me sleep, please?"

"Fine. Whatever."

Chapter 5

I arrived at the high school before most of the students, although a few were walking up the steps to the front entrance. I pulled the black and white police cruiser with the red cherry on top around the side of the school and up to the bus garage. Two other vehicles were already here. One was Robert Payne's '69 Chevelle, his pride and joy. The black muscle car with the 396 cubic inch engine was the envy of every teenage male in the high school, not to mention a good number of grownups in town. This alone made Robert Payne the favorite principal of all time at Molalla, but he also had a sense of humor that the kids loved. Unfortunately, the matter at hand was no joking matter.

The other vehicle belonged to the mechanic and maintenance man for the school district, Wes Strohmeier. His '77 Chevy truck looked rather plain alongside Robert's Chevelle, but the 427 Corvette-engine that Wes put in his truck would challenge the fastest of the fast. Wes was seven or eight years younger than Robert, but both were still kids at heart. I expect some night I'll find them drag racing outside of town.

I pulled up alongside the Chevelle and left plenty of space between us—a door-ding would mean a homicide for sure. I got out of the cruiser that hadn't even had a chance to warm up yet, and walked across the loose gravel to the door on the left side of the garage.

Once inside, I heard Robert and Wes talking, but I couldn't see them right away. They were at the front end of the bus, the only one in the garage. It looked pretty much like any other garage, only larger. It was big enough to park the school's two busses with plenty of room on either side. Wes' workbench, located in front of the bus, looked organized and clean. He took pride in his work and the condition of his tools and equipment. I came around the bus and saw the two men talking.

Robert turned away from Wes.

"Good morning, Chief. I didn't hear you come in. Come on over here and see what we have."

Wes didn't talk much, but he did respond.

"Hey, Chief."

"Mornin', Robert, Wes," nodding slightly to each one.

I followed the two over to a spot by the big garage door.

"So what ya got here?" I asked, not knowing why I asked it. It was pretty obvious what they had.

On the gravel floor between them was a fairly large patch of some kind of fluid, reddish brown in color. It covered an area about the size of my small throw rug back at the house. It sure looked like blood. To the right was a smaller wet patch, not nearly as large as the other.

"Wes got here this morning to do a little maintenance on this rig. He called me first thing, as soon as he saw this."

I took in the scene before me, looking not only at the fluid soaked in the gravel, but also at the front of the bus, the work bench, and the wall behind it.

"Is this the way you found it, just like it is now?"

"Yessir. I didn't touch nothin'," Wes responded. "I came in and turned on the lights. It takes a while for them to come on.

When it was light enough to see, I went up to my bench to get the tools for the job. I walked to the back of the bus and saw this spatter here on the wall. I thought it might be transmission fluid or somethin', although I couldn't imagine how it coulda got there. Then I walked over to where we're standin' right now, and saw this. I went over there an' got a quart of tranny fluid and poured it right here to see if it looked the same. It doesn't, but o' course this here ain't dry yet, but still, it don't look the same."

I looked at the two patches. Wes was right. They didn't look the same, and I was pretty sure we were talking about blood.

"You looked in the bus yet?"

"I opened it up and walked to the back. Nothin' different in there. Not that I could tell. I looked around in here—didn't see nothin' else 'cept what we already talked about. I went outside and walked all around the building, but didn't see nothin' out there either. Robert drove up right when I came around from the back."

"Who's the last one to leave this place at the end of the day?"

"I usually leave around five, but when there's an activity bus runnin', it's that person. Last night it was Sandi Riggs. She's usually the one driving it anyway."

"What time's she done with that?"

"Six or so I guess. I'm not usually around here at that time."

"Anybody seen her this morning?"

Robert answered this time, "I tried calling her this morning after I got here, right after I called you. I didn't get an answer. She should have been here by now."

"Where's she live?" I asked. I know who she is. It's a small town. But more people live outside of town than in it, and I still don't know where everyone lives, probably never will.

"Up above Dickey Prairie, a couple of miles past the store, right there on the river." Payne answered.

"What's she drive?"

"A '77 Ford pickup. It's blue."

"So, Wes, can her Ford take your Chevy?"

"You gotta be kiddin'. Not a chance, man." He seemed offended that I would even suggest it. "You know Fords—Fast Only Rolling Downhill."

"That, or Fix or Repair Daily."

In Molalla you were either a Chevy guy or a Ford guy or gal, one or the other. Fights were started more than once over that argument down at the White Horse.

"So did she drive it to work yesterday?"

"Yeah, it was here when I left, not this morning though."

"So we have a whole lotta blood from something, but not a body or a carcass that has been discovered. We're assuming its Sandi's blood, but we don't know that. Keep everyone outta here. I'm going back to the station to call the state police and report a possible homicide. After that, I'll take a drive up to Sandi's place and see if I can find her. Robert, could you get her address for me?"

"Yes. I'll have to go over to the office to get it. What should I say to the staff, because they will be asking?"

"I'll go over with you to get her address. Tell them what we know so far. Maybe one of them has had contact with her since yesterday. And keep trying to get in touch with her. I'll be back after my drive up there. Just make sure you don't let anyone come out here and mess up the crime scene, if that's what we have."

"Would you advise us to cancel school today?"

"That's your call, but it would probably be best."

"I agree. Let's walk over to the school and get her address. Wes, you stay here and make sure no one gets in here."

"Okay, Boss. Will do."

Chapter 6

Nicole was able to sleep another thirty minutes, until the bus pulled up to the curb in front of the school. The winter wonderland at the Parker residence had turned into a cold, wet, and gray day. There was no snow here in town.

"C'mon, let's go," Sherry said, as she elbowed her friend's shoulder.

"I'm coming, I'm coming."

Sherry stepped into the aisle and Nicole scooted across the seat to stand up beside her. Kayleen was still curled up into a little ball, oblivious to the kids noisily leaving the bus. Nicole smiled as she nudged Sherry.

"Look at her," she said, "isn't she just adorable?"

"Yeah, she really is," Sherry said, without a lot of conviction.

She wasn't too fond of children; at least not like Nicole was. The kids in the front filed off the bus, with Nicole and Sherry following. Sherry went down the steps with Nicole behind her.

"Nicole!"

She turned around to answer, but before she could open her mouth, Connie Williams looked at her in a way that gave her goose bumps up and down her spine. Her eyes revealed both fear and danger.

"Nicole, what did Kayleen say to you this morning?"

"Nothing really. She just said how sleepy she was—that she didn't get much sleep last night. Then she just curled up and went back to sleep."

Nicole didn't know why, but something told her not to include Kayleen's comment about her daddy and uncles making a driveway. She thought she noticed a slight look of relief, very slight, on Connie's face.

"Okay then, Nicole. Have a good day."

"Yeah, you too, Connie."

Nicole stepped down and out of the bus where Sherry waited impatiently.

"What was that all about?"

"That was weird. She wanted to know what Kayleen said to us. But she had a really strange look in her eyes. It gave me the creeps."

"Wuddaya mean, weird?" Sherry asked.

She glanced up at Connie who was still looking at them. She lifted her arm with an upward flick of her hand. It was Sherry's customary greeting and farewell.

"See ya later, Connie."

Connie responded with a nearly imperceptible nod of her head and a questioning look in her eyes.

"I don't know. It's probably nothing. It just seemed really weird."

They walked side by side and ascended the eight steps to the front door of the school. The door exploded outward as one kid chased another, nearly knocking the girls down. Neither of the boys felt that steps were a necessity as they continued their chase through the school yard.

Sherry grumbled, "I'm so sick and tired of this. I can't wait until we graduate and get out of this frickin' place."

Nicole laughed and started singing.

We gotta get out of this place
If it's the last thing we ever do
We gotta get out of this place
Girl, there's a better life for me and you

-*The Animals, 1963*

Sherry laughed as they walked through the doors and into the school. The office was on the left, where Nicole saw a meeting of sorts going on. The principal, Robert Payne, was in the middle of the group. Gladys Smith—short and round in her late fifties, an institution in the institution—stood by his side. Jim Woods, the superintendent of the Molalla School District, stood on the other side of Payne. It looked like most of the teachers were in the meeting along with the support staff.

On the right side of the entryway were groups of kids standing around, talking with all kinds of animation. One of the girls turned and saw Nicole and Sherry.

"Hey guys, have you heard what happened?"

Peggy Bass was the school gossip. A lot of kids left the "B" out of her last name when they talked about her. If you wanted to know anything about anyone, Peggy was the go-to gal.

Nicole was the one who responded.

"No, just got in the door, but obviously something's happenin'. Tell us, Peggy."

"Someone was murdered last night and they think it was Sandi Riggs," she said with a twinkle in her eye.

The news hit Nicole full force.

"What? Are you serious? Sandi Riggs?"

"That's what everyone's sayin'. But the weird thing is that they don't know for sure."

"Who is *they*, and how can *they* not know for sure?"

"The police, that's who, and there's no body. That's why they don't know. There's all this blood out in the bus garage. It was by the bus that Sandi drove last night and nobody knows where she is. I guess she didn't show up for her bus route this morning."

Nicole was shocked into silence. She thought back to the night before, waiting in front of the school for her dad to pick her up. She thought of her brief conversation with Sandi when she offered her a ride home. Nicole realized that she may have been the last one to talk to her. Maybe if she had accepted her offer, she would still be alive.

Sherry asked, "How do you know all this, Peggy? If it just happened last night and they just discovered all the blood—oh, never mind."

How Peggy got her information would always be a mystery. Most of the time it was fairly accurate, as would be the case in this situation.

The warning bell for the beginning of first period sounded, but none of the students left for class. The teachers were still in the office. The kids stood around and speculated about what may have happened.

Nicole couldn't believe that Sandi may have been murdered. She tried to believe that it wasn't so, that it was just a mix up.

"Hey, Nicole. Sherry."

A girl, Kim Williams, came up behind them. They knew who she was, but not much. She was younger than Nicole and Sherry—*a sophomore*, they thought. Nicole may have said hello once or twice, but she really couldn't remember. She was a small girl, had dark brown hair and large brown eyes. She couldn't weigh more that ninety pounds soaking wet.

"You sat by my little cousin on the bus this morning."

It wasn't a question. Nicole thought that she saw fear in her expression, and heard it in her quiet voice. She couldn't imagine why, though.

"You mean Kayleen? Yeah, we did. We usually do when she rides the bus with her mom. She's such a cutie," Nicole replied.

"Well, I don't know what she said to you this morning, but I've been given a message for both of you. Whatever she said, you didn't hear a thing. Just forget that you even sat close to her."

Nicole and Sherry looked at each other quizzically, and then back to Kim. Nicole responded again.

"What are you talking about? It was just another day on the bus. What's goin' on?"

"Just listen to me," she said urgently, making Nicole more than a little nervous. "Forget everything that Kayleen said. Don't talk to anyone about it. Don't talk to each other about it. Just forget it totally! I'm telling you this for your own good. If you keep quiet, it will be okay, nothing will happen."

Nicole felt a chill crawl up her spine, and it wasn't from the winter weather that had revived its efforts outside.

"Would you please tell us what you're talking about?"

"Listen, the less you know, the better. I'm talking about what happened last night. Sandi was killed—murdered—and they're going to say that Steve Carlson did it. If you say anything to anyone, you could end up the same way, your families too. This is bigger than you can imagine. It's big, really big."

With that, Kim turned and walked away without another word. Nicole and Sherry just stood there in shock. Neither knew what to say, and even if they did, they were too rattled to say it. They stared after Kim as she walked quickly down the hall and around the corner. She didn't look back.

The PA system crackled to life.

"May I have your attention please?" The voice was Principal Payne's. "Classes are canceled for the rest of today. The busses will be here in a few minutes to take you back home. There has been an emergency, a police matter, but there is no danger to students, teachers, or staff. Classes will resume tomorrow. Thank you."

"No danger?" Sherry spoke this time. "Maybe for them! I'm outta here!"

Chapter 7

I pulled away from the bus garage about the same time the busses came to take the students back home. I stopped by the station to call the Oregon State Police. They're the ones you call when there's been a felony homicide, if that's what this is. They'll come out and do some tests to determine if the fluid is blood, or something else. If it is blood, they'll test it to see whether it's from a human, or some other animal. I'm not even sure that there has been a crime committed, although it certainly is beginning to look like it.

I left the station, got back in the cruiser, and drove down Molalla Avenue to the four-way blinking light and made a right-hand turn. I passed the White Horse and headed toward the Andrews' ranch at the east end of town.

I passed the Y Drive-In and thought I might stop there and have lunch a little later. I'd put on a few too many pounds over the years, but the thought of country-fried steak, mashed potatoes and gravy, hot rolls with real butter and fresh strawberry jam, followed by hot homemade pecan pie smothered in ice cream was too hard to resist. That was the special every Wednesday, all for $2.25 and a twenty-five cent tip. It doesn't get much better than that. I was getting used to the small-town style of living. Now I wondered if that would change after this morning's events, and the day was just getting started.

I headed out toward Feyrer Park and crossed the Molalla River, then turned right onto Dickey Prairie Road. The house was just a couple of miles past the old country store on the right-hand side of the road. The river ran behind it. There wasn't much snow up here, just a little slush on the side of the road and some snow on the grass, though not enough to cover it. The address numbers were stenciled on most of the mailboxes, but not all of them, so I had to slow down to see which house was Sandi's. I spotted the number on the mailbox and turned into the gravel driveway that was more mud than gravel.

There were no other cars parked here, and it didn't look like I would find anybody home, either. There were some tracks in the mud, most likely from Sandi's truck. I parked on the other side of them so I wouldn't disturb what might turn out to be evidence. When I stepped out of the cruiser, my foot sunk into six inches of slush and freezing cold water, which immediately filled my low top shoes. This didn't happen in L.A.! The ground was firmer over where Sandi parked, so there were no footprints over there.

Behind the house, the river made a dull roar, moving swiftly, but not overly high. That could change fast, though, with a heavy rain in the mountains.

It was a nice little house, but in dire need of maintenance. The roof looked to be shingled, but I couldn't be sure for all the moss that covered it. The wood porch didn't look too sturdy, but I stepped onto it, not using the steps. They didn't look like they could handle a big guy like me.

Both the house and the porch desperately needed a fresh coat of paint, or two, or three. The existing paint was faded so badly that it was hard to tell it was yellow. And where you could see that it was yellow, it was peeling off, revealing bare plywood. I figured Sandi didn't have a man around to take care of the place, or that home maintenance just wasn't her thing.

I rapped my knuckles on the door and looked through the single-pane window in the door. There wasn't anyone around. I stepped off the porch and went to the back of the house, not finding much there, either. I walked back to the front, stepped up on the porch, again avoiding the steps. I tried the door and found it open, so I stepped inside.

There were a few pieces of furniture—a threadbare flowered couch with a matching loveseat scooted next to it. A cheap coffee table stood next to the couch. The carpet was burnt- orange shag that was so popular in the seventies. A stand held a 19-inch color T.V.—an Admiral— with rabbit-ears on top. The curtains were halfway open to let the morning light in, but there would be no sunshine this morning.

The kitchen was small. A guy my size could barely turn around in it. There was an electric range and a small refrigerator next to it. A large microwave sat on the Formica countertop. A black rotary-dial telephone was next to the microwave and a recorder next to the telephone. A red zero on the recorder showed that there were no messages. I pressed the message button and heard Sandi's voice and the standard greeting, *"I'm not able to come to the phone right now. Please leave a message and your name and number, and I'll get back to you as soon as I can."* There were a few dirty dishes in the sink, but other than that, everything seemed relatively clean. A small table just out of the kitchen area with two straight-backed chairs scooted next to it served as the dining room.

I walked down the dark hallway. There was a door on the right which turned out to be the bathroom. It was, without a doubt, cleaner than mine. A door on the left side of the hall opened to Sandi's bedroom. The bed was made, no indication that it had been slept in last night. A clothes hamper was half full, but no clothes were lying on the floor, unlike my bedroom. On the right side of the bed was a small night stand with a clock radio sitting on top. It was coming up on nine o'clock—8:57, to be precise—according to the bold red numbers shining brightly.

Next to the radio was a picture of a couple who looked very happy. The gal was Sandi, and the smiling young man was Steve Carlson. Sandi was a cute gal, dark hair, tall and slender, with legs that went on forever. I thought back to last summer, remembering the short shorts she wore around town. I'm sure I wasn't the only one who noticed. She was nice-looking, no question about that.

I met Steve a few months ago. He had been in the Marines when I became Chief, and had just come back home last summer. He seemed like a nice guy. He grew up in Molalla. I heard that he was a pretty decent athlete, but gave it up after graduating from high school.

The couple had been living together out here, but there was some trouble. He hit her, doing some damage, and that was it. She gave him the boot. I figured that paying him a visit would be a good idea. I would do that a little later.

I walked out of the bedroom and looked in one more door, which turned out to be the laundry room, complete with a Maytag washer and dryer standing side by side. There was a small load of colored clothes in the dryer, and a small load of whites in the washer, waiting to be dried. I thought to myself that I should probably separate my laundry, like Sandi did, but I never had, and I never would. I just let it accumulate for a week and then threw it all in together. I hate doing laundry.

I went back through the house one last time, but there was nothing that looked unusual or out of place. It didn't appear that

Sandi had slept here last night. The fifteen-minute drive out here and a look around the house didn't reveal anything that would explain what may have happened back in town. I walked out the way I came in, not using the rotted steps, and careful to avoid the muddy slush.

I drove back to town and over to the school again. A dark-colored sedan, with a *State of Oregon* insignia on the driver's door, pulled into the parking lot just head of me. I parked alongside it and got out of the cruiser. I walked over to introduce myself.

"Hi. Frank Thomas. I'm the chief of police here in Molalla."

"Glad to meet you, Chief. I'm Trooper Gary Collins. This is my partner, Lee Warren. We're field investigators with the major crimes division of the Oregon State Police."

"Good to meet you. Let's go inside and I'll show you what we have, or I guess I could say, what we don't have."

It was twelve fifteen by the time Troopers Collins and Warren pulled out of the parking lot, taking with them the collected evidence. Should the fluid samples turn out to be human blood, a full-scale investigation would kick in and crime teams from the state police would descend upon Molalla High School like a flock of geese. After determining that the crime was indeed a homicide, the state's Homicide Investigation Tracking System unit—HITS—would go to work collecting evidence and comparing them to other crimes of a similar nature. They will share this information with the field investigators, who in this case were Collins and Warren.

This all would take time, of course, and I didn't want to sit around waiting. For one thing, I would like to find Sandi Riggs, hopefully alive. Yet, I had a feeling, a familiar feeling that came from being involved in hundreds of homicide investigations in

LA. I felt that this wasn't going to have a happy ending. Still, I hoped for the best, this being Molalla and not LA.

Before I did anything more with my own investigation, I had to answer the *get me something to eat* call coming from my gut. The Y Drive-In had phoned in to my stomach around noon. I pulled into the almost-full parking lot and saw a car that was just then backing out—another satisfied customer. I pulled into the vacant spot, got out of the cruiser, and walked over to the drive-thru window. Violet Jones motioned for me to come inside, mouthing that it was way too cold to open the window.

She and her husband, George, owned the Y. She was the cook and really knew how to throw together a home-cooked meal. George was a logger and had been most all of his life. He never finished high school due to the death of his father, who was killed in a logging accident. George dropped out of school when he was sixteen, the oldest of five siblings. The responsibility to provide for the family fell to him.

He and Violet started dating when he was still in high school, and continued to date until her graduation from Molalla High. They married shortly thereafter. Twenty years and five kids later, Violet had the notion to open a restaurant. The Y became a reality a year later, and success followed.

I walked into the crowded dining room. Booths, that lined one wall, were all filled up at the moment. There were four, small, round tables set up in the middle of the room with four chairs around each. Two large, rectangular tables were set up in the back. Those tables were occupied, as well. I felt as though every eye was on me, causing me to feel a bit conspicuous. There were three empty stools at the counter, all in a row. I chose the middle one and parked myself there.

"Hey Chief, whatcha havin' today?" Violet asked.

"Oh, come on, Violet! You know exactly what I want," I said, smiling.

"Well, I thought maybe you wanted to try something different today, maybe not be so predictable."

"Maybe another day—I've been thinking about that country-fried steak since early this morning. You can't do better than perfection."

She continued to do her magic at the grill, situated within speaking distance from the counter where I sat.

"Order ready!" she called out.

Star, the waitress, retrieved four heaping plates and delivered them to the salivating customers sitting at the round table behind me.

"Okay, Chief, the special it is. Say, what's the latest on the murder investigation? That Sandi Riggs sure seemed like a nice girl. She used to stop here quite often and eat dinner after her bus run. You know she went by here on her way home. She lived on the river up past Dickey Prairie."

News got around fast in a small town, but not always was the gossip accurate.

"Hold on, Violet. We don't even know if there's been a murder yet. And even if it is a murder, we don't know who the victim is. There's a lot more questions than answers right now."

"I'm just sayin' what everybody else is sayin'. Who would do something like that anyway? She seemed like such a nice girl."

"That's what we're trying to find out, Violet, the answers to those questions."

I knew it would be futile to attempt to squelch small-town gossip. I heard plenty of it growing up in Puyallup, with my own mother being one of the gossip ring leaders.

This was big news for a small town and the talk would

continue for quite some time. Violet heaped the food on my plate, and even gave me extra mashed potatoes and gravy. She carried it over to me.

"Here ya go, hon. Enjoy."

I did.

Chapter 8

"Nicole, what are we gonna do?"

The two friends were in Sherry's bedroom. The old, two-story farmhouse was empty, except for the three dogs and two cats that were inside more than out. Her mom was at work. Sherry's radio was playing The Police in the background…

Every move you make…

"I don't know. Maybe it's all a mistake. I say we just keep quiet about this and wait to see what happens. Maybe it's not what we think."

Nicole knew that it was just wishful thinking.

"I heard gunshots last night while I was waiting for my dad, just after you went back in the school. I thought it was from the play, but now I don't know. I think—I think maybe I heard…" Her voice drifted off as she stared at a spot on the wall.

"You really think that's when Sandi got killed? Don't you think we should go to the police or something? Maybe we should go talk to Mr. Payne."

"We can't. You heard what Connie and Kim said. We can't tell anyone or we could get killed, our families too."

"You don't really believe that, do you?"

Sherry really wanted Nicole to say that she didn't believe it.

"Do you?"

"Do I what?"

Every step you take...

"Believe it—do you really believe we could get killed?"

Nicole's silence gave her the answer that she didn't want to hear. They spent the rest of the afternoon trying to imagine what could have happened. For now, they wouldn't tell a soul, especially not Nicole's mom, who couldn't keep her mouth shut for nothing.

I'll be watching you!

Chapter 9

I finished off the pecan pie, left two bits on the counter, and got up to leave.

"See ya later, Violet—just put it on my tab. That was the best, as usual!"

"Will do. Go catch the bad guys now."

I smiled at her as I walked out the door. It was still cold outside, but now the sun was shining brightly. That's how it is in the Pacific Northwest. It can be snowing, raining, hailing, and the sun shining, all at the same time. If you wear shorts, sandals—with socks on, of course—and a parka, all at the same time, you live in Oregon.

Catch the bad guys. I thought that was a good idea, too, but who were they? As of yet, there were no suspects. There wasn't even a victim, yet. I decided to take a drive over to Brazier Forest Products. It was only a few minutes from the Y, and I wanted to have a talk with Steve Carlson. Maybe he knew where Sandi was. I could only hope.

I pulled into the parking lot that was used by visitors and walked into the main office. The receptionist asked if she could be of some assistance. Her name was LeAnne, according to the name on the desk. I asked if Steve Carlson was working and, if so, could I have a few minutes to talk with him. She informed me that Steve worked swing shift and wouldn't be in until later. Before I could respond, Luther Heinrichson walked out of his office.

"Chief Thomas, come on in for a few minutes."

"Hi, Luther. It's good to see you again."

Luther was the superintendent of Brazier Forest Products. White hair, broad shoulders, and wearing a plaid, red and black Pendleton shirt, he invited me into his office. We were close to the same age as far as I could tell. I had talked with him on a handful of occasions since my move to Molalla.

He had served in the Navy during WWII and had plenty of stories for anyone who would listen to them. He was a nice guy— loved sports. Hanging on the wall was a picture of an athlete wearing a University of Oregon track outfit. This was his son, he informed me, who had set a world record throwing the shot put some fifteen years earlier.

"Have a seat, Chief. What brings you out here today?"

"I don't know if you've heard anything or not about what's going on over at the school…"

"Well, the girls in the office have been telling me all the local gossip—murder? Are there suspects?"

"News travels in a small town, doesn't it? Here's the thing. We don't even know if we have a murder."

I told him the story, but that we wouldn't know anything until the results came back from the state police.

"What about that tall dark-haired gal that wears her shorts too short?"

Luther wasn't good with names, but he could pretty much describe anyone and you would know who he was talking about. Whether her shorts were too short was a matter of opinion.

"Sandi Riggs. I still haven't found her. I'd like to talk to her. I went up to her place this morning, but she wasn't there. That's why I came out here. Seems she's friends with one of your employees, Steve Carlson. I thought he might know where she is. Your gal, LeAnne, informed me that he works swing shift."

We talked in his office a good hour, much longer than I intended. We talked about *The War*, the Ducks, and the Trail Blazers, in that order. It took time. I didn't tell him I was a Huskies fan from way back. I finally stood and said that I really needed to go. He stood too. We shook hands like men from our generation did.

"Thanks for your time, Luther."

"You're welcome, Chief. Now, go catch the bad guys," he said with a broad smile as I left his office.

It seemed everyone in Molalla wanted me to catch the bad guys. LeAnne just smiled and said goodbye. I was really glad she didn't say it, too.

"Oh, I almost forgot. Could you give me Steve's address?" I asked LeAnne.

"Sure, Chief." She wrote it out on a piece of paper and handed it to me. "There ya go."

"Thanks, LeAnne."

I smiled at her and turned to walk out of the office, wishing I was forty years younger.

I pulled out onto the highway behind a log truck that was throwing up water and mud. That combination, with the glare of the sunshine, made it nearly impossible to see. The wipers were still on from before, but all they did was smear the mess. I turned on the washers, which helped a little, but not much. I thought it would be a good idea to take the cruiser through the car wash, but I knew it wouldn't do any good, not until June anyway, maybe July.

I crossed the railroad tracks that paralleled North and South Main. The trains here didn't carry people—they carried lumber, but the tree-huggers were lobbying to shut down the timber industry. If they succeeded, all the mills would shut down. Molalla would become a ghost town, but the Spotted Owl population would grow dramatically.

Driving out on West Main, I took a right onto Leroy Street. Wally's Market stood on the corner. I thought about stopping in, but decided to wait until after I talked to Steve Carlson. The Carlson home, a modest single-level, was located across the street from the grade school. Several trees in the front yard provided welcome shade in the summer afternoons, but they were stripped bare at this time of year.

I parked at the grade school and stepped out of the cruiser, just as the school bell sounded. The district's two busses were waiting for the children, who would soon be coming out the doors. I crossed Leroy Street and walked up the sidewalk to the front door. I rang the doorbell, which set off a melody that could be clearly heard while standing outside. I heard footsteps coming toward the door, and a moment later, a pleasant-looking woman opened the door.

"Good morning, Ma'am, I'm Chief Thomas. Are you Mrs. Carlson?"

She smiled, looking past me to see if there was anyone along with me.

"Yes, I'm Mrs. Carlson, but you can call me Jennie. Is there something I could help you with?"

"Well, I hope so. I stopped by to see if I might talk to your son. Is he here?"

"No, I'm sorry. He left about twenty minutes ago to run some errands before he goes to work this afternoon. Why do you want to talk with him?"

"I'm just trying to locate an acquaintance of his and thought maybe he might know her whereabouts."

"Oh? Who would that be?" Mrs. Carlson asked.

"I'm looking for Sandi Riggs. Do you know her, or, better yet, where she might be?"

"Of course I know Sandi. She and Steve used to be together, you know, a couple. But they had some issues last fall and broke up. That's when Steve moved back into his old bedroom. I really liked Sandi. I was hoping that one day she might be my daughter-in-law."

"What happened with them, anyway?"

I thought I would just listen a while. Mrs. Carlson—Jennie—seemed more than willing to talk, and, I was sure, could provide some good information.

"Would you like to come inside? It's cold out there. Would you like some coffee?"

"Yes ma'am, to both."

We talked, or rather, she talked, for a good hour. I didn't come any closer to finding out where Sandi might be, but I got plenty of information about both Sandi and her son. A clock somewhere in the house chimed four times, and I thought I should be going.

"Well, Mrs. Carlson—Jennie—thank you for your hospitality and the conversation."

You're welcome, Chief Thomas. I sure hope Sandi's okay. She really is a nice girl."

"You can call me Frank, and I hope she's okay, too."

I smiled and tipped my hat, wishing for the second time that day that I was younger—this time, about twenty years younger.

After my visit with Jennie, I drove back into town and to the police station. I hadn't been back all day, although my reserve officer was there when I pulled into the parking spot that was reserved for the chief. I walked in, and Mike Benson was talking on one of the two phones in the office.

Mike had been a reserve for about six months now. He was a local kid—twenty-four years old—who had gone through the academy in Monmouth a year and a half ago. He came back to Molalla and stopped by one day to see if there might be a place for him. He was looking for a paid position, preferably full-time, but budget constraints wouldn't allow it. I thought that I could use some help, though, so I made available a reserve position. I told him that I would work with the city clerk to get a full-time position added into the budget come July. Mike took me up on the deal, and he's worked out well so far. The kid and the old man get along pretty well.

I went to my desk and sat down on my well-worn office chair that had tears in the Naugahyde upholstery. The chair belonged to the previous chief, and probably the chief before him. Mike hung up the phone.

"Hi Chief. That was CAU, the Crime Analyst Unit."

"Yeah, Mike, I know what the CAU is. What'd they say?" I asked, not surprised that the results had come back so fast.

"It looks like we have a murder here. It was 100% human blood. I guess there were two troopers here earlier?" he asked.

I nodded.

"They'll be back out tomorrow, along with a detective—said they'd be here at eight."

"Sounds good. When did you come in?"

Mike has a part-time job, in Oregon City, at the car wash by Fred Meyer. His hours aren't regular, so I never know for sure when he'll be in.

"It was around two, I guess."

"How about goin' out to Brazier with me. I want to talk to Steve Carlson, and he should be there by now. You probably know him, don't you?"

Mike got up and headed toward the door. I guess he wanted to go along.

"Yeah, I know him some," he said.

I followed Mike out the door and to the cruiser, while he continued to talk.

"He was a senior here at Molalla when I was a freshman, so I never hung around with him or nothin'. He was a good athlete— football and baseball—and pretty popular with the girls. Seemed like a nice guy. D'ya really think he might have something to do with this? Hey, can I drive?"

Mike had a habit of asking two, or more, unrelated questions without giving the opportunity to respond to any of them. I threw him the keys in response to the last question and answered the first.

"Don't know, but he and Sandi Riggs used to live together after he got out of the service. I guess they did before he went in, too. Anyways, something happened, and they broke it off. I just want to see if he has any idea where she is."

It was already dark when Mike backed out of the chief's reserved parking space.

"Why don't you drive by Dickens' Thriftway?"

The store was just down a few blocks from the station.

"Why? What are ya thinkin'? You think maybe her truck's there?"

One word answered all three questions, "Yup."

Mike drove through the parking lot, but there was not a blue, '77 Ford truck.

"Oh well, just a hunch. Once in a while you get lucky. Let's get out to the mill."

He pulled out of the parking lot and turned right onto Francis Street, then took another right, heading north on Molalla Avenue. Mike turned right at Brinkman's corner, named for the Brinkman farm located at the corner. Fortunately, this wasn't August, or the odor from the farm's silo would be overwhelming.

We came to Highway 211 and turned east toward Meadowbrook. He pulled into the mill and parked in the same space that I had parked in earlier. We got out of the cruiser and walked up to the gate. There was a guard shack, complete with a guard, who was reading a book and listening to the tune on the radio—*I Shot the Sheriff* was playing, the Eric Clapton version. We walked up to the window that was very much like the drive-up window at the Y.

"Good song," I said to the old guy who was doing a good job guarding the mill. To be honest, he was close to my age.

"I didn't do it, though, Sheriff. Really!"

A big smile revealed tobacco-stained teeth and a couple of vacancies where there were no teeth.

"You sure about that?" I asked, smiling. "I'm Chief Thomas. I need to talk to an employee—Steve Carlson. Is he here tonight?"

"Well, I think so. Let me take a look-see."

He stood, stuck his head out the window, and looked in the employee parking lot that was just on the other side of the gate.

"Yup, he's here. That's his truck, right over there—that Chevy. By the way, my name's Frank." He pulled back through the window and stuck his right hand out.

"Good to meet you, Frank. My name's Frank." He laughed and I did too. "So, can we just go on out there?"

"Here, put these on. OSHA, ya know."

He gave two blue hardhats to us with *Visitor* stenciled on them.

"Just head out that way. Keep going straight 'til you see the chain on your right. He should be up there pulling lumber."

Mike and I followed Frank's directions and soon found the planer chain. There were eight guys that were pulling lumber off the chain that never stopped moving. The lumber just kept coming. It looked to me like three guys were doing most of the work, while the others pulled off a board here and there. There were three other guys standing up at the front where the lumber came out of the planer. They were marking the appropriate grade on the lumber.

Steve was on the catwalk, third from the front. I walked up the steel I-beam on which a series of rollers were situated. When a load was full, a *puller* would step on a lever, which would release the load. It would then go down the roll case to a waiting forklift that would take it to the *bander*. Steve had just done that and was starting a new load when I walked up behind him. He was pretty busy and hadn't seen me. It was noisy, too.

"Steve!" I yelled, but not loud enough.

WHACK! A board landed right beside me and right behind Steve. He turned around to communicate to the puller behind him, using sign language that even I could understand. That's when he saw me.

"Steve, can I talk to you a minute?" I said it loud enough to be heard over the planer, which was painfully loud.

"Sure, just a second."

He went into overdrive, grabbing his boards and stacking them with seemingly no effort. He worked his way up the catwalk to the guy ahead of him. He must have asked him to cover for him, because Steve motioned for me to follow him. I walked down the roll case very carefully. Steve skipped down them, again with no effort, but I took a little longer. I finally made it to where Steve and Mike were. It was a little quieter here, but not by much.

"I'm Chief Thomas."

I put out my hand. He took off the leather mitt he was wearing and shook my hand. It was cold outside, but his hand was still sweaty. Steam was rising from the t-shirt he was wearing, and sweat rolled down both sides of his face. *Hard work*, I thought to myself, and was glad that I had never worked in a mill.

"Hi Chief. What's up?" His voice was elevated above the whine of the planer.

"I understand that you know Sandi Riggs. Have you seen her lately?"

"No, not lately. We broke up a few months ago. I don't see her much anymore, just around town once in a while." He looked at his watch. "She's probably on her bus route right now. Why ya lookin' for her, anyway? She's okay, isn't she?"

"I guess you haven't heard anything."

"I guess not. I was in Portland most of the day getting some business done. I got home, to my mom's place, changed my clothes, and came to work. Is something wrong?"

Steve had a worried look on his face. Was there something else? Fear, maybe?

"No one's seen her since yesterday. She didn't show up for work, and I spent most of my day trying to find her."

"And no one's heard from her?"

"No, and there's something else. At the bus garage this morning, the maintenance guy found a whole bunch of what looked like blood, lots of it. I called in the state police and they ran tests on it today. Just found out that it is human blood, but whose? We don't know. The rumors are flying around town that its Sandi's blood, but we just don't know. That's why we're trying to find her."

Steve looked like someone sucker punched him. He just stared at something behind me with a *deer in the headlights* kind of look in his eyes.

"You sure you don't know where she is?"

"What? No, I don't know where she is. I gotta get back up there. The guys are getting hammered."

He turned and walked away. Mike and I looked at each other and started walking toward the main gate. When we got out of range of the whining planer, Mike spoke first.

"He looked pretty shook up, didn't he? You think he knows something? You don't think he did it, do you?"

Mike fired off his volley of three questions. One answer wouldn't suffice this time.

"Yes, he looked shook up, and yeah, I think he knows something, more than he's lettin' on, anyway. And the question I don't know the answer to is the last question. I don't know if he did it. Let's go take a look at his truck while we're here."

We looked around the truck, but didn't notice anything unusual. I shined my flashlight in the cab, but that didn't reveal much of anything except for a couple cans of chewin' tobacco and some fast-food garbage.

Mike drove us back to the station and I told him I was calling it a day. What a day it was, too. This is Molalla, not L.A. There wasn't supposed to be days like this, not here. What I didn't know was that the days ahead would be more bizarre than this day had been—bloodier, deadlier, too. I got out of the cruiser, walked around to the driver's side, and got in.

"See ya tomorrow, Chief."

"Okay, Mike. Take care."

"Yeah, you too."

I drove to my place on Toliver just across the railroad tracks. The temperature was dropping rapidly, but a nice cold beer sounded good, anyway, and I just happened to have one in my fridge. I walked in the house, switched on a light, and turned the thermostat up for the oil furnace. I got a Hungry Man dinner out of the freezer and a beer out of the fridge, turned the oven to preheat, and took my beer to the easy chair.

It was Wednesday. I looked in the TV Guide to see what was on—*The Fall Guy*, Lee Majors. I liked him. He played a stuntman, but was also a bounty hunter when stuntman work was slow. I fell asleep in my chair halfway through the show and woke up during Johnny's monologue. I got up, turned off the oven, and put the uncooked dinner back in the freezer. I went to bed and slept a dream-filled sleep. I don't usually remember dreams, but I did on this night. I dreamt about *The Fall Guy*, but Lee Majors wasn't the actor. It was Steve Carlson.

Chapter 10

Nicole Parker would not sleep well on this night—not at all. After staying the afternoon at Sherry's place, she had come home around dinner time, but not too late that her mom would bombard her with questions—*where have you been? Who were you with?* Instead it was the usual—*You need to get your chores done soon as you eat,* and, *Soon as your done with your chores you need to get your homework done.*

"I don't have homework, Ma."

Nicole had recently taken to calling her *Ma,* mainly because Janice Parker was annoyed by it, and Nicole usually enjoyed annoying her mother.

"You sure?"

"Yes, I'm sure, Ma."

"Then you can clean your room and get your laundry done after your other chores. And stop calling me *Ma.*"

It was the same thing every night, but tonight, Nicole didn't mind. She didn't want to be in the same room with her mother, let alone talk to her. Nicole really did love her mom, but she had a knack for getting on Nicole's nerves. Her dad was pretty cool, though. He didn't get too excited about things, and served as a calming influence for his wife, and for Nicole too. Yet she couldn't say anything to her dad either.

Ma had actually fixed a decent dinner tonight—pork chops, mashed potatoes and gravy, steamed carrots, and her favorite, Pink Lady Jell-O. After dinner, she did her chores, as Ma requested, and then went to her room. She would make a feeble attempt at cleaning it, but mostly, she thought about the day's events. It started out in a normal way. The snow wasn't that unusual for this time of year, but from the time she got on the bus, things went from weird to freaky, and then, to downright terrifying.

Now what? She and Sherry decided that they wouldn't say anything to anyone, at least not until they saw how things played out. She opened her door to say goodnight to Ma and Dad. They were watching *The Fall Guy* on TV.

"Night, honey," her dad said.

Ma was too much into the show to hear her.

"Good night, Dad."

Nicole turned out her light a little after ten, but her mind continued to race. She finally fell asleep, but it was a dream-filled, restless sleep…

> *"Nicole, who ya gonna tell?" Sherry was walking next to her. It was a dark, moonless night, and they were on a country road that she didn't recognize. It was cold. She could see her breath as she exhaled. "Who ya gonna tell?" Sherry was annoying her, asking that same question over and over. A set of headlights appeared. A vehicle, larger than a car, came around a corner about a quarter mile ahead. As it drew closer, Nicole could see that it was a school bus. "Nicole, who ya gonna tell?" She turned to answer Sherry, but it wasn't Sherry*

any longer. It was Sandi Riggs. She had no life in her one eye, she just stared straight ahead and asked, "Who ya gonna tell?" Sandi slowly turned her head to look at Nicole. "Who ya gonna tell?" Nicole opened her mouth to scream, but nothing came out. The right side of Sandi's face wasn't there. There was a bloody mass where her eye should be. Pieces of shredded and burnt skin fell away from its usual place, revealing bone and brain matter. There was matted hair, blood, and mud mingled together, which was intended to cover the entire mess, but failed to do so. Nicole wanted to run, but her feet were glued to the gravel road. She wanted to scream, but her tongue seemed swelled to ten times its normal size. The bus pulled up to them and stopped. The doors opened slowly, revealing the driver. It was Connie Williams. "Hi girls, need a lift?" Seated in the seat behind her was Steve Carlson, who smiled too. "Hi Nicole," he said. Connie smiled at them and asked, "Who ya gonna tell, Nicole?" She reached under her seat to get something—a gun! She pointed it at Nicole. Then a brilliant white flash—Nicole believed she was dead, but realized she was still standing beside Sandi. This time, though, when she looked, Sandi's face was totally gone, a bloody pulp was all that remained. A voice oozed from the mess, "Nicole, who ya gonna tell?" as Sandi grabbed her shoulders and shook her—"Nicole!"

"Nicole, Nicole! Wake up!" Pete Parker shook his daughter's shoulders. "Nicole, wake up."

She slowly opened her eyes, realizing it was all a dream.

"Nicole, you were screaming in your sleep. You were having a nightmare. You're all right."

Ma was standing next to her husband with a worried look on her face. He turned to her and assured her that Nicole was okay, that it was just a dream.

"What were you dreaming, honey?" he said. I nearly messed my pants when you screamed."

Nicole stammered, "I don't know. I can't remember."

But she did remember, and she was scared and wanted to cry, but she didn't. And she thought, *how could a typically boring life turn into a nightmare in one day?*

Chapter 11

There was at least one other person in Molalla who didn't sleep well that night. The shift ended at one o'clock, but Steve stayed after for another thirty or so minutes to clean things up, stack some un-pulled lumber, and restack a load that the forklift knocked over.

It was one thirty-seven when he punched out on the time clock and walked out to his truck. The parking lot was empty except for the security guard's heap and another wreck next to it. Someone parked there and didn't bother to come back to pick it up.

The streets were empty too. He didn't pass one car all the way home, and that included driving right through the middle of town. Even the White Horse was vacant and dark. Most nights after work he'd go home, grab a beer, and try to find something on TV, usually an old Western. He rarely finished watching the show before he would head for bed.

But tonight there was more on his mind. He saw Sandi yesterday, well, technically, two days ago, since it was now Thursday morning. Not only did he see her, but he had been with her. He hadn't talked to her in months, but there she was, and she looked really nice in tight-fitting blue jeans and a black sweater that was tight, too. She came by the house around one o'clock, just when Steve was heading out the door to run a few errands in town. He could tell she had been crying and was upset about something, but all she did was come up to him, put her arms around his neck, and held on. The errands could wait.

She let go and took his hand, leading him to her car, her eyes asking him to get in. She backed out of the driveway and drove down Leroy toward Wally's Market at the end of the street. They turned left, heading toward town.

Neither of them said a word. He was ready to listen if, and when, she wanted to talk. She went straight through the four-way, turned right at the Y, and continued toward Dickey Prairie. She was going to their place. It used to be their place—no longer—but he still liked to think of it as their place.

He opened his mouth to say something, but nothing came out. He cleared his throat and tried again.

"Sandi, I have to go to work in a while. Mind telling me what's goin' on?"

She turned her head, her eyes still moist.

"I just wanted to see you, to be with you for a while. I miss you."

She continued driving, eventually arriving at the place they had shared, and pulled into the driveway. She looked at him and asked him to come in, without saying a word. Again, her eyes did the inviting.

"I don't think..."

The driver's side door opened. Sandi got out and shut the door without looking at him. "... it's a good idea," he said only to himself.

She unlocked the door to the house and walked in. Steve got out of the truck and walked to her as she waited just inside the door. He stepped inside. It was warm. Sandi liked to keep the heat on so she could always come into a warm home. He shut the door behind him as she moved toward him, and he remembered the first time he'd seen her. It seemed like an eternity ago. She stood facing him, their lips just inches apart as she put her hand softly on his face, gently pulling him the last few inches until their lips met. It was suddenly very hot inside the already warm home.

That was thirty-six hours ago. Steve thought of Chief Thomas and his deputy as Andy Griffith and his sidekick, Barney Fife. They stopped by work yesterday—Wednesday—wanting to know where Sandi was. Steve had no desire to talk to them, so he told them nothing about being with her, or what she had told him.

He listened to the ticking clock that sat on the end table next to the couch. It was mostly dark in the living room. What little light there was came from the streetlight that shone through the translucent curtains covering the picture window.

Where was she? He prayed silently to a God that he didn't believe in. He could only remember one other time that he had prayed. It was in Beirut, during the attack. *Where was God then? Where is He now?* he thought, and then drifted off into a dream-filled sleep that would soon turn into a living nightmare.

Chapter 12

Saturday morning, January 26

Steve groaned when he rolled over in his bed and looked at his alarm clock. The obnoxiously-bold, red digits glared—9:31. He figured he might as well get up since he couldn't sleep anyway.

The night before had been a rough one at work, and he was feeling it this morning. Mike Bennett, one of his co-workers, decided to get an early start on the weekend—two days early—and had called in sick. One less guy makes ten times the work for the rest, at least that's what it felt like to Steve. But that wasn't the reason for the uneasy sleep. He hadn't seen or heard from Sandi since Tuesday afternoon. He was afraid that she was in serious trouble, or worse. Yesterday afternoon, some detectives from the state police came by the house to question him. They were asking about Sandi and if he knew where she might be.

"No, haven't seen her or talked to her," was all he said, with a little too much of an edge in his voice.

They asked him where he was on Tuesday between five and midnight, and Steve produced the easy answer.

"I was at work from five 'til one."

He didn't tell them that he was nearly late to work due to his being with Sandi that afternoon, and that she was nearly late for her activity bus run.

"You can check it out with my foreman, Ken Peterson."

They said they would indeed check it out, and Steve couldn't help but think that he was involved in an episode of *Dragnet*. This was Sgt. Joe Friday and his partner, Bill Gannon, detectives in plainclothes. It was Andy and Barney on Wednesday. Steve smiled ruefully and thought that maybe he watched too much TV growing up.

He shook his head, still on the pillow, and thought again about getting up. He swung his legs out from under the covers and sat on the edge of the bed. His feet touched the cold floor, and at the same moment, the doorbell rang downstairs, as though he'd set it off with his feet. It was probably those kids on bicycles with the white shirts, black ties, and short haircuts. His mom would answer it if she was home and, if not, he would just ignore it. He heard his mom talking and smiled to himself as he envisioned her trying to get rid of them.

He stood up and walked around the bed to his dresser. He took out some clean underwear, faded blue jeans, and an Oregon State t-shirt. He was just about to open his door and walk down the hallway to the bathroom. There was a rap on the door.

"Steve, are you awake? There's someone here who wants to talk to you." Her voice cracked a little as she said it.

"Wait, just a minute. Let me get my clothes on."

He slipped into the jeans and t-shirt and opened the door. "Who is...?"

That's all he got out before he saw his visitors, and they weren't Mormons. It was Joe Friday and Bill Gannon.

Detective Friday spoke, "Steve Carlson, you're under arrest for the murder of Sandi Riggs."

Their department-issued Smith & Wesson Model 15 revolvers were pointed at him.

"Take two steps back and put your hands behind your head," Friday said.

Detective Gannon, the taller, older one, slipped through the door and stepped behind Steve. He pulled Steve's right hand down, behind his back, and put the cuff on. He did the same with the other hand.

Friday read the Miranda rights to Steve as he was being cuffed, "You have the right to remain silent. Anything you say can be used against you in a court of law. You have the right to have an attorney present now and during any future questioning. If you cannot afford an attorney, one will be appointed to you free of charge if you wish. Okay, let's go."

Steve walked through his bedroom door and past Friday. Jennie Carlson was down the hallway by the bathroom door. She was crying, an anguished look on her face. Their eyes met. Steve felt as if a knife was cutting out his broken heart. He couldn't stand to see the pain on his mother's face.

They marched him down the stairs and out the door, no shoes or socks on his feet. When they walked him past his truck parked in the driveway, he saw what appeared to be dried blood smeared on the passenger-side window, a lot of smeared blood. The fear of being set up hit him full force, and the knife pierced deeper into his heart.

A uniformed officer opened the rear door and directed Steve into the back of the Clackamas County police car, holding his head down to avoid an accusation of police brutality. It looked like today's cop show was going to be *Adam-12*. The shorter of the two deputies, *Pete Malloy, the veteran,* slid in the driver's side. The other deputy, *Jim Reed, the rookie,* shut the back door and climbed in the front passenger seat, a metal screen separating them.

He was glad, for his mom's sake, that there were no neighbors outside and that it was a Saturday. The grade school, across the street, was empty. They drove down Leroy and turned left on Toliver, went a mile, and then turned right on Highway 213. The Clackamas County Jail, in Oregon City, was a twenty-five minute drive from Molalla.

Friday and Gannon—Steve never did learn their real names— had stayed behind, hopefully to comfort his distraught mother. Jennie Carlson was a tough woman. She was also a loving, loyal mom who didn't believe for a minute that her son had murdered Sandi Riggs.

They arrived at the county jail on Kaen Road. They slowed for a couple who were walking four dogs. After the couple and their pack of dogs crossed the street, the car turned left into the driveway and proceeded through a gate that shut behind them. They backed up to a receiving bay with deputies awaiting their new guest.

Steve climbed out of the car and was promptly escorted to a holding area. It was an oversized cell with concrete walls, a door in the back, a concrete ceiling with a single light in the center, and an ice-cold concrete floor. Steve shivered as a deputy told him to sit down. Another deputy applied shackles to his ankles, as if he was going anywhere.

It was fifteen minutes before the door opened and he was instructed to get up. They escorted him inside where they issued him his jail clothes. He was fingerprinted, photographed, and assigned to the cell block that would be his new home. Steve changed into the jail clothes, all in stylish orange, with black letters stenciled on the back—Clackamas Co. Jail.

One of the deputies escorted him to his cell. The door clanged shut, and he sat, and thought. There would be plenty of time for thinking. And the gnawing pain and anxiety inside him continued to grow.

Part 2

Chapter 13

Saturday morning, June 30, 1985

I would try to sleep in on most Saturday mornings. But after years of sleeping six hours or less, I couldn't stay in bed later than seven o'clock. It was nine thirty now, and I headed out the door to go down to the station for a while. I fired up the chief's cruiser—that's how I liked to refer to it—backed out of the driveway, and drove the short distance to the station, less than a mile away.

It looked to be a beautiful day. There were just a few wispy clouds far off to the south, and the sun was already warming things up. June weather in Oregon is always iffy, but today would be a nice one, in the mid-eighties. The humidity was low—a perfect day.

The Molalla Buckaroo's first showing would start tomorrow and run through the Fourth. The equipment for the carnival came in last Wednesday, along with the crew to set it all up. The rest of the carnies stumbled in on Thursday and Friday, in time to open up the rides and booths for the weekend.

The rodeo contestants started coming in yesterday, and more

would be arriving today. This was big-time for Molalla, attracting lots of people from the Portland and Salem areas, and of course, the locals. Two groups of people live in Molalla—those who stay home over the Fourth and those who decide to get out of town until it's all over. Me? I don't have a choice.

Today would be the calm before the storm. Tonight, things would start to hop around here, which meant that Mikey and I would be hopping, too. The Fireman's Ball, which occurs tonight, gives a whole new meaning to the term "ball". It's nothing at all like Cinderella's. Drunken cowboys liked to fight, and they don't need much of a reason to start one. It might be over a woman or two, or it might be over who had the best horse. Or, it might be over who had the best ride—not referring to a car, of course, but to a ride on a bucking bronco or a Brahma bull.

I knew what was in store for this evening based on prior experience, so I had called in some other law enforcement types from other nearby towns—Canby, Silverton, Oregon City, Woodburn— as well as the Clackamas County Sheriff's Department. They all kindly responded by pitching in with some manpower, some of whom would be coming this evening.

I unlocked the back door to the station, which was just in front of the chief's parking space. Mikey wouldn't be in until late afternoon, which meant that I'd have a quiet office, and hopefully, an uneventful morning, to get caught up on some paperwork.

It had been quiet in and around Molalla the last few months, ever since the disappearance of Sandi Riggs back in January. I say *disappearance* because her body hadn't been found. There had been no luck finding her car, either.

The state's official investigative unit determined that there most definitely had been a violent crime committed. After that determination, they handed the investigation over to the HITS unit, led by field investigators Gary Collins and Lee Warren. They were very thorough, discovering incriminating evidence that led to the arrest of Steve Carlson. The evidence was submitted to the Clackamas County District Attorney, James Harrison, who determined that there was enough evidence to try Carlson for murder in the first degree. It will be the first time in seventy years that an accused murderer would be tried without the evidence of the victim's body.

For a while, after the disappearance, I took drives up past Dickey Prairie to Sandi's place, but found nothing. She had disappeared—vanished—as if a magician waved his magic wand, and *poof*, she was gone. But this was no magician's trick. My instincts told me that this was of a sinister nature.

On Friday afternoon, the week of the disappearance, I took a drive to Sandi's hometown, Mill City. It was a little over sixty miles from Molalla. The small logging community was very similar to Molalla in both its size and its cultural makeup. From what I could gather from the DMV, Sandi's mother still lived there. I decided not to call ahead. Sometimes you get better results if you show up unexpectedly. Of course, I was hoping to discover that Sandi was just fine, that she had gotten a case of homesickness, and just wanted to see her mother.

I remembered the day clearly…

I drove into the town. Snow was piled a couple feet high on the sides of the road, but the driving lanes were clear. I found the post office on South First and Kingwood and went inside to get directions to the Riggs' residence. Turns out I wasn't too far away, just turn left out of the post office parking lot, go three blocks on Kingwood, and turn left onto Fourth. It would be the third house on the left.

The driveway was clear. Someone had shoveled off the snow, probably a neighborhood kid wanting to earn a few bucks. An old Buick was parked in the driveway in front of the one-car garage that was detached from the house. It looked like there was someone home. At least it wouldn't be a wasted trip. I walked up the three steps to the porch and rang the doorbell. It didn't play a melody or make any other sound that I could hear. So I rapped on the door three times and looked through the glass panels on the front door. It was that yellow-colored glass that didn't allow you to see anything, but I heard footsteps approaching and saw a shadow coming to the door. The door swung open to reveal a dark-haired woman who looked to be in her 50s, an inquisitive smile pasted on her face. She wore tight jeans and a sweater, and I couldn't help but notice the resemblance between mother and daughter.

"Good morning, Ma'am, my name's Frank Thomas, chief of police in Molalla."

I tried to be as pleasant as possible, but when a policeman comes to your door, especially a cop from where your daughter lives, well, Mrs. Riggs went into high anxiety mode.

"What's wrong? Is something wrong with Sandi? Did something happen to her?"

She started shaking. I thought she might fall over, so I offered my arm for her to lean on, which she gratefully accepted. I tried to calm her.

"I'm sorry to alarm you, Mrs. Riggs. I drove down to ask if you have seen or heard from Sandi in the last couple of days. She didn't show up for work on Wednesday, or yesterday either, and now today. People are concerned. She didn't tell anyone that she was leaving and there's no one at her house. So I decided to take a drive out here and pay you a visit. I'm sorry that I alarmed you like I did."

I didn't mention the blood at the bus garage, at least not yet. I was still standing on the porch.

"Please, come in."

I stepped into the living room that looked lived-in, but in no way messy.

"You can sit here if you like," offering a recliner, not unlike the one in my living room.

I sat down. She sat across from me, and continued.

"I talked to her on Sunday afternoon, that's the last time. She didn't say that she was going anywhere."

"I thought maybe she might have come to see you. Can you think of anywhere else she might have gone, maybe just to get away for a few days?"

"Well, not that I can think of."

Mrs. Riggs seemed to be calming somewhat, but the worried expression in her eyes was still evident. She continued.

"Of course, Sandi hasn't lived here for around five years or so. That guy—Steve, Steve Carlson—he swept her off her feet. He talked her into moving to Molalla. So she did, and moved in with him. Of course I was totally against that and let Sandi know about it. The more adamant I was, the more determined she was to go live with him, so that's what she did. I'm afraid we haven't had much of a relationship since then."

Her eyes teared up.

"What about her father?"

"Harold passed away almost ten years ago, when Sandi was a sophomore in high school. He died of cancer. He fought hard, but after two years of chemo and radiation, well, it finally took him. It was really hard for Sandi, for me too. Sandi had a wonderful relationship with her dad. She really loved him. She was his little princess, and always would be. She took it really hard."

A tear clung to the corner of her eye. She brushed it away with the sleeve of her sweater. Mrs. Riggs was a lonely woman, and now she was worried, too.

"I only met Steve a couple of times when Sandi brought him with her to visit me, but she came by herself most of the time. I tried to talk her into coming back here to live when he went into the Marines, but she wouldn't do it. She's always been so independent. I suppose you heard about what Steve did to her, didn't you?"

I nodded.

"Well, I thought for sure she would come back home then, but no, she wanted to stay there," she said sadly.

Mrs. Riggs continued talking for another forty-five minutes. I didn't have to be much of a conversationalist. It was clear that she had no idea where Sandi was. I finally stood to leave when there was a slight pause in her monologue, trying not to be rude. I promised that I would let her know of any news, and she promised that she would do the same if she heard from Sandi. I gave her my card and said goodbye.

I've talked with her a handful of times since then, but with no news of Sandi's whereabouts. The back door opened, jarring me from my thoughts, and in walked Mikey. He was getting paid now, a full-time employee of the City of Molalla. The new fiscal year had just begun, and I was able to get a deputy position added into the new budget. He deserves it. He's a good kid. And now, he can finally quit working two jobs.

"I thought you weren't coming in 'til later?"

"Ah, I was going to, but decided to come on in anyway. What have you got goin' today?"

"I was just going to do some paperwork this morning. After

that, I thought I'd go see how things are going down at the carnival. I was just thinking about the Sandi Riggs case when you walked in."

"So they're really starting the trial on Monday? I thought they'd wait 'til next week, at least until after the Fourth."

"You would think so, but it sounds like Judge Maurer wants to get the show on the road."

"What about the jury? He won't hold them over the holiday, will he?"

"Nah, just picking the jury will be challenging enough, Steve being a local boy and all. And with the publicity this thing is getting, I wouldn't be surprised if they changed the venue to another county. I don't think that's what Maurer wants though. He likes the publicity."

"You gonna go? To the trial?"

"Of course I am. I've been subpoenaed to testify on behalf of the prosecution, but I'd be there anyway, even if I hadn't been subpoenaed."

"So tell me, just between you and me—do you think he did it?"

"Well, they seem to have a solid case against him, so, yeah, I think they'll convict him," I said without conviction.

"Let me ask you again. Do *you* think he did it? What's that gut of yours telling you?"

I didn't answer right away. I started thinking about all that had happened since that snowy, January day, and got lost in my thoughts.

Mikey cleared his voice, "Well, do you?"

"I guess, I, uh, well...." I was having a hard time saying what I really felt. "I guess my gut feeling is that he didn't do it. I'll wait and see what evidence the D.A. has. I know one thing he doesn't have, and that's a dead body."

"I knew it. I could tell. You're having a hard time with this one, aren't you?"

I changed the subject. "I'm gonna go see what's happening around town. Wanna come with me? The paperwork can wait."

"You bet, Chief."

Chapter 14

Nicole Parker lay in her bed, thinking about a lot of things, but the one thing that captivated the majority of her thoughts was the Sandi Riggs murder. She knew that Steve Carlson would be going to trial for a murder that he didn't commit. At least that's what Nicole believed, and with good reason. She thought back to that fateful day—the bus ride to school, the adult-child conversation with Kayleen Williams, Connie Williams' warning, and then Kim Williams' threat. Nicole rolled over to her other side, hoping that the move would take her thoughts in a different direction, too.

She and her best friend, Sherry, had finally made it through high school. The graduation had been three and a half weeks ago. They thought that the time would never come. It did, though, and here they were, still in this small hick-town named Molalla. Nicole wanted to leave the day after graduation, but she knew that realistically, it wouldn't happen then. But as soon as she could leave, she would, and that looked like it would be in the fall at the earliest.

A couple of weeks before graduation, she put in her application at Publisher's—one of the three sawmills in Molalla—and a week later, they called her in for an interview. Three days after the interview, she received a call from Mitch Brown, the personnel manager. He told her that they would hire her, and asked if she could start on Monday, working swing shift. School wouldn't be out yet, but the last week was pretty much a waste, anyway. She felt that way about high school in general, that the whole time was a waste.

She accepted the offer. It would be good money right out of high school. Mitch said she would start at the beginning rate, $5.65 per hour, two dollars over minimum wage. Nicole's plan was to earn enough money to move out with Sherry and take a few classes at the community college in Salem. It was only about forty-five minutes from Molalla, but, to Nicole, it seemed far away, and that was just fine with her.

The sun shone through her window and was doing its best to rouse her out of bed. She worked the night before and hadn't gotten to bed until one thirty, but this was Saturday. She would have two days off before having to go back on Monday afternoon. Nicole didn't want to sleep the day away, so she crawled out of bed around ten and went downstairs to the kitchen where her mom, Janice, was standing over the sink doing the breakfast dishes.

"Mornin', Mom."

Nicole had stopped calling her *Ma* after graduation. She thought that it sounded too much like something a redneck would say. And that was the last thing that Nicole wanted to sound like. Janice Parker was happy about that, too. She never did like it when Nicole called her that.

"Good morning, dear. Would you like some breakfast? How does French toast, eggs, and some hash browns sound?"

"Mmm, that sounds really good. Do we have any bacon? That sounds good too."

"I think we do, let me check."

Janice walked to the freezer and opened the door and looked inside.

"You're in luck, we have bacon too."

"Thanks, Mom. I think I'll go take a quick shower while you're making it."

Nicole was not like a lot of girls who took forever in the bathroom. She knew that breakfast would be ready when she was out of the shower and dressed.

Twenty minutes later, Nicole sat at the table with a full breakfast in front of her. Since she had been working at the mill, her appetite had increased dramatically, but she worked hard enough that she hadn't gained any weight. Nicole was no stranger to hard work—she had been raised on the farm. That meant a multitude of chores from the time she could remember.

"How was work last night?"

"It was work, about like any other night. At least I'm learnin' how to pull the lumber from the chain and to stack'em on the right load without gettin' my ass buried. It's getting easier. The guys are treating me better, too, now that they see I'm a hard worker."

Janice Parker cringed. "It sounds like you're starting to talk like them, too."

"Sorry, Mom, but believe me, they talk far worse than that!"

Mrs. Parker was not thrilled about her daughter working at the sawmill.

"So what plans do you have for today?"

It used to really bug Nicole when her mom would give her the third degree, but now she just let it go.

"I thought I would call Sherry and see what she's doing, maybe go into town, mess around at the carnival or something. Can I use the car?"

"That's fine, but before you go, would you vacuum and run a load of laundry?

"Sure, Mom."

After breakfast, Nicole called Sherry and asked if she wanted to go into town and see what was happening there. Sherry said that would be awesome. Nicole said she would pick her up at one thirty.

It was one thirty on the dot when Nicole pulled into the Johnson's gravel driveway that looped around a tall Douglas fir. It was surrounded by blazing red geraniums. She honked the horn just as Sherry opened the front door and stepped outside. She did a silly kind of walk out to the car, opened the door, and plopped herself down in the passenger seat.

"Hey, girl, how's it going?"

Sherry seemed all too bubbly for the mood that Nicole was in, but deep down, Nicole knew that a *pick-me-up* in the form of Sherry was just what she needed.

"Wow. You sure seem happy today. You need to get out more."

"Sorry Miss Down-in-the-Mouth. It's a beautiful summer day, the Fourth of July is this week, we graduated, and we have our whole future ahead of us. What's not to be happy about?"

"That sounds like the graduation speech that you didn't get to give—our whole future ahead of us—brother!"

"Jeez, Nicole, sorry I was born. Maybe you can just take me into town and then you can go cry a river somewhere."

"I'm sorry, Sherry, it's just been bugging me so much that I can't think about much else. I can't believe the trial starts on Monday."

"C'mon, Nicole, it bugs me too, but there's nothing we can do about it that doesn't put us in danger, not to mention our families.

At first, I didn't think that it would happen, but when Steve got arrested, I started to believe it actually could."

"I know. Me too. I keep telling myself to just forget about it, but I can't. We have to do something. There has to be someone we can trust."

"Nicole, there's nothing we can do. There's no one we can trust. Let's just focus on making enough money so we can get out of this place."

"I guess, but it just doesn't feel right."

"I'm right, Nicole. We have to get out of Molalla. Now, let's just forget about it today and go have a good time. Maybe after we mess around in town for a while, we can go to the mall. I'll give you some money for gas."

Sherry talked nonstop, about anything and everything, for the rest of the way into town. Nicole just listened and shook her head every now and then, attempting to appear interested. She still was thinking about *it*. They came into Molalla on South Molalla Avenue and drove past the front of the high school. They came to the four-way stoplight in the center of town. Turning right, they passed by the White Horse.

"Nicole, check it out," she said, laughing, and pointed at the stallion.

Sherry finally succeeded in getting Nicole to laugh. They laughed every time someone *decorated* the underside of the horse, which averaged out to be three or four times a year. No one had ever been caught, and if truth be known, the owners probably liked the publicity. There was only one time that Nicole knew who did it. Christy Yoder, a girl one year ahead of her in school, blabbed about how she and some friends had done the *dirty deed*, as she called it. That was a couple of years ago, around Thanksgiving.

They drove past the White Horse, out to Francis Street, and

turned left toward the Buckaroo and the fairgrounds. They parked in front of the Zimmer place. Nicole knew they wouldn't care if they parked there. They got out of the 1980 Chevy Citation, locked the doors, and started walking the quarter-mile to the carnival.

Quite a few people were already out and about. It was a beautiful day—the kind of day that almost made up for the rain that Oregonians must suffer through for a good portion of the year.

Some things never change, and the carnival was one of those things. There were hundreds of them, all across the country, taking place on this Fourth of July holiday. This was Molalla's version. The two girls walked through the main gate. There was no admission charge because the money would be made on the rides and the games that only a few would win. There were some people walking through the park with huge stuffed animals, but they were just *plants* to make others believe that they really could win one, too.

Nicole and Sherry barely got through the gate when the first hawker challenged them to make three baskets, shooting an oversized ball into an undersized hoop.

"Only one dollar, girls, for three shots. C'mon girls, step right up."

Clyde the Glide Drexler couldn't even make a shot in one of those baskets. But that attraction always got plenty of business because the guys were always trying to impress their girls.

The next hawker challenged them to throw three plastic rings around the necks of Coke bottles placed close together. It looked easy enough—it did every year—so Sherry thought she'd give it a try. She handed him her dollar as he handed her the three rings. She flipped the first one Frisbee style, which landed in the middle of the bottles but not around any necks.

She employed the same throwing technique for the next two tosses, but without success.

"Good try, young lady, you almost got it. Give it another try for only a buck. I'll even throw in an extra ring for you cuz I want you to win! Just one more time."

They passed the throw-the-dime-in-the-dish challenge. They didn't want a cheap dish or glass ash tray anyway. The cool oil lamps, one of the other prizes, each had an invisible plastic film over the top to which no dime would ever stick.

Next was the dart throw. The challenge here was to throw three dull darts at a cork board with rows of underinflated balloons pinned to it.

Next to the dart throw was the softball toss. One dollar would give the sucker a chance to throw three softballs at six bottles. Each bottle weighed about ten pounds apiece. The contestant had to knock over all of them.

Nicole and Sherry walked by all of these, ignoring the hawkers' pleas. *Maybe later,* Nicole thought, as they continued to walk through the carnival. Neither had eaten lunch and the aromas started to entice the both of them— caramel corn, corn dogs, cotton candy, elephant ears.

Sherry exclaimed, "Wuddaya say we go get something to eat? It all smells *soooo* good!"

"I think we should go on some rides before we eat anything," Nicole said.

"I guess, but I am really hungry," Sherry said, laughing out loud. "I know why you want to wait. It was that time in the seventh grade when I puked all over your back. That's it, isn't it? Isn't it?"

Nicole started laughing too, "How can I forget that, Sherry? That was bad, and you even laughed after you did it. You're lucky you're still my friend, but don't try it twice! By the way, has anyone ever told you how annoying you are?"

They both laughed and started toward the rides. They would start off slowly with a ride on the Ferris wheel, followed by a ride on the *Deluxe Swing Chairs*, and then the *Go Gator* roller coaster.

After those three, they would be more daring. *The Pirate Ship* guaranteed an upset stomach. *The Paratrooper* got the stomach churning. And finally, the dreaded *Roc-o-Plane* would cause those with weaker stomachs to hurl.

They went for the triple-whammy. It was a good thing that Nicole had used good judgment, waiting to eat until after they went on the rides. It took a few minutes to get their legs back and their stomachs under control. They looked at each other at the same time.

"Elephant ears!" both screamed together. They raced toward the stand.

There were a lot more people now, and several of their classmates could be seen milling around in groups of two or three, or more. They would stop and talk, see what they were doing with their summer, which was usually not much. Some were working, most weren't. Some were planning to go away to college in the fall. Others seemed content to make money by logging or at one of the sawmills in the area. Some continued to work on the family farm with parents, brothers, and sisters, something they had been doing as long as they could remember.

Nicole and Sherry told everyone that they would soon be moving out of Molalla, and planned to attend UCLA. Their friends wouldn't believe them, but they insisted it was true. They didn't tell them that this UCLA was not the university in Westwood, but the community college in Salem that they referred to as the *University of Chemeketa on Lancaster Avenue*.

It was a good day, bringing back memories of a dozen or more Fourth of July celebrations that they had spent together. Nicole had forgotten all about *it*, as she and Sherry wandered through the carnival again, ignoring the hawkers, stopping here and there to visit with friends.

"Hey Sherry, Nicole…how's it goin'?"

It was Peggy Bass, the school gossip. Nicole cringed on the inside, but managed to smile on the outside, appearing to be happy.

Nicole said, "Hey, Peggy, I'm doin' all right. How about you?"

"Doin' good. I'm starting this fall at Clackamas. I hear you two are going to UCLA. That's pretty impressive."

They decided not to let her in on the joke since she always has her nose up in other people's business.

"Yup," Sherry replied, "movin' down there in September. We can't wait."

"Wow, that's cool. So what do you think about the Steve Carlson trial? You know it starts Monday, don't you?"

"Yeah, I knew it was coming up, I just wasn't sure when it was," Nicole lied, showing little interest.

"How could you not know? It's all over the news, and everyone's talking about it?"

"I don't know, Peggy, I guess I don't get around like you do. You have a gift."

"Yeah, that's what everybody says."

She didn't have a clue about what everybody really said, Nicole thought.

"So are you going to it, Peggy? I mean the trial?" Sherry asked.

"Of course—I wouldn't miss it for the world. You gonna go, Sherry?"

"Yeah, I'm goin'. So wuddaya think, Peggy? Do you think Steve did it?"

"Well of course he did it. Who else would have done it?"

"But they don't even have a body!" It was Nicole who spoke this time.

"I know that, but who else could it be? It has to be Steve. You know he beat her before, right? She kicked him out, ya know? He had to move back in with his mom. How embarrassing is that? I figure he tried to talk to her and she wouldn't have nothin' to do with him. So he killed her. You know he was in the army, right?"

Peggy wouldn't stop talking, and Nicole shifted her weight from one foot to the other. She was uncomfortable talking about it with anyone, especially Peggy the Mouth. Nicole watched people as she half-listened to Peggy, interjecting a word or two periodically.

Three girls walked by. Kim Williams was one of them. A chill crawled up Nicole's spine, even in the eighty degree heat. She had successfully avoided Kim for the rest of the school year. They had no classes together, and whenever they would cross paths in the hall, Nicole would pretend to be distracted and not notice her.

But this time, she wasn't on guard. She wasn't expecting to see her on what had been a great day up until now. Seeing her was bad enough. Making eye contact was worse. If looks could kill, Nicole would have keeled over right then and there. But it wasn't just the look. Kim raised her hand toward Nicole, as if firing a gun, then looked away and kept on walking with her friends. It was then that Nicole heard that song playing from somewhere in the distance, that song by The Police—*Every Move You Make.*

"What do you think, Nicole? You're being kinda quiet, aren't you?" Peggy asked.

"What? Quiet about what?"

"The trial—Steve Carlson, Sandi Riggs—we've been talking about it. Hello?"

"Oh, that. I just don't think about it."

Nicole noticed another friend, Jim Greer, and walked over to talk to him. She got away from Peggy, but the look in Kim's eyes and the gun gesture was imprinted on her mind. She couldn't get away from that. She had no idea what she could do about any of it, nothing really. And she knew she wouldn't sleep tonight, again.

Chapter 15

Monday morning, July 2

Monday morning rolled around. The town of Molalla was left relatively unscathed from the weekend's festivities. The Fireman's Ball was a mostly calm affair, which was a nice change from the last couple of years. Mikey and I made our presence known around town on Saturday afternoon, and in the evening, we used the divide and conquer strategy. He patrolled the center of town, which meant the White Horse. I stayed close to the fire station on North Main, where the big party was.

The outside help arrived early in the evening and patrolled the other areas around town. A fight nearly broke out a couple of times, but cooler, and more sober, heads prevailed, and peace was restored. Mikey reported that the crowd at the White Horse seemed to be a relatively peaceful bunch. Sunday was uneventful, at least from a cop's perspective, which was just fine with me.

Today looked to be interesting, unrelated to the holiday—jury selection would begin in the Steve Carlson trial. It would begin at nine o'clock at the Clackamas County Courthouse in Oregon City, down on Main Street, in the lower and older part of town.

I got to the station about seven thirty and finished up some paperwork from last week. Mikey came in at eight thirty, even though his shift didn't officially start until eleven. He was anxious, as usual, to get started.

"Mornin', Chief. Sleep well last night?"

He was his usual, chipper self, but not annoyingly so. I was beginning to really like the kid.

"Mornin', Mikey."

I had started calling him "Mikey" a few weeks ago and found out that it was a nickname that he liked.

"I slept as well as I usually do, which means I got about six hours sleep. How was your day off?"

"It was good. I went to church, and then we had a barbeque afterwards. The ladies made some really good pies, too. You should come with me sometime, Chief. I think you might like it."

"Uh, thanks, but I probably won't take you up on that one. Not that I really have anything against church, just never had much interest. It seems kind of boring to me," I said, wishing he would stop talking about it.

"Did you ever go to church growing up?"

"I went to Sunday school once in a while at the Baptist church in Puyallup, but Mom and Dad didn't go. I never got into it. I stopped going altogether when I got older."

I started feeling that Mikey was pressuring me, but really, he was just being friendly, so I didn't let it bother me. He didn't bring it up anymore anyway, after he told me that the invitation was always open. I didn't tell him, but there was one time when I started praying, and thought I might even start going to church. That was when my partner, and my best friend, Dickey Cook, got shot. I prayed for him to live, and he did, but I forgot about going to church and stopped praying too. I guess I'm probably like a lot of other folks.

"So what do we have going today? Are you going in for the jury selection?" Mike asked.

"Yeah, I'm headin' in there pretty soon. The questioning of the jurors probably won't start right away, so I'll wanna be there by nine thirty or so."

"Sounds good—do you have anything in particular you want me to do?"

"Why don't you set up out by your church and check for speeders this morning, and then hang around down by the carnival later on. Most people are working today, but there'll be plenty of kids messing around. Try to keep 'em outta trouble."

"You got it, Boss."

Mikey left the station at eight fifty to set up shop at the Baptist church, located on the outskirts of town. I finished the paperwork and left twenty minutes later.

I enjoyed the drive in on Highway 213. It's one of those drives you don't mind because of the beautiful scenery, especially for one who had been in L.A. for so many years. Mt. Hood loomed to the east in the light blue sky. And today, you could see steam rising above the crater of Mt. St. Helens, situated farther north in the Cascade mountain range. St. Helens erupted on May 18, 1980, an infamous date for those living in the Northwest. A lava dome had been forming inside the crater, oozing lava and boiling mud, rising several hundred feet from the base of the crater. I was now seeing the steam from that formation, some fifty miles away as the crow flies. It was a gorgeous day.

I arrived at the courthouse at nine thirty on the dot. I prided myself for being on time. There was no problem finding a parking spot. It would be different, however, when the actual trial started. Everybody and their brother would be on hand for the event.

I entered the courthouse on the lower level in the back of the building. The only ones allowed in this entrance were officers of the law. One lone guard stood at the entrance. He checked my credentials and then let me pass. I went up the steps to the first floor—the main floor.

A small group of people stood to the left, a dozen or so, who were waiting in line to pay their fines and tickets. To the right of that line were a kid and his fiancé—they couldn't have been much older than eighteen—standing in front of a window where they would get their marriage license.

On the wall to the right were several large and very old photographs. One featured Willamette Falls, taken before the mills were built that stood on both sides of the river. Another featured the original elevator that connected the two levels of the city. A third photo showed the bridge that spanned the Willamette River, connecting Oregon City and West Oregon City, now known as West Linn. John McLoughlin, the first governor of the Oregon Territory, had his own special place in the center of the other photos.

Farther to the right, down the corridor, was the main entrance that was used by the general public. There was a line there now. Men were taking everything out of their pockets and placing them in plastic dishes. Their brief cases and coats, and just about everything that they owned, were placed on a small conveyor belt. Women placed their purses, some as large as small suitcases, on the belt that would carry them through a scanning device. The added security was due to several acts of violence occurring across the country, courthouses and other government buildings being the target.

The two largest courtrooms, A and B, were on this floor as well. They were on the other side of the corridor, opposite the photos. I walked over to the reader board that had the day's docket posted on it. It was at the top of the list.

State of Oregon vs. Steven Lane Carlson

Courtroom A 9:00 A.M.

Judge Franklin Z. Maurer

I walked over to the doors of the courtroom and peered through the small glass windows. A deputy opened the door as I stepped back, pointing to a seat in the first of five rows. I sat down as the attorney for the defense questioned one of the potential jurors. I learned later that the defense attorney was court appointed, which surprised me some.

There were ten potential jurors in the courtroom right now, including the one being questioned. Several more were sitting in the juror room, awaiting their turn. Each potential juror had already filled out a questionnaire that asked about their background, and now they waited. Attorneys from both sides, as well as the trial judge, could question them to determine if they would be objective and fair-minded. If either attorney considered a prospective juror's views or opinions to be biased against his or her client, they could challenge their inclusion on the jury.

I had sat through a number of these proceedings while a detective in Los Angeles, including the Rodney Alcala murder trial. I didn't sit through the entire process then, nor would I today, just long enough to get a feel for how this trial might go. I listened, hardly noticing the time. Then Judge Maurer declared that there would be a lunch break and the jury selection would resume at one thirty. I had heard enough and decided to head back to Molalla.

I waved to Mikey as I drove by the speed trap he had set up. When I got back to the station at twelve thirty, I radioed him and told him to come on back. Ten minutes later, he entered through the back door.

"Well, how did things go?"

"It's moving along pretty fast, faster than I expected."

"How many jurors did the defense attorney let go?"

"That's the strange part. Except for a few jurors who said they had a strong opinion on the case, all the others survived the first cut. Fourteen were retained and three got to go home. At this rate, the jury will be selected by tomorrow. That's really fast, especially for a murder trial."

"Did Steve's attorney use up any of his strikes?"

"No, not one, and that surprised me, too. It didn't seem like he did his homework. I guess that's what you get with a court-appointed attorney."

"Court-appointed? Are you serious? If I was in Steve's shoes, I'd want the best attorney I could get. I think any attorney worth his salt would be licking his chops to get a case like this. Think of the publicity he would get."

"Yeah, you're right, but that's not the way it's looking right now. They'll have their jury by tomorrow. The judge will give the rest of the week off and start next Monday. At least that's what I think. I could be wrong. So how was your mornin'?"

"Pretty slow—I did ticket one guy that was doin' forty five well into the twenty five mile zone. That was it. He was from California, so I didn't mind giving him a ticket."

"Have you eaten anything yet?" I asked, knowing that he hadn't.

"No, been out there the whole time you were gone."

"Wuddaya say we go out to the Y? I'll buy."

"I love those two words. Let's go."

Chapter 16

Chester and Lester Williams, twins, and the eldest of eight siblings, were always expected to set the example of a good work ethic to the younger kids. There were six of them— four brothers and two sisters. They had grown up in Molalla on the family farm south of town, up in the Wilhoit area. It wasn't a large farm, not by any means. They had a few dairy cattle that supplied their large family with all the milk, cream, and butter that they would need. There were always some beef cattle that they would butcher as often as they would need to. With six hungry boys in the family, plus their cousin Billy, who was in their home more often than not, they went through a lot of meat.

They stayed out of trouble, for the most part, while growing up. They drank a little, and if they could find a girl or two to drink with them, well, that would be even better. They both played on the football team, though it was unusual that their father allowed them the time. Chores were always more important than some foolish game. Yet for some unknown reason, he let them play football, and football only. That was the extent of their extra-curricular activities and, even though they complained about their circumstances, they knew they were lucky to even be playing football.

Neither of the twins graduated from high school. It was the summer of their junior year that their dad, George Williams, Jr., keeled over and died, just like his dad, and his grandfather before him. George Jr. was out in one of the fields working on a fence when his time was up. He was only fifty two years old. Apparently, bad hearts were common in the Williams family. With his passing, it meant that Chester and Lester would now be running the farm.

That was it as far as school was concerned. They dropped out, continued to work the farm, and helped their mom raise the younger kids. Mrs. Williams wasn't much help after George Jr. died, though. She never seemed to get past it and move on, so the responsibility fell on Lester and Chester. Even though they lived through the Great Depression, the Williams family always had enough to eat and enough clothes to wear.

Both met girls on the same day, the Fourth of July, 1932, at the Buckaroo, and both brothers got married on the same day, November 23, of the same year. It was a double-ring affair at the little white church called Smyrna, and friends and family from all over the county crowded into the small sanctuary with hard, wooden pews. Some had to watch from outside the doors because there was no more room.

The brothers did everything together, and that didn't stop after they got married. Both couples lived on the family farm along with their siblings. It was one, big happy family, at least that's the way it appeared to those on the outside. Over the years, Chester and Lester became the patriarchs of the large family, none of whom ever moved out of the area.

They both served, at various times, on the city council, and also on the district school board. Lester even ran for mayor just after the war was over, but somehow lost to a veteran who had just come home from Germany.

Chester and his wife had four kids, and not surprisingly, so did Lester and his wife—two boys and two girls for each of them. Over the years, the Williams family bought up a lot of land, to the point where they owned a good portion of Molalla.

In 1962, when they turned fifty, they bought the bus company that served the Molalla School District. Nobody really knew why they did it, but folks were happy about it. The two brothers seemed happy as clams about the purchase of the business. It wasn't a money-maker, but they didn't really need the money anyway. The family, with Chester and Lester as the double head, had become a rags-to-riches story. There were many theories as to the source of the riches, but no one really knew.

The people of Molalla loved the twins. *Grandpa and Grandpa* and *two of the sweetest men you'll ever know* were titles that many used in reference to them. The twins lost their wives to cancer in the same month—May—and the same year—1979. The townspeople grieved with them.

But there were things about the large family that were not known by most people. It was true that several generations of the Williams men had suffered from bad hearts. Chester and Lester had bad hearts as well, although it wasn't the organ that pumped blood through their arteries that was bad. Their bad hearts were of a sinister nature, dark and cold—bad hearts that drove the family to a darkness that few would have believed.

The black phone with the rotary dial rang three times before it was picked up. It was still a couple of hours before the sun would sink below the horizon and, even then, it wouldn't be dark yet. But in this house, all the shades were drawn, with a single light on in the kitchen. In his younger years, Chester would have picked up the phone almost before it rang, but now, in his early seventies, it took him a little longer. He was expecting the call from his twin brother, Lester.

"Hello?" Chester answered quietly, even though there was no one in the house who would hear him. It had been five years since his wife, Tillie, had passed.

"It's Lester."

"How'd it go?"

"Perfect, just as planned."

"That's good. When will the jury be complete?"

"Maybe tomorrow—for sure by Thursday, with Wednesday being the Fourth and all. It's a done deal."

"Good. That's really good. So everything's going according to plan?"

"That's what I said. It's gonna be fine. Bingo, bango, bongo, as the Shonz would say."

Both brothers had been Trailblazer fans since the beginning of the franchise in 1970, and play-by-play announcer Bill Schonely's phrases were a regular part of their speech.

"Rip City! But what about that girl—she keepin' her mouth shut?"

"The Parker girl? No problem—she's scared. Kim's keeping track of her—saw her at the carnival the other day. Better yet, the girl saw Kim. That girl's sharp, just like her old man. She said the girl was freaked out. Don't worry, she won't say nothin'. Look, I gotta go now—headin' over to Paul's place to discuss events."

"You sure things are okay?"

Chester had always been the worrier of the two. He worried plenty for both of them.

"I'm tellin' ya, Chester, it's all going fine."

"But what about..."

The line went dead. And Chester had a bad feeling, despite his brother's assurances.

Chapter 17

Wednesday, July 4

The Fourth of July turned out to be another warm and cloudless day. The locals couldn't remember better weather for the Independence Day celebrations. The festivities began with the all-you-can-eat pancake breakfast at the Methodist Church, on the east side of town.

The parade started at ten, or close to it, anyway. The route began two blocks south of the high school on East Heintz Street. From there, it took a jog left for a block, then turned west again on Robbins Street. At the intersection by the local grocery store, the parade would turn north onto Molalla Avenue and then left on Toliver, a few blocks later.

Three-quarters of a mile later, the route turned south on Ridings by the Smith house. There was always a crowd that watched the parade in front of their house.

The route continued to West Main and turned east toward the center of town. This was the longest stretch without any turns, ending at the high school baseball field out on East Main. The entire route was just over three miles in length.

Horses and their riders, members of the Molalla Saddle Club, were always at the head of the parade, proudly bearing the American flag, with the Oregon state flag next in line. The spectators on both sides of the street stood—the men removed their cowboy hats and baseball caps as the flags went by. Veterans from the local VFW marched behind the flag bearers, proudly saluting the flag that they had fought to defend.

The Buckaroo Court came next, led by Queen Robin Gorbett, who was riding a chestnut quarter horse, which the horse-lovers adored. Princess Sheila and Princess Connie flanked her on either side.

There were clowns on crazy-looking cycles with any number of wheels, some on the pavement, others sticking out at all angles from the frame. The clowns threw candy and balloons, and the children would scramble to pick up all they could.

The Molalla High marching band played Queen's *Fat Bottomed Girls* and *We Will Rock You* and several other favorites. And of course, the Molalla High fight song was played several times along the route.

Grave's Logging Company had one of their trucks carrying a log so large that one was all the truck could carry. The log was over nine feet in diameter, and over thirty feet long. The mills in the town, Publishers, Brazier, and Avison, also proudly displayed their products on large flatbeds.

Lots of little kids threw candy from floats—decorated trailers pulled by tractors—that represented area churches. Cute little girls twirling—and frequently dropping—their batons, followed after the floats.

The last entries in the parade were always the emergency vehicles—police cars, gleaming red fire trucks, ambulances—all with their lights flashing. An occasional blast from the sirens came from the various vehicles, much to the delight of the crowd.

Mike Benson was driving the police car, an '83 Chevy Impala that had just come to the department the previous September, and Chief Frank Thomas was driving his favorite, the '84 Chevy Blazer, black with crazy rims and a souped-up 350 cubic inch engine. It's doubtful that the chief of police in L.A. had a ride like that!

The parade was a grand time for young and old alike. Families gathered along the route, some standing, and others, sitting in their lawn chairs. Mike had been to every one of the parades while growing up in Molalla, but this was the first one that he'd actually been in. He turned left onto Toliver and thought about what should have been his first speeding ticket...

He was in his first car, a bright, cherry-red, '72 Chevelle. It had a 350 cubic inch engine with an Edelbrock Performer 4-barrel carb, four-speed with a competition clutch, headers, and wide tires with mag wheels. It had locks on the front corners of the raised hood—the Edelbrock was a hot item.

He was eighteen and, like most guys, he liked to drive fast. Mike decided it was a good time to drive fast. Sammy Hagar's new song, I Can't Drive 55, was blaring on the radio and it just felt right.

He turned left on Toliver Road, stomped on the accelerator, and by the time he passed the old Yoder place, he was up to seventy five. The speed limit was twenty five. He passed the Christmas trees that were just tall enough to hide the cop car from speeders coming from either direction. The cop pulled out from his hiding place, lights flashing and siren blaring. That's when Mike saw him in his rear view mirror—a big black and white with a cherry on top. He coasted all the way to Leroy Street and pulled in front of the house where Mr. Fox lived, his high school football coach.

The cop pulled in right behind him. He got out and walked toward the open window of the Chevelle. Mike fully expected the worst—a mega-ticket, suspended license—he might even get thrown in the city joint, as Sammy had just sung.

> Go on & write me up for 125
> Post my face, wanted dead or alive
> Take my license n' all that jive
> I can't drive 55! Oh No! Uh!

Mike turned off the radio as the cop got to the window. What could he say? He knew it would be bad.

"May I see your license?"

Mike already had it out of his wallet and handed it to the officer without saying a word. "Davenport" it said on his nameplate. After a few seconds that seemed like minutes, Officer Davenport spoke.

"Benson, huh? You any relation to Warren?"

At that point, Mike had to make a quick decision—to lie or not to lie. Warren was his older brother. Was that a good thing or a bad thing in Officer Davenport's eyes? He took a chance.

"Yeah, he's my brother."

A drop of sweat tracked down his nose and dropped off the end.

"Really," he said, "How's Warren doin' nowadays?"

He wanted to make small talk? Now? Really?

"Uh, he's doin' good."

Another drop took the same path to the end of his nose and plopped on his already drenched tee shirt.

"Good. Glad to hear it. We worked together at Avison. Where's he livin' nowadays?"

Sweat streamed down Mike's face now—no longer a single track— much to the delight of Officer Davenport.

"He's up in Clarkes, just east of the Four Corners."

"Where's he workin' now?"

Did Davenport really like his brother? It seemed like he did. He prayed that he did.

"He works for Pioneer Title Company in Milwaukie."

"Well that's good to hear. I really liked Warren. Glad he got out of that mill."

Thank God, Mike thought, and it really was a thank you, not a "taking God's name in vain" kind of "thank God".

"You know, you were going kinda fast back there.

Mike acknowledged that yes, he did know that. Judgment was nigh.

"Slow it down. Are you hearing me?"

"Yessir. I'll slow it down."

"And next time you see your brother, tell him Willy gave you a break."

He turned and walked back to his car—no city joint, no ticket, no written warning. Just, slow it down.

"I will," he said weakly, not even sure that Willy heard him.

He felt like he had just been through daily doubles in August. He was wiped out, and he knew that he would owe his brother for life.

Mike snapped back to the present and slowed to a stop as the parade stalled, again. He was on the same stretch of road where Officer Davenport had hidden. But now it was Mike driving the police car. No one would ever have believed that. Life's funny sometimes.

Even funnier than being a police officer was the fact that Mike was now a Christian, too. His old high school buddies were amazed and couldn't understand why he didn't go out and get drunk with them anymore. "Ol' Mike got religion," they would say sadly when they thought back on their partying days. A lot had changed since then.

They were only about a third of the way through the parade route. Mike's thoughts turned to the Steve Carlson trial. As the months passed since Sandi Riggs' disappearance, he was feeling more and more that something wasn't right. Steve didn't seem like the type who would do something like this. Maybe he was just getting his first hunches as a cop, but it didn't feel right.

The Fourth of July holiday had been a nice diversion for many of the town folk, for Chief Thomas, and for Mike, too. But tomorrow—Thursday—jury selection would be wrapping up and the trial would most likely start on Monday. He decided that he would talk to the chief about his hunches. Yeah, he'd talk to him, maybe tomorrow.

For today, he'd forget about it as much as possible. He would enjoy the rest of the day, which would end for most people with the fireworks display around ten thirty that night. It wouldn't end for everyone, though. The White Horse would still be open into the wee hours. After all, it was Molalla on the Fourth. The parade started moving again.

Chapter 18

Nicole and Sherry sat in the car waiting for the first of the fireworks show. There was a great place, just east of town with a little elevation, where they could see, not only the fireworks in Molalla, but the ones in Canby and Gladstone too.

They had been together the whole day, beginning with the parade, followed by the barbeque at the Christian Church. They went to the matinee performance of the Buckaroo, and then they drove to the Y to get something else to eat, as if they needed any more. After that, they went to the carnival, bought some cotton candy and split it, and then walked around for a few hours, mostly talking with friends. They bought a couple of elephant ears and Cokes to take with them. They drove to the vantage point where a few other cars were already parked.

It was a good day for Nicole because she was able to forget, for a little while anyway. But as she sat in the car, nibbling on the elephant ear and sipping her Coke, her mind once again went back to it. She hadn't slept well ever since she saw Kim Williams at the carnival four days ago.

It was during those sleepless nights that she decided to do something about it. She wasn't sure quite what that plan was, but she couldn't just do nothing. She decided it would be best to leave Sherry out of it. For one, Sherry had a big mouth and, secondly, Sherry had a really big mouth.

Who would it be safe to tell? How would she tell her story? How could she tell anyone without the wrong people finding out? And what did she know, really? A little girl had said seemingly innocent things. But then came the warning from the girl's mother. And then there was Kim Williams and what she had said about the murder, and, of course, the threats.

Steve Carlson was being framed for murder and the Williams family was right in the middle of it. Was Sandi Riggs' body really under a slab of concrete at the Williams' place? Nicole knew that Paul's dad and uncle ran the bus service for the school district, a couple of sweet old men. Everybody loved them.

"Hey, wuddaya bein' so quiet about?"

Sherry startled her out of her thoughts.

"Nothin' really," Nicole lied. "I'm just thinking about being out of high school and wonderin' what it's going to be like. It's kinda scary."

That much was true. It was kind of scary. She didn't have to lie about that.

"Yeah, I know what you mean. We've been in school seems like forever and living at home with our parents and our families. But don't forget that we couldn't wait to graduate, and now we have. It's gonna be cool."

The first firework exploded in front of them a few miles away, and before the sparks faded away, two more went off. Nicole turned down the radio so they could hear the explosions that came several seconds later. They sat in silence, taking in the sights, lights, and sounds. It was sometime during the grand finale that a plan started to form in Nicole's mind.

Chapter 19

Monday, July 9, 1985
Day 1 of the Trial

The Fourth of July celebrations were over and Molalla was back to normal. Not really normal though—the trial was starting this morning in Oregon City and I planned to be there. Jury selection had finished up last Thursday. Both attorneys would be making their opening statements this morning. I sat in Courtroom A on the hard brown benches that I felt could really use some padding. Some might say, though, that I had enough padding on the back-side, but still, these benches were really hard!

I arrived at eight, wanting to get a good seat, close to the front where I could see the defendant's face, at least from the side. I also wanted to see the jury without my head having to do a three-sixty, like Linda Blair's did in *The Exorcist.*

By eight fifty, the courtroom was full. No more spectators would be allowed inside. I looked around and saw many faces that I recognized, even if I didn't know all their names. If I had to guess, most of the locals were there in support of Steve Carlson, but it would be the jury that would either convict him or set him free. At precisely nine o'clock, the county clerk stood at the front.

"All rise for the Honorable Judge, Franklin Z. Maurer," he said with a strong voice.

Everyone rose to their feet. The judge entered and told us all to be seated before I made it all the way up. I sat back down on the hard bench.

The jury then entered—every eye was on them. If all the questions that were being thought in those moments could be heard with the ear, there would be a deafening cacophony roaring throughout the courtroom—who's the leader? Who'd be the bleeding heart that wouldn't be able to cast a guilty vote without pressure from her peers? Whose eyes were steely and hard, a guilty vote already forming in his mind? Who would be a surprise—maybe to the prosecution, maybe to the defense, or maybe to both? Those questions would be answered in the days ahead, and a man's fate would be determined.

The judge pounded his gavel and spoke with a firm voice, "The People may proceed with their opening statement."

Eric Holton, Deputy District Attorney, stood up wearing a dark gray, three-piece suit, white shirt, and a multicolored tie that went well with the rest of his attire. He approached the podium which was placed between the prosecutor's table and the defense table. He would address the jury from there. He paused for a moment, and began.

"Thank you, Judge Maurer." He then looked at the twelve men and women seated in the jury box, and said, "Good morning, ladies and gentlemen of the jury, Your Honor, defense counsel," making eye contact as he spoke to the different parties.

Holton began his statement, and the show was on.

"Sandi Marie Riggs had her whole life in front of her. She

enjoyed life in a small town like Molalla where she could work hard, and play hard, and have a lot of friends. Sandi would have loved to be a part of this year's Fourth of July celebrations—the Buckaroo, the parade, the pancake breakfast, the Fireman's Ball, and the fireworks that lit up the sky and the accompanying *ka-booms* that echoed through the night air.

But it didn't happen this year, not for Sandi. Why? Because it was on January 22, a little over five months ago, that Sandi Riggs was brutally murdered on that cold winter night."

"It was a typical January day in Molalla. Parents went to work. Children went to school. Sandi drove the school bus, making sure that those children got to school, and back, safely. That night was no different for the children, who arrived safely at their homes. But Sandi would not arrive home safely, not on that night. After the activity bus run, she drove to the bus garage on the north side of the school building where her former boyfriend, Steve Carlson, waited inside."

The jury and the rest of us in the courtroom were hanging on his every word. I glanced toward Steve, who watched the prosecutor with sad, but intense, eyes. At least to me, they looked sad.

Mr. Holton continued.

"Mr. Carlson had been waiting for Wes Strohmeier to leave the bus garage that afternoon. Wes is the mechanic for the school district. When Mr. Strohmeier left that day, around five o'clock, Steve Carlson entered through the side door that had been left open. He waited in the darkness. At approximately six o'clock, Sandi Riggs arrived at the garage, opened that large door, and pulled the bus into the darkness. She exited the bus and went to the large door and closed it. She turned and saw something move, maybe thinking that some rodent or other small animal was trapped inside. That wouldn't be the case. The only one left alive that knows what was said at that moment is sitting right over there." He turned and pointed his index finger at Steve. "Or maybe nothing was said. Only *he* knows."

"Here was a star-crossed lover, scorned, rejected by the girl of his dreams. He tried to hold it together. He tried to get over her. But months went by since their break-up, and it didn't get any better. In fact, it got worse. It got so bad that on that afternoon, Steve Carlson took his .44 Magnum from the gun safe in his mother's home, along with six rounds of ammunition. This brutal act was not the result of a blind rage. It was a cold and calculated act. How do we know it was well-planned? Sandi Riggs' body was somehow disposed of without ever being found, to this day. That takes planning. Most murderers attempt to get rid of the murder weapon, but not Steve Carlson. No! Steve Carlson disposed of her body. How? No one knows. That secret is locked in his mind and his only."

"In the coming days, the prosecution will prove, beyond a shadow of doubt, that Steven Lane Carlson planned, and committed, the bloody, gruesome demise of Sandi Riggs. He disposed of her body. No closure for her loved ones. The prosecution will provide overwhelming evidence, facts, to prove Steve Carlson's guilt. At the end of these proceedings we will ask you to return a guilty verdict based on the evidence. We ask you to find this defendant guilty of a murder, a murder of passion."

Eric Holton nodded his acknowledgement to the jury, then to the judge, and finally, to the defense, as he returned to the prosecutor's table. It was quite a performance. He had the "audience" eating out of the palm of his hand. If the trial ended here and now, Steve Carlson would be convicted of first-degree murder, even without the victim's body.

I looked at Steve at times during the opening statement, and now again at its conclusion. He remained stoic, yet somehow, I again sensed a pained sadness. Was it guilt? Was it that Sandi was gone forever as a result of his rage? I wondered, *what was going through his mind?*

Chapter 20

He listened as the thirty-something, young-buck attorney made his opening statement of his trial. Even after all these months, it still seemed impossible to him that he was accused of Sandi's murder. And after listening to this guy, he almost believed that he, in fact, was guilty—almost.

What had gone so wrong? Did he have a break with reality that caused him to snap? *No way!* he screamed silently inside his own head, just as he had several times in the past five months. He thought to himself that if he had snapped, he would at least know where her body was. *Wouldn't he?* Of course, he would. In the space of a few seconds, he once again asked himself, his lips silently forming the words, *What went wrong?*

Steve's mind went back to that afternoon, the last time he was with Sandi—he could see her, hear her, feel her, smell the perfume she wore that day. He told her, over and over, that he was so sorry, that he wanted to help her, not to hurt her. And she had forgiven him. He had renewed hope. But now all that was left was profound sadness and confusion.

That day in January would be a new beginning, or so he thought. Up at the river, at the house that seemed like their house once again, Sandi asked him to help her. She was afraid— more than afraid—she was scared to death. He vowed that he would let nothing happen to her, that they would leave together. He told her that they would start a new life together.

But that seemed an eternity ago. "Together" now seemed a cruel word, one with no hope attached. Sandi was gone before the plan could be put into place. And here he was, accused of her murder, being tried by a jury of his peers, just like all the trial novels said.

His attorney, Bill Baker, was about to give his opening statement. Would his statement be as persuasive as the prosecution's? He hoped so, but even then, the evidence against him seemed insurmountable. He was set up for this and saw no way out. His life was over.

While he was in jail, he decided he would start praying—it couldn't hurt. But none of his prayers were ever answered. He doubted more than ever that there was a god, or even some higher power. If there was such a being, he must not be powerful enough to do much of anything. He thought of Beirut and his friends who died that day at the hands of terrorists, claiming it was for Allah, their god.

Steve thought of the starvation, disease, and death in the world. Why would a loving god, if there was such a thing, let a little child die of cancer? Why would a loving god let Sandi be murdered? No, there was no god, he had decided. His mind was flooded with memories, stirring up intense emotions, when his thoughts came back to the present.

Chapter 21

"**Mr. Baker, the** defense has no obligation to make an opening statement. Do you wish to make one at this time?" Judge Maurer asked.

"Yes, I do, Your Honor. Thank you."

"You may proceed."

"Thank you, Your Honor. Good morning, ladies and gentlemen."

He approached the podium.

"I have to confess that I'm just a little nervous. Yes, this is a big trial. A man's life is on the line. There are a lot of people here, but the only audience that matters are you twelve jurors. You hold Steve Carlson's fate in your hands. And I'm nervous because it's my job to defend my client from the allegations directed at him. The prosecution believes that these allegations are true, and that they will be able to prove them."

I settled in to my uncomfortable pew, wondering what the game plan would be for the defense. Attorney Bill Baker seemed to be off to a good start, and his humility seemed to move the jury in a good way, judging by their facial expressions and body language. But Mr. Baker would have to be really good, not only in his opening statement, but in the entire defense of his client. You could hear a pin drop in the courtroom.

"This is a case about a good man. He grew up in Molalla, delivering newspapers there when he was twelve. Some of you may have been his customers. He went to the grade school and graduated from the high school, where he was an okay student and a better-than-average athlete. He stayed out of trouble—kept his nose clean.

After graduation, he worked at a sawmill for a few years, and then joined the Marines. He knows hard times. He was in Beirut when the Marine barracks were attacked, and it was only by fate that he survived. He came home after an honorable discharge, and has been working hard at Brazier Forest Products ever since. His work ethic is impeccable, as is his attendance—he doesn't miss work. Steve Carlson is a good man and a hard-working man. Any one of you would be proud to have him as your own son."

"The facts will show, ladies and gentlemen, that Mr. Carlson is being prosecuted for a crime that they say was committed while he was at work. Now that's something. I've always wished that I could be in several places at the same time. And if you believe the prosecution, that's exactly what Steve Carlson has learned to do. I see the defendant sitting right over there, and I'm wondering where else he might be right now—maybe at the beach, maybe he's hiking Silver Creek Falls, maybe he's fishing for salmon on the Columbia—he must be a real magician. The prosecution believes he is."

A few members of the jury chuckled at this, along with several of the people in the courtroom, including myself. It seemed that Mr. Baker was up to the challenge of defending his client. He knew how to play the audience, pausing just long enough to let his words sink into our minds, especially the minds of the men and women sitting in the jury box.

"And speaking of magic tricks, how about the *disappearing body* trick? It is true. There is not a body. The prosecution is asking you to believe that Mr. Carlson brutally murdered a person who mysteriously disappeared after the attack. Was she put into a magic box with Steve waving his wand over it and, *abracadabra*, it's gone? No one saw anything. No one heard anything—just *poof*, and the body is gone. He must be a master magician."

"Just one more trick, ladies and gentlemen, and this may be the most impressive trick of all. Sandi Riggs was allegedly murdered sometime Tuesday evening, January 22. And between the time of the alleged murder and the time when Steve Carlson was arrested the following Saturday, he behaved as he always did—dependable, helpful, considerate. He worked hard and long at the mill. He found time to help his mother, too. He did some maintenance around the house, split wood, and filled the wood box. And nobody, not even his mother, saw any change in his behavior, nor did his fellow employees, or his foreman. No one saw any change of behavior. Not even a magician of Steve Carlson's caliber could pull that off."

"The truth is, ladies and gentlemen, we do not know what happened that night. We do know there was a lot of blood on the gravel floor in the bus garage on Wednesday morning, January 23. And yes, it was determined to be human blood. But whose is it? The prosecution assumes it belonged to Sandi Riggs, but in my experience, when I assume something...well, you know the saying."

Chuckles were heard throughout the courtroom.

"We do know that there was a crime committed, and it is assumed that it was the defendant who murdered Sandi Riggs. Assumptions—ladies and gentlemen—that's all the prosecution has is assumptions. The accused has been locked up at the county jail for over five months, all based on these assumptions. A man's future is at stake. His life is in jeopardy. Steve Carlson deserves better. He is being prosecuted for a crime that is based on nothing but assumptions, including the identity of the missing body of the assumed victim. I hope, ladies and gentlemen, that you will listen to the evidence, or lack thereof, and do the right thing. End this man's nightmare. Thank you very much."

Bill Baker nodded his head to the jury and then to the judge as he walked confidently back to the defendant's table. There was an immediate and growing buzz generating throughout the courtroom.

Judge Maurer struck his gavel a couple times and ordered the people to settle down. He didn't seem too upset about the disturbance—it had been quite a performance by both attorneys—but if I'm the judge, I say round one goes to the defense. He hit his gavel one more time for good measure, and then announced that there would be a recess and that proceedings would resume at one thirty.

"Mr. Holton, will you be presenting the state's case?"

"Yes, I will, Your Honor."

He didn't seem quite as confident as he had after delivering his opening statement, certainly not as smug.

"Are you ready to present your case and bring forth witnesses at that time?"

"Yes sir, I am."

"Very well. Court is adjourned until one thirty."

I stood and looked over at Steve. There was no discernible expression on his face. But there was something in his eyes. Did the jury see that too? He certainly didn't look like a cold-blooded killer to me, and I've seen a few in my time.

I stood, slowly. It took a little bit to get moving again after sitting for a while. I moved slowly toward the exit, planning to go back to Molalla for an hour or so to see how things were there. Maybe Mikey had nabbed a few speeders. I'd make sure to be back in time to get a good seat though. It was too good to miss. I might even be called to testify, although the district attorney had not talked to me about it. The sun was shining bright outside the courthouse as I walked to my cruiser.

Chapter 22

Steve exited the courthouse through the same door he had entered. They would take him back to the jail and to his own cell since it was just a few minutes away. As the patrol car left the parking lot, Steve saw the chief of police, Chief Thomas, walking toward his cruiser. Was he friend or foe? Steve didn't know. Was there anyone he could trust? The only one who came to his mind was his own mother, but no one else. And what really happened? He wanted to know more than anybody. He thought that his lawyer had a good opening statement, but would he be able to convince this jury that he was innocent, or at the least, that there was reasonable doubt of his guilt?

The ride back to the jail was short and uneventful. The automatic gate slid open as Officer Smith proceeded through it and to the back entrance of the jail, where three guards awaited his arrival. Most of the inmates were in their cells, some sleeping, some reading, or just talking until it was time for lunch. Several called out to him as he walked past the cells.

"Hey Steve, how'd it go?" or, "Steve, I'm pullin' for ya, man."

Even the guards treated him well. They didn't do that to many of their *clients*.

All the support was nice, but the fact was, none of it mattered. Only the jury mattered. He knew he was innocent, but would they see through the drummed-up evidence? He didn't feel good about it.

They passed through B block. He shuffled to his cell in C block. C14 was open and he walked in. One of the deputies entered with him to remove the shackles while two other deputies watched.

"We'll be back for you around twelve forty-five. Get somethin' to eat."

"Sure, thanks," he said, somewhat sarcastically. He had no interest in food even though he hadn't eaten anything since breakfast.

He lay down on his bunk and closed his eyes, ignoring the oppressive heat and the constant noise from the inmates.

Chapter 23

Chester Williams sat in the back seat of his nephew's Pontiac Le Mans. They were parked in the Napa Auto Parts parking lot a few blocks from the courthouse. His brother Lester sat in the passenger seat while they waited for Paul to come. The windows were rolled down, letting a warm breeze flow through the car. The vinyl seats were blistering hot, matching Chester's mood.

"What the hell happened in there? That lawyer made Eric sound like a fool! I thought this was going to be a slam dunk. Tell me what happened in there!"

Paul got into the car and looked back at his uncle, hissing at him, "Would you just shut up? I could hear you all the way down the street. What are your shorts all up in a wad about, anyway? It was just the opening arguments."

Paul started the car and backed out of the spot and turned on to Main Street, turned left on 15th Street, and then right again onto McLoughlin, driving toward Gladstone. They rolled up the windows as the AC started to cool the car down and, at the same time, Chester started cooling down some too.

"It's just that the defense lawyer, what's his name?"

"Baker," Lester and Paul answered in unison.

"Yeah, Baker—he had the jury eating out of his hand. What's going to happen when the arguments start?"

Lester spoke, "Chester, how many times do I have to tell ya? It's all under control. Frank knows what he's doing, and Ted will take care of the jury. Eric will come through, too. But if you keep opening your big trap when we're sittin' in a car with the windows down, it won't be under control. Just calm down, you old fool."

Sometimes Lester just wanted to slap his twin brother.

Paul turned into the Burgerville parking lot. Maybe, he thought, a Tillamook cheeseburger and a fresh strawberry shake might calm his dad and uncle down. The last thing he wanted was the two of them to start throwing punches, although the thought did bring a smile to his face. They had always been like this according to the stories that he heard growing up. Grandma used to say they were holding each other's necks when they came out. He thought she was joking at the time, but the older they got, the more Paul thought that maybe she wasn't joking!

Paul reasoned with them, "Listen, we can't talk about it in there, or anywhere in public. Just believe me, things will go our way. You two just need to be the sad employers of the victim. Right? The rest is taken care of."

The three of them got out of the car and walked to the counter where the young girl took their order. She smiled broadly at Chester and Lester, with a twinkle in her eye, as if she were thinking that they were just about the cutest little old men she had ever seen. The twins had that effect on most everyone. They should have been actors.

Chapter 24

I stopped at the Big Burger on the west side of town. Big Burger has a great cheeseburger and thick shakes. It would be another month before the blackberries were ripe, so I got a fresh strawberry shake to go with the cheeseburger. I sipped hard on the thick shake as I drove back to the station, saving the cheeseburger until I got there. Mikey was there eating his sack lunch that he had packed that morning.

"Thanks for thinking of me, Chief. I appreciate your thoughtfulness," Mike said sarcastically.

"Sure. No problem, Mikey. I haven't eaten the burger yet but the milkshake is great."

"I'm sure it is. So, on to other things—how'd it go this morning? Anything exciting happen? Did they produce the body? Did Steve confess?"

"No, no, and no. It was just opening statements for both the prosecution and the defense. Both speeches were well done and well-rehearsed. The prosecutor, a kid by the name of Eric Holton, went first, and I think the jury would have convicted Steve then and there if they had had the chance."

"Wow. How did Steve react?"

"I watched Steve and the jury, going back and forth from one to the other. Every one of the jurors hung on the prosecutor's words. But Steve...uh, well, he didn't so much as blink an eye, no emotion, except..."

"Except what?"

"Except that I'm pretty sure I saw sadness—maybe it was regret. At least it wasn't the look that you'd expect to see from a cold-blooded killer."

"So maybe he's feeling remorse over what he did. Maybe he actually has a conscience."

"Could be. I guess we'll see, won't we."

I finished eating my cheeseburger and slurped the last of my shake, at the same time Mikey finished off his PB&J.

"Do you think you'll be called as a witness?"

"Wouldn't surprise me. I received a subpoena, but that doesn't necessarily mean they'll call me. If they do, it's probably just about going to the bus garage that morning, and what I saw there. I'm okay with it if they do or if they don't call me. Anyway, I need to get some of this paperwork done before I head back."

"Then I won't bug you anymore. I think I'll go take a drive through town and set up somewhere. I'll see you later, Chief."

"See ya, Mikey...hey, hold on a second."

Mikey turned to look as I reached into my back pocket to get my wallet.

"Here's a five. Go get yourself something at Big Burger. It's on me."

"Gee. Thanks, Chief," he said with a broad grin. "See ya."

I worked at my desk for a half hour or so and then decided to get back. I locked the station and drove the thirty minutes to the courthouse. I again found parking in the back, and went through the same routine, entering the building, as I had in the morning.

The courtroom was again filling up, so I found the best seat I could. I made a weak effort to stand up all the way when the judge entered at one thirty-two. The jury came into the courtroom and was herded into the jury box. Then Steve entered, escorted by an officer of the court, once again in shackles.

The prosecuting attorney, Mr. Holton, was up to bat, so to speak. He would now be calling witnesses to testify for the state. He would also introduce physical evidence that he hoped would prove his case against Steve Carlson. The defense attorney, Bill Baker, would have his opportunity to cross-examine each witness and challenge any evidence that was presented. I thought about the many times that I'd sat through these things, hundreds of times, over the course of my career. And you never know which way it's going to go.

Judge Maurer, in his baritone voice, spoke firmly and loudly.

"Before Mr. Holton calls his first witness, I would like all of you who have been subpoenaed as witnesses, to please stand for the administering of the oath. You will all stand together and answer together. This is as binding as it would be if you were to each do this individually. Please rise."

I stood, the others did too. The county clerk spoke so fast that you could hardly understand him.

"Do you solemnly swear that the testimony you are about to give in the case pending before this court will be the truth, the whole truth, and nothing but the truth, so help you God?"

We answered in unison, "I do."

"Are you ready to present your case, Mr. Holton?"

"Yes, Your Honor, the prosecution is ready." It sounded as if Mr. Holton had his swagger back again. You could hear it in his voice and his body language exuded confidence.

The judge was ready. It was show time, and that meant

publicity. And most judges loved to be in the spotlight. Judge Maurer was no exception.

Before the witness could be called, Mr. Baker stood up and announced, "Your Honor, I am requesting that 'the Rule' be invoked."

I expected that this might happen. Either attorney can request this at any time during a trial, but it usually occurs before the first witness testifies. Judge Maurer responded.

"I ask that all witnesses who have been subpoenaed to please stand once more."

We stood.

"'The Rule' requires that all witnesses are to leave the courtroom, except for the defendant, if he indeed does testify in this case. You are to remain outside the hearing of any of the proceedings, and you are not to discuss your testimony with anyone, except for the attorneys involved with this case. If you fail to comply with the court's instructions, you may be held in contempt of court, fined, and/or become unable to testify. Do you understand these instructions?"

We all answered yes in unison and began filing out the back of the courtroom. I was hoping that I wouldn't miss any of the testimonies, but it wouldn't happen this time. With any luck, I would be one of the first witnesses called, and then be allowed to hear the rest of the testimonies. One of the deputies led us out and down the corridor to another room. We followed him inside.

"This room has been reserved for you. There is coffee, hot water for tea, soft drinks, and ice water. You don't have to stay in here, but I can assure you that you will be most comfortable here. If you do leave this room to use the restroom or whatever, do not leave the courthouse. You need to be available as soon as you're called. Any questions?"

"Yes, I have one." Robert Payne, the principal of Molalla High School asked, "After testifying will we be allowed to stay in the courtroom?"

"That generally is the procedure, although I can't guarantee it. That's the judge's call. Most likely, though, you'll be able to. Are there any other questions?" There were none. "I'll be here if you need anything."

The door opened, and another deputy entered the room.

"Mr. Wesley Strohmeier, you are called as the first witness. Please come with me."

Wes put down the glass of ice water that he was holding, wiped his mouth with the back of his sleeve, and walked out the door. It made sense that he would be the first witness since he was the one who discovered the body—no, there was no body. He discovered the blood.

Eric Holton would ask him general questions to establish his relationship with Sandi Riggs, the assumed victim. He would establish a timeline, from the few hours before the crime to the next morning, when Wes arrived at work at the bus garage. Holton would attempt to put it in the jurors' minds that Sandi was, indeed, the victim.

"So, Chief, how have things been going in town? Was it an eventful Fourth?" Robert Payne came over with two cans of Coke. "Have a Coke and a smile, Chief," and handed me one of the cans.

"Thanks, Mean Joe, I mean Robert." I popped the tab and drank the ice-cold drink. "That hits the spot. I always have preferred Coke to Pepsi."

I answered his original question. "This Fourth was probably the least eventful since I've been here, at least from a cop's perspective."

"How long have you been here now, two or three years?"

"Comin' up on two years now," I said, nodding my head.

The small talk continued for another ten or fifteen minutes. I asked him how things were at the school without saying anything about the proverbial elephant in the room. I asked about the coming football season.

He laughed and said, "Well, we're going to be pretty small, but we sure are slow! It looks to be another typical football season for Molalla High."

About the time I finished my Coke with a stifled belch, the fetching deputy opened the door to the witness room.

"Mr. Robert Payne, you have been called as a witness. Would you please come with me?"

Robert set his nearly finished drink on the table that we stood next to.

"Well, here I go. It was nice talking to you, Chief."

"Nice talking to you too, Robert."

I watched him go through the door and hoped that I might be up next. At least that's the way it appeared to be going, since I was the third one to know about it. I looked at my watch. It was two fifteen already, and I thought, *time's fun when you're having flies*—I always got strange looks when I used that one.

I got to thinking that I might not be called until the next day, given the time of the day. I sat down at the table on which Robert's Coke can sat, and began to reminisce, thinking back over my life. I guess I was just in one of those melancholy, reflective, kind of moods. I thought about Dickey, and I decided that I would call him tonight. I hadn't talked to him in a while. It would do me good to talk about the good ol' days and get caught up on his life. I know him well, that he'd feel the same way.

It turned out that Robert Payne was the last witness of the day. We were instructed by the resident deputy to return to the courthouse tomorrow, no later than eight forty-five, and that we were to report back to this room.

Then Judge Maurer came into the room. *How did he get in here?* I wondered. Then I noticed the door on the far end of the room. He must have entered there.

"Thank you, witnesses, for your cooperation in this case."

Like we had a choice? I thought to myself.

"I need to once again tell you to talk to no one about this case. The only exception to that is if one or both of the attorneys in this case contacts you. Now, do you have any questions?"

There were none and we left the room without talking. I went out the back of the building to my cruiser and drove back to town. I thought that I'd go back to the station for an hour or so, and then to the Y to see what Violet had cooked up.

Chapter 25

"You did what?" Nicole was pissed. "Why did you do that? You're a jerk. You're gonna get us killed!"

She was nearly hysterical, yelling into the phone.

"Really, Nicole? I love you, too! Just calm down."

"I just can't believe you went."

"Nicole?" Her mom yelled up to her room from downstairs. "Are you all right? Who ya talkin' to?"

She didn't answer her mom, and Mrs. Parker continued her dusting. The last thing Nicole needed was her mom questioning her. She needed to calm down.

Sherry continued on the other end of the line, "Why shouldn't I? No one said that I couldn't go to the trial. It's only the biggest thing that's ever happened around here. I want to see what's goin' to happen."

"Okay, okay. I'm sorry. It's just that this thing has me all messed up. It's all I think about. Doesn't it get to you?"

"Sure it does, but I'm not going to let it ruin my summer, or my life. You shouldn't either. Nothing's goin' to happen."

"But what if Steve's not guilty? What if he gets convicted?"

"Nicole, he's getting a trial and he's got a really good lawyer. You should see him. He's really cute."

Nicole rolled her eyes and wondered if Sherry could hear it over the phone.

"Okay, so what happened anyway?"

Sherry told her how the day had gone. If there was one thing that Nicole knew about her friend, it was that she was very detailed. She described not only what was said by both lawyers and the judge, but what they were wearing, too. Nicole, on the other hand, could care less what anyone was wearing. It amazed Nicole how she and Sherry were such good friends, and yet so much the opposite of each other. Sherry rattled on and on, describing the courtroom, the people who were there, and what they were wearing.

"Sherry, just tell me, does Steve look guilty?" She wondered what "guilty" looked like.

"Well, I wouldn't say he looked guilty necessarily, but I don't know that he looked "not guilty" either. I don't know. He did look kinda sad though, like he was sorry about...I don't know; he just looked sad."

"What about the lawyers? What did they say?"

She wanted to get a feel for how the trial was going, even though it had just started.

"Well, the prosecuting attorney told the jury why the defendant was guilty, and the defense stood and said why his client was innocent. After the lawyer against Steve spoke, I thought for sure Steve was guilty. But after the other lawyer, Steve's lawyer, talked, I thought he was innocent. I can't really tell."

It seemed to Nicole that Sherry was more interested in fashion statements and the body-build of the attorneys. Did she care that a potentially innocent man could go to prison for years? The only other information Nicole got from Sherry was that the prosecution had called two witnesses. The girls knew both of them. They didn't provide any more details than what Nicole already knew. That was it for the day, with the trial resuming on Tuesday. They talked for a while longer, and Nicole knew one thing for sure. It was a good idea not to let Sherry know what she was planning.

"Hey, Sherry, I gotta go to work pretty soon. Some of us have to work, you know."

Nicole hoped the dig would get to Sherry, but it either went right over her head, or she didn't really care, or most likely, both were true statements.

"Okay, Nicole. I'll call ya tomorrow and let you know what happens."

"Yeah, and what everyone is wearing, too," she said sarcastically.

"Of course."

They hung up at the same time. Nicole looked at the clock on the wall and realized that she better get going or she would be late for work.

Chapter 26

I was finishing up and about ready to leave when Mikey came in through the back door.

"Hey, Chief, how'd things go today? Did you have to testify? What do you think? You think he's guilty?"

It was Mikey's usual barrage of questions that was characteristic of him. This time, though, it was four instead of three.

"It went okay, interesting," I answered the first. "No, I didn't have to testify, but most likely will tomorrow, and I don't know what to think. What was the fourth question?"

He had to think a second before responding, "Oh, do you think he's guilty?"

This time I had to think a bit.

"I wish I knew the answer to that one! But I think the prosecutor is going to have a hard time convincing the jury without the proof of a body, let alone, not knowing whose body it is—or isn't. You know what I mean."

"But who else could it be? I mean, all that blood, right? And no one's seen or heard from Sandi since then. It has to be hers, right?"

Usually Mikey's questions didn't bother me, but right now

they were. I guess it was because of the conflicted feelings I was having. At any rate, before I could answer this latest batch of questions, the phone rang, and I gratefully answered it. I hoped someone was double-parked and I could tell Mikey to go write a ticket. It turned out not to be a complaint.

"This is Chief Thomas," I answered.

"Hi Chief. This is Bill Baker, Steve Carlson's attorney. Do you have a few moments? I'd like to ask you some questions, if you don't mind."

"Sure, I have a few minutes. Hold on a second, though."

I covered the mouthpiece and told Mikey that this might take a while, and that he could go home if he wanted.

"Isn't the All-Star game tonight?"

That's tomorrow night. But I think I will head'er on home. See ya, Chief."

Mikey looked a little like he got his feelings hurt, but I really didn't want to answer a bunch of his questions.

"Sorry, Mr. Baker. I just was telling my deputy to call it a day."

"No problem, Chief."

"Isn't it about that time for you, too?" I asked, guessing that he wasn't getting much sleep this week.

"No, it's not a day yet, not for a while—maybe in a few weeks," he said with a chuckle.

"Well, what can I do for you?"

We talked for a good half-hour. He asked what I had done, officially and un-officially, concerning this case. I told him about going to the mill and talking to Steve and about the limited search of his truck afterward. I told him about talking to Steve's mother. I told him about going up to Sandi's place on the river, and about taking a drive to Mill City for the one-sided conversation with her mom.

The defense attorney asked a few questions here and there, but mainly, he listened. He knew I was a witness for the prosecution, but he listened closely, trying to determine if I might be a help for his client's defense. It was nearly six o'clock when the conversation ended, and my stomach was rumbling. Breaded veal cutlets at the Y would take care of that.

Chapter 27

"**Grams, this is** Nicole."

"Who?—I can't hear you. Who is this?"

"Grams, it's me, Nicole," she yelled into the mouthpiece of the phone. Grandma had a hard time hearing under the best of circumstances, and the noise inside the mill was deafening.

"Nicole?"

"Yes, Grams—it's Nicole."

This clearly wasn't working.

"Grams, can I come over and see you tomorrow? I can be there around ten."

"Ben? Who's Ben?" she asked, becoming more confused by the second.

"Grams, turn down Jeopardy so you can hear me better."

Nicole could hear Alex Trebek in the background, even with the noise of the saws and machinery all around her. Her Grandma loved this new game show, which had just come out earlier in the year.

"Hold on, I'm going to go turn down Jeopardy so I can hear you better."

"Good idea, Grams."

"There, that's better, but it still sounds staticy."

"I'm callin' you from the mill. It's noisy here."

"Now what did you say about a Ben? Is that someone you work with?"

"No, Grams. I was wondering if I could come and see you tomorrow. I could be there around ten."

"Oh, ten—yes, that would be fine. I walk in the morning, but I'll be home by then."

"I love you, Grams. I'll see ya tomorrow."

"Okay, honey."

Nicole hung up. She loved her grandma to death. At seventy-nine, though, her hearing was getting worse and worse. But fortunately, for Nicole, Gram's wisdom was not affected by her loss of hearing, and Nicole really needed her wisdom right now. She walked out of the break room and down the stairs. She stepped up on the catwalk and saw the endless stream of two-by-fours flowing down the length of the chain—*like a Douglas fir river*, she thought.

Chapter 28

The jail door clanged shut with an echo sounding off the concrete walls. Steve had returned to his cell after the first day of the trial. Just thinking of it made the tuna-fish sandwich he'd just eaten churn in his stomach. He sat down on his bunk, put his elbows on his knees, and rested his head in his hands. He was alone. His cellmate—*cellie*—was working in the kitchen and later would be doing janitorial work for most of the night. That was fine with Steve. He just wanted to be alone with his thoughts, terrifying as they were.

The day had gone as well as could be expected, at least he thought so. He still wasn't thrilled about having a court-appointed attorney, but there was nothing he could do about it. There's no way he would have his mom take out a loan on her house, even though he knew she would if he asked her. His lawyer seemed pretty good, though—really good, actually. And that was a good thing, since only one in ten of these court-appointed attorneys were worth their salt. He thought that, just maybe, his prayers would be answered this time. He smiled a crooked smile that really wasn't a smile at all. There was nothing funny about it.

How could he say anything without getting other people hurt, or even killed? And how could he find out what really happened? It certainly didn't go like he'd planned, and there was nothing he could do about it. The way it looked now, unless his lawyer could miraculously get him off, he would be convicted for murdering Sandi. The more he thought about it, the more depressed he got.

He saw the mystery novel that his cellie had been reading lying on his bunk. He picked it up and, after reading the first page, put it back down. It wouldn't help his anxiety and his depression. It was about a "crime of passion". A jealous husband was accused of beating his wife senseless and killing her lover. It just didn't sit right with Steve, kind of like that tuna sandwich that still hadn't settled down.

There was a Bible on the shelf that was attached to the wall. It was one of those little green ones that people hand out at schools and hospitals, and jails. He took the small Bible in his hands. He didn't even know where to start—at the beginning? That's usually where you start a book. He opened it to the book call Matthew and read the first line…

"The book of the genealogy of Jesus Christ, the Son of David, the son of Abraham."

It didn't sound too interesting, but he kept reading anyway. After some time, he fell asleep, and then woke up when his cellie came back from his work detail. It was a little after two in the morning. The Bible was lying on his chest. He put it back on the shelf, rolled over, and went back to sleep. For the first time in many nights, he had a restful sleep—dreamless.

Chapter 29

Tuesday, July 10
Day 2 of the Trial

I didn't get to the courthouse as early as yesterday, since I wouldn't be in the courtroom anyway, at least not at the beginning. We witnesses were instructed yesterday to return to the same room no later than eight forty-five, so I walked in, went over to the carafe filled with hot coffee, and pumped myself a cup, black. Coffee wasn't made to have all those foreign ingredients like cream and sugar—the blacker, the better. I thought of that television show with Eva Gabor and Eddie Albert—*Green Acres*—and the thick goo that Lisa Douglas called coffee. I thought, maybe not quite that strong, but almost. The theme song played in my mind...

Green Acres is the place for me
Farm livin' is the life for me...

I took my coffee and sat down on one of the stiff plastic chairs. I sat in an orange one. There was only one other person in the room when I arrived. It was Warren, but that wasn't his first name, it was his last name, and that's why I remembered it. His first name escaped me, but later I got him to say it—Lee. He was one of the field investigators that arrived on the scene of the crime on the day after the murder. He had his back to me when I walked in, reading the day's calendar for Clackamas County Courthouse. He turned and recognized me.

"Chief Thomas, right?" he asked. He couldn't remember my first name either.

"You're right, but call me Frank," I said, hoping he would say his first name.

"Lee Warren, state police," he answered.

He walked over and we shook hands. He chose a green chair.

"Hi, Lee. I guess you'll be testifying today?"

"Well, I hope so—soon, I hope. I don't want to be sitting in here all day."

"Are you plannin' on staying around after you testify?" I asked.

"Nah, I have another case I wanna get to—guy beat his wife to death out in Scio. My partner's out there. Gary Collins, you remember him?"

"Yeah, I remember him," I answered, but I didn't know where Scio—pronounced "sigh-o"—was.

"Well, he's on his way out there right now. You stayin' around?"

Other witnesses started coming into the room.

"Yeah, I am. I'm hoping to testify first thing, too, so I can hear the rest of the witnesses."

It was getting close to nine o'clock, so the proceedings would start soon. Lee and I talked, while the other witnesses got coffee and sat in the green and orange chairs. The deputy came in. Neither Robert Payne nor Wes Strohmeier was in the room since they had testified yesterday. I wondered if they would stay around for the trial, thinking that they probably would.

The deputy spoke loud enough to get our attention.

"The court session will begin shortly. I assume that you all followed Judge Maurer's instructions from yesterday. If anyone attempted to contact you other than the attorneys in this case, let me know as soon as I'm finished. After you testify, you will be able to stay in the courtroom for the rest of the proceedings. Do you have any questions?"

No one did.

"Okay then, if you need something, I will be here. Thank you for your cooperation."

The clock on the wall read nine fourteen when the second deputy from yesterday opened the door.

"Chief Frank Thomas, you have been called as a witness. Would you please come with me?"

I stood, happy that I would be the first witness called that morning. Lee Warren groaned, but there was a good chance that he would be called as the next witness after me.

I followed him out the door and through the double doors of Courtroom A. I walked down the aisle and stood before the witness stand. Judge Maurer instructed me that I was under oath, that yesterday's swearing in was still in effect. He asked me if anyone had contacted me in regards to this case other than one or both attorneys. I answered that no one had contacted me. He then asked if I had discussed this case with anyone since yesterday, and I answered that I had talked to the defense attorney, but no one else.

"Please take the stand."

I walked through the little swinging gate, stepped up one step, turned and sat down. Deputy District Attorney Eric Holton stood at the prosecutor's table and walked toward me. The jury members were all in their places on my left.

"Good morning, Chief Thomas."

"Good morning," I responded.

He started by asking my name and occupation, both easy questions.

He continued, "Please give me an account of your involvement in this case."

I told him of the early morning phone call from Robert Payne, when he asked me to come down to the bus garage. I told my story—about my visit out to Sandi Riggs' place on the river, and going to Brazier Forest Products to talk to Steve Carlson.

Holton asked me follow-up questions as to what I found at the place on the Molalla River, and then about the conversation with Steve Carlson. He asked me if I had done any other work on the case. I told him of my visit to Carlson's mother and then later to visit Sandi's mother in Mill City.

"Have you been successful in any of your attempts to locate Sandi Riggs?"

"No, sir, I have not."

It appeared that he was done questioning me, but I knew that Bill Baker would have a cross-examination.

"Your Honor, I am finished with my questions for Chief Thomas."

Judge Maurer responded. "Mr. Baker, do you have any questions for this witness?"

Baker stood, "Yes, Your Honor, I do."

"You may proceed."

Chapter 30

Nicole rolled over and looked at the alarm clock on her bed stand. The digits read 9:33, and she said, "Oh crap" out loud to no one. She was supposed to be at her Grandma's place in Canby by ten o'clock. Rolling out of bed, and then getting vertical, she raced to get ready. She pulled clean clothes out of her dresser, choosing something cool, as the day promised to be another warm one.

She went out of her room and down the stairs to the only bathroom. Nicole had always wanted to have a sister, but with only one bathroom in the house, she figured it was probably best that she didn't. Thank goodness she had Sherry. She started the water, got out of her lightweight pajamas, and stepped into the shower. Any other day, she would enjoy a long, hot shower, but not this morning.

She shut the water off and reached for the towel to dry off. She let her hair dry naturally, which is what she did on most days. Nicole wasn't one to spend much time in the bathroom. Her mother, on the other hand—there was a knock on the door.

"Nicole, why are you in such a hurry this morning? You want to have some breakfast?"

"No thanks, Mom. I'm headin' over to see Grams. I told her

I'd be there around ten." She spoke over the bathroom fan, getting dressed at the same time.

"Why are you going over there?"

What is this, 20 Questions? she thought to herself, but didn't say out loud to her mother.

"I just haven't seen her since graduation, and want to go see her." That was the truth, but not the reason for this visit.

"Well, you should eat something before you go," her mother persisted.

Nicole opened the door and, walking past her mother, said, "Mom, it's Grams. You think she'll let me go hungry?"

"I guess you're right about that."

She went back up to her room and slipped into her pink flip flops. She grabbed the keys off her dresser and raced back down the stairs, two at a time.

"See ya, Mom. Love ya."

She crashed through the front screen door and out to the Citation. She got in and started it up, the radio set to the station she had left it at—*92.3 KGON. Cheap Sunglasses* by ZZ Top was playing...

When you wake up in the morning and the light has hurt your head
The first thing you do when you get up out of bed
Is hit that streets a-runnin' and try to beat the masses
And go get yourself some cheap sunglasses

She reached for hers from the visor and put them on, adjusted them, and made the forty-minute trip to Canby.

Chapter 31

Attorney Bill Baker got right to business. After our conversation last night, I knew which track he would take.

"I have several questions for you, Chief, but before we get to them, I would like to take a few moments to establish your credentials and your history in law enforcement. You are the Chief of Police for the City of Molalla, correct?"

"That is correct."

Easy questions again, but something told me it was going to get more interesting.

"And how long have you been the Chief?"

"Comin' up on two years now."

"What did you do before becoming the Chief?"

"I was a police officer for the Los Angeles Police Department."

"How long were you employed with the L.A.P.D.?"

"Just a tad over 30 years."

"And what was your position with the department."

"I drove a patrol car for the first ten years and then got a promotion to homicide. I was a detective for twenty years, give or take."

"You were a homicide detective for the L.A.P.D?"

At this point, the Assistant D.A. stood and addressed the judge, "Objection, Your Honor. Chief Thomas isn't interviewing for a job here. I don't believe this line of questioning has any relevance to the case at hand."

Baker countered, "Your Honor, I just want to establish the fact that Chief Thomas is highly qualified to conduct a murder investigation. He knows what to look for after twenty years as a homicide detective. I will be asking about his investigation and findings directly."

"Objection overruled. Please continue, Mr. Baker."

"Thank you, Your Honor. I'll continue with the rest of my cross-examination." He turned toward me. "Chief Thomas, you told the court earlier that you went out to the house where Sandi Riggs lived, is that correct?"

"That's right."

"And what day was that?"

"It was the same day that the blood was discovered in the bus garage, on that Wednesday morning."

"January 23?"

"Yes, that's correct."

I saw Eric Holton out of the corner of my eye. He seemed to squirm a bit in his chair at the prosecutor's table. He knew what his adversary was up to, and there wasn't a thing he could do about it.

"Please tell the court what you saw when you arrived at her house."

I was ready for the question and answered, "I saw the address on the mailbox and drove into the driveway. There were some tracks there, so I parked well away from them, not wanting to disturb anything."

"How many sets of tracks did you see in the driveway?"

"Just one set, that's all."

"Then what did you do?"

"I got out of my cruiser and promptly stepped into about six inches of slush and mud. It filled my shoes."

Mr. Baker chuckled, as did several in the courtroom, including the jury. I continued.

"I walked over by the tracks that were already there. It was firmer over on that part of the driveway, so there weren't any footprints that I could see."

"One set of tracks and no footprints, correct?"

"Yessir."

"Then what did you do?"

"I walked around the back of the house. I didn't see anything unusual, so I went back to the front and stepped up on the porch. I didn't use the steps because I didn't think they would support me." I looked down briefly at my belly, and that elicited a few more laughs.

"So the steps were intact when you were there?" he asked.

"Yes, they were. I avoided them when I left the place, too."

I'm not sure if Eric Holton had introduced any evidence the day before, but Bill Baker was using my testimony to systematically refute at least some of the prosecution's evidence, even before he introduced it.

"Okay. Did you go inside the house?"

"Yes, I did. I knocked on the door a few times, but no one answered. I tried the door and it was unlocked, so I went in."

The fact that it was unlocked didn't really surprise me. People were still pretty trusting in these parts. L.A. is a different story altogether.

"And what did you discover once inside?"

"There was nothing unusual. It looked lived in, but really pretty clean, cleaner than my place."

"Did you find anything that made you think someone other than Sandi had been there, at least recently?"

I had racked my brain the night before, trying to remember everything I saw, but there just wasn't anything out of the ordinary.

"No, I really didn't. There was a load of laundry in the dryer, and another in the washing machine, waiting to be dried. The clothes looked to be a woman's, if you know what I mean."

Baker looked a little amused.

"Yes, I believe I do."

For a young buck, he was pretty good. He was hungry, wanting to make a name for himself.

"Did you notice any photographs in the house?"

"There was only one that I noticed."

"And what, or who, was in that photo?"

"It was a picture of Sandi Riggs and Steve Carlson. They looked to be happy in that picture."

"Where was this picture?"

"It was on a stand by her bed, right next to the clock radio."

"And it was all there, on the night stand I mean?"

"Yes."

"Was the picture frame or the radio broken at all?"

"No, they were both in one piece. I even remember the time on the clock. It read 8:57."

"On the night stand, right?"

"Yessir."

"Was there anything else that you can remember about your time in the house?"

"Only that it all looked perfectly normal to me."

"What did you do after you left the house?"

"I went back to town and got a bite to eat at the Y Drive-In.

Then I went over to Brazier Forest Products to see if I could talk to Steve Carlson, but he wasn't there. He worked the swing-shift. I got his address from the secretary and drove over to see if he was there. He wasn't at home, but I talked to his mother."

"Did you ever talk to Steve?"

"Yes, that night. Well, it wasn't really night, around five thirty or so, but you know how it is around here that time of year. It was dark. My deputy and I drove out to the mill."

"And what did Mr. Carlson say?"

"Not much, really—when I told him why we were there, he acted as though he didn't know anything about what happened at the bus garage, about where Sandi Riggs might be, nothing."

Eric Holton wasn't going to let that one go by. "Objection, Your Honor. The witness is drawing a conclusion for the court."

"Sustained…Chief Thomas, just tell what he said, not what he was thinking."

Bill Baker took over again.

"So what did Mr. Carlson say?"

"Well, I asked him if he'd seen Sandi Riggs lately. He told me that they had broken up a few months before and hadn't seen her. He asked why I wanted to know. I told him what we had discovered out at the bus garage, and that we were just trying to find her. I told him that she didn't show up for work that day, and that no one had seen or heard from her."

"And how did he respond when you told him that?"

"Well, he didn't say anything—kind of looked like he'd been sucker-punched, and stared at something, or nothing, behind me."

"Did he say anything else?"

"I just asked him again if he was sure he hadn't seen her. He said no, he hadn't, and then said that he needed to get back to work. That was it. Then we left."

"Did you do anything else before you left the mill?"

"Yes. We went to the parking lot to look at Steve's truck."

"How did you know which one was his?"

"The guard told us which truck belonged to Steve before we went and talked to him. It was a '64 Chevy."

"And what did you find when you examined the truck?"

"Again, there was nothing unusual. We looked all around the outside of the truck. We shined our flashlights in the cab, but nothing unusual inside, either—just a few cans of chewin' tobacco on the seat and some other garbage—a typical guy's truck, messy."

"But nothing else?"

"No sir."

"Chief Thomas, did you see any blood on the outside of the truck?"

"No, there was no blood."

"In the bed of the truck?"

"No sir."

"Did you see any blood when you looked inside?"

"No, no blood anywhere."

"And this was on that day, January 23, the day the blood was discovered in the bus garage."

"Yes."

"Thank you, Chief Thomas. I'm through with my cross-examination, Your Honor."

"Very well, the witness may step down."

I stood up and felt kind of stiff from sitting, what seemed, a long time. The clock in the back of the courtroom said it was nine fifty-seven. I stepped off the stand and found an empty seat. There were few to choose from.

Judge Maurer announced that there would be a twenty-minute recess before the prosecution called its next witness. Most everyone stood at once and made a move for the doors at the back of the courtroom that the deputy had swung open. I didn't know it, but I would find out later that there were some very unhappy people in that courtroom, including Deputy District Attorney Eric Holton.

Chapter 32

It was not long after Frank Thomas stepped down from the witness box that Nicole pulled into her grandma's driveway. She always loved going to her grandma's, ever since she was little. Grams made everyone feel like she loved them the most, and, of course, that's what Nicole believed, that she was her Grams' favorite.

She parked next to Grams' Buick in the double driveway. Her car was in the garage most of the time, but she had driven to the high school track this morning to do her walking, along with her friends. After two miles around the track and saying their good-byes, she drove to Cutsforth's Thriftway to get a few groceries for their lunch today. She hadn't put the car back in the garage.

Nicole got out of her car and left the windows down so it wouldn't get so hot inside. Grams came around the corner of the house before Nicole reached the porch.

"Hi, honey," Grams said. "Come on around to the back. I was just pulling a few weeds before it gets too hot to do it."

Mrs. Parker, Pete's mother, had lived alone a good number of years since her husband had passed. Nicole was only three when her grandpa died, so she didn't really remember him, but she had seen pictures of her grandpa many times. Her favorite was of Grandpa and her riding on the small John Deere tractor-mower. She heard so many stories about what a wonderful man he was that Nicole thought she had her own memories of him, but she couldn't really be sure.

Grams still used that mower to keep the grass down on the junior acre that the house sat on. She did all the yard work—weeding, of course, trimming her roses, and "giving haircuts" to the various shrubs, as she liked to say. In the fall, she would borrow her son's blower that also served as a vacuum, picking up and mulching all the leaves from the shade trees in the front yard.

Grams kept the place looking nice, inside and out. When Nicole walked into her grandma's home, it always smelled so good. She always had something good cooking in the oven—pies, apple dumplings, cobbler made with berries that she had just picked, and bread pudding, to name just a few. If Nicole had a hero in her life, it was Grams. Nicole turned to greet her.

"Hi, Grams," Nicole said, giving her a monstrous hug.

"Whoa, honey...not so tight. You're going to break every bone in this old lady's body. Working in that sawmill has made you stronger than you realize."

Nicole let out a giggle and lessened her hold a bit, but still hugged her tightly.

Grams wasn't a big fan of Nicole working in a sawmill. She thought that it was man's work, and she had let Nicole know how she felt about it. But Grams also told her that she realized that this was a new generation, and things were changing. She said that she knew there were a lot worse things her granddaughter could be doing, and that she was proud of her.

Nicole finally released her hold and followed her grandma around to the back of the house. The white metal, round table with the green umbrella sat on the patio, the umbrella tilted toward the sun, which was rising to its mid-morning position. There were four chairs with overstuffed cushions positioned around the table. Sprinklers were watering the back yard.

"Nicole, why don't you just sit down here? Would you like something to drink?"

"Some ice water would be really good, but why don't you let me go get it?"

"Oh, no honey—you just sit. I'll go get you some."

Nicole loved being babied by her grandma.

Grams went into the house through the sliding glass door. Nicole pulled out a chair and positioned it so that the sun would shine on her back. She sat down, scooting it up next to the table. Grams came out the door with two glasses and a pitcher of ice water. She set them down on the table and then went back inside and brought out some banana bread, still warm from the oven, a small dish with butter on it, a butter knife, and two small plates with napkins on them. Grams pulled out the chair to the right of Nicole so she wouldn't be looking into the sun. Nicole poured two glasses while Grams cut two slices from the loaf, putting generous slabs of butter on each piece.

"Eat up, honey, it looks like you're losing weight. I need to fatten you up some!"

Nicole laughed at her grandma. She was always telling her that she was losing weight, and Nicole knew for a fact that she wasn't.

"Thanks, Grams," as she took a bite of the bread. "Wow, this is good. It's still warm."

"I had a few bananas that were getting a little ripe, so I thought I'd just make up some banana bread for you."

"You're the best, Grams."

"So how have you been? I haven't seen you since graduation night. Your dad tells me that you're going to Chemeketa this fall."

Nicole answered questions. She shared about her plans for the fall and beyond, talked about what she did over the Fourth, and so on. She didn't say, though, why she really had come over.

After a half-hour or so of chit-chat, Grams asked, "So, Nicole, I think you wanted to come over for more than just a visit, although that would be fine if that was the only reason. You want to tell me what's going on?"

She felt her eyes tear up a little and go blurry on her.

"Grams, I'm so scared, and I don't know what to do."

"Nicole, are you pregnant?"

"Grams! No, I'm not pregnant!"

She laughed and cried at the same time, which caused a snort, which brought on more laughter from both of them. Nicole figured that being pregnant was the worst thing that Grams could imagine, at least at this time in Nicole's life.

"Well, then, what is it?" she asked.

Nicole didn't know where to begin, so she just started from the beginning, from when she was sitting on the steps of the high school that Tuesday night last January, the last time she saw Sandi Riggs alive.

Grams listened attentively to the whole story, asking a few questions here and there for clarification. When Nicole was finished, Grams took a deep breath and let it out, looking at her with a grandma's concern. She scooted her chair back and stood up. Nicole did too, and Grams gave her a great big hug. This time, Nicole was the one who was hugged tightly.

"Well, that's quite a story, honey."

"Grams, you're the only one I can talk to. What am I supposed to do? I can't hold this in and let Steve go to prison for a murder that he's being framed for. But if I tell anyone what I know, they'll know for sure it was me. I don't know what to do."

"Nicole, right now I don't know what you can do. I want to make sure I tell you the right thing, once I figure out what it is. I know it may seem strange to you, but I need to pray about this. Jesus knows what you should do."

Nicole knew her grandma prayed and went to church—Nicole had gone with her several times when she was younger. She knew that her dad went to church when he was growing up, but had stopped going shortly after getting out of high school. Nicole's mom went to the Lutheran church once in a while, on Christmas and Easter, but that was about it. Nicole didn't know what she believed, whether there was a God at all, but she trusted Grams, and if she wanted to pray, it was fine with her.

"Let's go in and have a little lunch."

Nicole followed her inside to the aroma of roast beef cooking in the oven. The table was set. Grams went to the oven and took out the roast, which was already sliced, and put it on the table. She went back to the stove and brought a pot over, setting it by Nicole. She removed the lid, and steam rose from the mashed potatoes.

"I have some gravy to go with that, too," she added.

"Grams, I thought we would have just a 'little' lunch."

"It is a little and you're just too skinny, so eat up." Grams went to the fridge and took out the molded *Pink Lady* Jell-O. "I thought you might like this, too."

Ever since Nicole was a little girl, she would always eat the center out of the *Pink Lady*, the flower. Grams went back outside to retrieve the banana bread and set it down on the table, too.

They talked through the lunch, and after the lunch, and while Grams cleared the table and did the dishes. She wouldn't let Nicole help her—that's just the way Grams was.

"Well, Grams, I have to go back home and get ready to go to work."

"Nicole, Jesus will give us the answer we need. I'm going to pray after you leave, and all night if I have to. Call me in the morning when you get up and I'll tell you what Jesus tells me."

"Goodbye, Grams, and thank you for listening to me. I love you."

They hugged again and Nicole kissed Grams on her cheek. She went out the front door and walked to her car. She waved to her grandma, who was standing in the doorway, then backed out of the driveway. If Nicole ever wanted to believe there was a God that answered prayers, it was now. And if anyone knew how to pray, it was her grandma.

Chapter 33

When Judge Maurer dismissed the court for a ninety-minute lunch, I decided drive up to the upper section of Oregon City and stop in at Mike's Drive In. After moving to Molalla, it didn't take me long to find this place, and especially Mike's Special, which is prominently displayed in the middle of the menu.

This culinary treat consists of a half-pound, pure beef patty, on a bun that is well-suited for the meat. The large toasted bun was slathered with Mike's own special sauce, which had been kept a secret for years, I'm told. On top of the patty was not one, but two, fried eggs, done just well enough so the yoke stayed where it was supposed to, but only barely. On top of the patty and the eggs was a quarter-inch slab of melted Tillamook cheese. And imbedded into the cheese were four pieces of bacon, the thick-sliced variety. To make it healthy, a freshly-sliced tomato with a generous bed of lettuce was added. There was avocado, too, but I don't like those things and chose not to have one. Add to the sandwich a generous helping of curly fries, smothered in ketchup, and a thick chocolate shake to wash it all down, and you were well on your way to a major cardiac event!

On the way up to Mike's, I called the other Mike on the

horn—that's old-school talk—to check what was happening back in Molalla. Mikey was at the station eating his sack lunch. I didn't have the heart to tell him where I was and what I was about to eat. He hurled the usual volley of questions at me over the radio, and I told him of the morning's sessions. He was particularly interested in the testimony I gave, especially the cross-examination.

I told him of Lee Warren's time on the witness stand that occurred after the morning recess. Eric Holton introduced several pieces of evidence that the state's investigative team had discovered. This evidence would turn out to be the bulk of the prosecution's case against Steve Carlson. Mikey had more questions.

"So what evidence did he present? Did the defense question it? Is the jury buyin' it?"

"There's too much to tell right now. I'll be back to town after things are done here for the day. I'll tell ya all about it then, Pilgrim."

I said it in the best John Wayne impersonation I could muster, which honestly wasn't very good. I'm sure Mikey had no idea that it was an impersonation at all. I can't believe how little the younger generation knows about the good ol' days.

I pulled in to the drive-in and went inside the dining room. It was mostly full, but I saw an empty stool at the counter and decided that would work for me. After I ordered the Mike's Special, I got lost in my thoughts.

The waitress brought the food, and that brought me back to the present, for the moment. I started eating and went back to my thoughts, and to Lee Warren's testimony.

Eric Holton did the questioning and skillfully presented the evidence. He hoped that the preponderance of evidence would cause the jury to forget my testimony and what I observed, or more so, what I didn't observe. If Lee Warren had any thoughts of this being a short day for him, well, he had another thing coming.

The deputy district attorney had started by asking Warren about Steve's truck and what was found there. It was a bloody mess, inside and out, Warren had testified. The windows were also smeared with blood in a way that suggested a struggle had occurred, maybe from wrestling the dead body into the truck. The blood on the truck matched the blood that was found at the bus garage.

Certain items of women's clothing were also found in the truck—an Oregon State University sweatshirt stained with the same blood, one pair of tattered blue jeans that also had a fair share of blood on them. There were also a woman's undergarments consisting of a bra and panties.

I was amazed when the panties were entered into evidence. How they could cover anything was beyond me. I was sitting next to Robert Payne and whispered my observations in his ear, and he informed me that they weren't intended to cover anything. It made sense then. Still, I wondered, how much those things cost for the little amount of fabric that was there!

Holton then questioned Warren about what the investigation had turned up at Sandi Riggs' place up on the Molalla River. The prosecutor presented a plethora of evidence that was collected there, as well as a description of the inside of the house. Amazingly, to me anyway, there were two sets of tracks in the mud driveway, in addition to the ones left by my cruiser.

From Warren's observations, it sounded like WWIII had broken out right there in her living room, and then had moved into the bedroom. The picture of the happy couple was torn to shreds and the frame was smashed to bits. The clock radio hadn't fared much better as it lay in pieces on the floor.

Back in the living room, a Leatherman Tool—the rage of every sawmill worker in Oregon—was found on the floor next to the couch. It had the initials SLC engraved on one side and BFP on the other side—Brazier Forest Products. There was blood on the three-inch blade, which wasn't folded back into its proper place. The blood on the blade matched the blood in Steve's truck, and of that in the bus garage. Of course, one could only surmise what had taken place in that house, but this evidence, combined with the evidence found in Steve's truck, painted a pretty dark picture. Of course, Steve's fingerprints were found everywhere, when supposedly, he hadn't been there in months.

As I listened to the testimony, I could hardly believe that we had been to the same place and seen the same truck. Now, I know my eyes aren't what they used to be, and maybe my powers of observation aren't either, but I know what I saw. It didn't look anything like the description that Warren gave.

Eric Holton seemed to have a powerful case, and he was presenting it well. The jury seemed, once again, to sway toward a guilty verdict, at least according to my incredibly feeble observation skills.

Holton then said, "No further questions, Your Honor, but I would like to reserve the right to recall the witness if necessary."

"Duly noted." Judge Maurer responded.

"Thank you, Your Honor."

Court was adjourned for lunch. Bill Baker was on deck.

I came back to the present and realized that I had eaten most of the Mike's Special and hadn't even remembered it, and that ticked me off. There were a few fries left that were cold now, and half of my once-thick chocolate shake.

I laid a couple of bucks on the counter and went to the register

to pay for it. I had another half-hour to kill—pardon, the pun—
before court would be back in session. I decided to go walk off
the meal that I had just consumed, but had very little recollection
of consuming it. I only know that I felt stuffed and empty, both
at the same time.

Chapter 34

In another part of town—in the lower part—the Williams twins were having another one of their heated arguments, which would have ended in fisticuffs in their younger years. Both of them were displeased with the way things were going inside Frank's place, as they referred to the courtroom. Although both agreed that the young kid had done a decent job of presenting the evidence, Chester was still in a foul mood. Rather than causing a public disturbance, Lester tried to calm down his brother.

"Okay, I agree that it's not going as well as we all were hoping, but we'll be fine."

"So, how's Eric going to explain the timing thing? That Frank Thomas is really screwin' us over. Why the heck didn't Eric think about that when he called him as a witness, for cryin' out loud?"

Chester's voice started getting louder and also took on a higher pitch.

"Would you keep your damn voice down, Chester?" Lester said in a hoarse whisper, wondering who might have overheard his idiot brother in the Shari's restaurant.

Chester spoke, looking around like the guilty old man he was, "Let's get out of here. I don't want to be here."

"You go ahead, but I'm going to eat. Walk your butt back to the courthouse." Lester said, checking to make sure he had the keys.

Chester didn't go anywhere, and pouted through the rest of the lunch. Lester left a two-dollar tip on the table and paid the tab at the register.

"Have a nice day, guys," the cashier said, smiling broadly.

"You too, sweetheart," Lester answered, but Chester said nothing.

"Too cute!" she thought as they walked out the door.

"So, how's it looking?"

"Right now it could go either way, especially with the setup they're springing on the defense."

"What's his attorney like—any good?"

"His name's Bill Baker, court-appointed, of course. That's usually not good news. Most of them just do the bare minimum, talk their clients into accepting a plea, and collect their fees. But this guy seems different—hungry. He's young, but he's good."

"Okay. Same time tomorrow—you'll call?"

"Sure."

Chapter 35

The walk did me some good, and now I was anticipating a cross-examination that could make or break the case. Robert was already in the courtroom and, kindly, had saved a seat for me. I sat down and told him what I had for lunch.

"Chief, if you keep eating like that, you'll be heading for an early retirement, if you know what I mean."

"Yes, dear," I replied, as if I knew what it was like to have a wife that cared about me.

He laughed.

There was a low murmuring going on throughout the room. No doubt, most of them were anticipating Bill Baker's cross-examination of Lee Warren.

At exactly one thirty, Judge Maurer entered the courtroom, and the clerk said, "Please rise."

Mike's Special held me down, and I didn't even bother to stand this time. It all happened so fast.

Judge Maurer began, "The court is now in session. Mr. Holton, you are finished with your examination of Mr. Warren, correct?"

"Yes, Your Honor, I am."

"Mr. Baker, would you like to cross-examine Mr. Warren?"

"Yes, I would, Your Honor."

"Mr. Warren, please take your place on the witness stand, and remember that you are still under oath."

Lee Warren stood and walked to the witness stand. Bill Baker pretended to examine some papers at the defense table for a few seconds, then stood and approached the witness stand.

"Good afternoon, Mr. Warren," he said, without giving time for a response. "Could you tell the court how you first became involved with this case?"

"Yes sir. When there is a homicide, or strong evidence that there has been a homicide, the state police are called in to conduct the investigation."

"And is that the process that took place in this case?"

"Yes, that's what happened."

"What day were you made aware of this incident?

"It was Wednesday morning, January 23."

"1985?"

"Yes, this year. The incident was reported early that morning to the Oregon State Police. After receiving the call, my partner, Gary Collins, and I, were apprised of the situation, and then prepared for the trip to Molalla."

Baker's questions were establishing that the proper procedure had taken place and, more importantly, establishing the timing.

Baker continued, "Do you know who reported it to the state police?"

"Yes. We were told that Chief Frank Thomas reported the crime, or what appeared to be a crime."

"And what time, approximately, did you and your partner arrive at the alleged crime scene, at the bus garage?"

"It was shortly after ten o'clock."

"Was Chief Thomas there when you arrived?"

"No, well, we pulled up to the garage about the same time. He pulled in right behind us."

"Did he say where he had been?"

"Not right then. We introduced ourselves and then Chief Thomas took us inside. Later on, he said that he had driven out to Sandi Riggs' place to check it out."

"Did he tell you what he found?"

"Yes, he said that he didn't find Sandi, and that it appeared that she hadn't been there the night before. He said that it all looked normal, nothing out of the ordinary."

"Please tell the court what you and your partner did while at the bus garage."

Warren told of the procedure that had taken place. They looked at the patch of blood. Then they had looked for other evidence, a weapon, anything that didn't belong. They questioned Robert Payne and Wes Strohmeier.

Baker got a few chuckles from those in the courtroom when he asked Warren if he and his partner had looked for a body during their search. Then the defense lawyer shifted into bulldog mode.

"After conducting your search, collecting the evidence, and doing your interviews, did you drive out to Sandi Riggs' place to have a look yourself?"

Baker made it sound like that would have been the logical and prudent thing to do.

"No. We took the blood samples to the lab in Salem to determine the nature of the blood."

"Do you mean whether it was human blood, or some kind of animal, a deer, maybe?"

"That's right. At that point, we didn't even know if there had been a crime, or not."

"I see. So the murder investigation didn't start until when?"

"It was later that day that the report came back from the lab. It was determined to be human blood and, judging from the amount of blood, that person would no longer be alive. That's when it became a murder investigation."

"So, Mr. Warren, when did you and your partner finally get out to the residence of Sandi Riggs? Was it that same day?"

"No, it wasn't until Thursday, the morning of the twenty-fourth."

"So what you're saying is that Chief Thomas was out to that residence a full twenty-four hours before you and your partner."

"That would be true."

"And, of course, no one knew if it was actually Sandi Riggs who had been murdered, correct?

"Yes, that's true. She was still just a missing person."

"And she's still missing. The body that had contained all that blood is still missing, right?"

"Yes."

Lee Warren was doing fine with the line of questioning. He and his partner had done everything by the book.

Baker continued, "So when you and your partner did go to Sandi Riggs' residence, is that when you found all this evidence that you testified to earlier?"

"Yes, sir, it is."

"Were you surprised at what you found?"

"Somewhat."

"And why was that?"

"Well, because of what Chief Thomas had told us the day before, that everything appeared normal when he was there."

"And presumably the alleged crime had already been committed by the time Chief Thomas went there the day before."

"Yes, that is the assumption."

"How do you explain that?"

"The perpetrator must have gone back to the house sometime after the crime had been committed."

"And trashed the house, smashing pictures and radios and conveniently leaving his bloody knife there for you to find—is that the way you see it, Detective Warren?"

"I suppose it must have been that way. Criminals aren't known to be the sharpest tools in the toolbox."

Now Baker was getting under Warren's skin, and Holton was really beginning to squirm.

"So, a man's life is on the line, sitting right over there." He pointed at Steve Carlson. "And the prosecution is basing their case on suppositions? That's what..."

"Objection, Your Honor!" Holton's voice squeaked a little when he said it. "Mr. Baker is asking the witness to form a conclusion on the state's case against the defendant. That is not his job."

"Sustained—the jury is instructed to disregard Mr. Baker's last question."

Judge Maurer seemed a bit perturbed, and the jury, although instructed to disregard the question, couldn't help coming to some conclusions themselves.

"I'm sorry, Your Honor. I'll withdraw the question. Let me continue. So what did you do after your time at the house?"

"After collecting the evidence and taking several pictures of the interior of the house, we went back to Salem to discuss the evidence, particularly the Leatherman Tool with the blood on it. We sent it to the lab, along with the other evidence. We also made two molds of each of the tire tracks that were in the driveway."

"And then what did you do?"

"We waited for the results."

"Which took how long?"

"It was late Friday afternoon before we had the report back. The blood on the knife matched that of the crime scene. The initials on the knife, SLC, proved to be those of Steven Lane Carlson. We reported our findings to our superior and determined that Steve Carlson was the prime suspect."

"Prime suspect of what, in particular—of trashing a house?"

"No, he's the prime suspect of murder, because of the blood on his knife."

"I see. Then what did you do?"

"We tried to get a warrant for his arrest which proved to be a bit difficult."

"How so?"

"Well, it was Friday evening by that time, and we were having difficulty locating a judge who could sign the warrant," Warren said, turning different shades of red.

"So when did you get the warrant?"

"Not until Saturday morning."

Baker gave that incredulous kind of look and said, "You have to be kidding me. You have a murder suspect, at least you think it was murder, and you didn't get the warrant until Saturday morning."

"Yes," he answered, his face no longer red, but now, a pretty shade of purple.

Baker let that sink in for the jury and then said, "Oh, I almost forgot. When did you discover the blood that covered Steve Carlson's truck, inside and out?"

Warren hesitated, then mumbled, "Saturday morning."

"I'm afraid that the jury may not have heard your response. Could you please repeat that?"

"It was Saturday morning."

"When you made the arrest at Mr. Carlson's residence?"

"Yes."

The defense attorney rolled his eyes.

"Mr. Warren, were you aware that Frank Thomas had already checked that truck two and a half days earlier, the day after the alleged murder of someone whose body is still missing? And at that time there was no blood, no female clothing, no signs of a struggle, nothing, other than that Steve Carlson was guilty of chewing tobacco?"

"OBJECTION!" No squeaking this time. "The defense is badgering the witness!"

"Sustained!" Judge Maurer said, perturbed. "Mr. Baker, I order you to refrain from this badgering. You're treading on thin ice, so I suggest you redirect your questioning."

But it sure got the attention of the court, especially the jury.

"I'm sorry, Your Honor, I will not go there again."

"Ladies and gentlemen of the jury, you will disregard the last exchange between the defense and the witness."

But the damage was already done.

"So, you discovered the blood on defendant's truck on the morning of the arrest?"

"Yes."

"And that was some sixty hours after Chief Thomas had checked that same truck that was free of blood and no women's clothing in it."

"I guess so."

"I have no further questions, Your Honor."

The defense was through with Lee Warren.

"Mr. Holton, do you have any questions on re-direct?"

"Yes, Your Honor, I do."

Judge Maurer was giving the Deputy DA an opportunity to save face and stop the bleeding, so to speak. Holton would only be allowed to ask questions related to what the defense brought up in the cross-examination. I'm guessing he would attempt to give some explanation for the discrepancies between what I saw and what Lee Warren saw.

"Proceed."

Holton stood and walked to the podium. He asked Warren questions, hoping his answers would give a plausible explanation for the blood, first noticed on Saturday morning, on the inside and outside of Steve's truck. He attempted to explain the difference in the condition of the interior of Sandi's house from when I had been there. It wasn't working. I wasn't buying it, and I doubted that the jury was either.

Holton sensed it as well, and said, "I have no further questions, Your Honor."

His attempts to explain the discrepancies fell short of being successful. I looked at the clock and was surprised to see that it was already a quarter past three o'clock. Judge Maurer told the badgered witness that he could step down, and I thought to myself, *with his tail between his legs.*

"Court is adjourned until nine o'clock tomorrow morning."

I didn't move for a few minutes while everyone around me stood to leave. Robert didn't move either.

"Wow!"

That's all the usually very proper principal could say.

We stood and left the courtroom. We were the last ones out except for the two old men sitting in the back, Lester and Chester Williams. I thought to myself that this must be hard on the old guys. Little did I know.

Chapter 36

"Close the door," he said, sternly.

The twins stepped into Judge Maurer's chambers. Neither Lester nor his brother had ever been inside Frank's office. The first thing Lester noticed was Frank's desk—a deep, rich mahogany that must have weighed a ton and a half. The thick-pile carpet was a burgundy that was close to being black, which made the desk look even more magnificent. The walls were a lighter color paneling, probably birch, which contrasted nicely with the darker colors of the carpet and the desk. Paintings of historical figures decorated the walls—George Washington, Abraham Lincoln, and John McLoughlin, the original Oregon pioneer who was given the title, "Father of Oregon". There was a window, kind of small, that let in some natural light, and through which one could see the sun sparkling on the Willamette River.

The twins were in awe of their surroundings, a far cry from the office, if you call it that, where they ran their legitimate business, the Molalla school district bus service. Lester was the first to speak after Frank's order to close the door.

"Never been in here, Frank—this is impressive," he said

He and Chester continued to gaze at the extravagant surroundings.

"Lester, I couldn't give a rat's ass what you think about my office. Sit down, both of you."

They sat in two high-back chairs, also of mahogany, with a mauve-colored fabric covering the seats and backs of the chairs. Chester said nothing, but felt like he was a small boy in the principal's office in school. It didn't matter that the Honorable Franklin Z. Maurer was their brother-in-law, married to their youngest sister, and several years their junior. Chester was intimidated. Lester was, too, but wasn't as obvious about it.

Maurer continued, "You two are the biggest jerk-offs this side of the Mississippi. Do you realize what is happening in that courtroom?" waving his arm in that general direction. "Do you?"

The brothers just sat there, Chester turning a deeper shade of red than Lester, but neither shade went well with the mahogany. There was a question floating around, waiting for one of them to answer, but neither did, so Frank continued.

"I can't believe I'm related to you two dickheads. If you had just let things go, we, YOU, wouldn't be in this pile of shit right now. I'm doing everything I can to get the two of you out of this mess and save the family business, but it's not going well. Have you guys figured that out yet?"

Chester sat there, but Lester talked.

"Isn't there still a chance that Carlson will be convicted? I mean, we got Eric." Eric was Chester's and Lester's great-nephew. "He's doing a good job with the evidence and Ted can turn the jury, right?"

Ted Campbell, the head juror, was their cousin's oldest son.

"Lester, I can only do so much, Eric too. Frank Thomas really hurt the case, and I'm not sure the damage can be reversed.

Ted can't do magic with the jury. You guys are getting screwed, and the defense hasn't even called their witnesses yet. You need to be aware that there's a good chance that Steve Carlson will go free. And let me warn you, if you do anything, and I mean ANYTHING, your heads will roll, and you can take that literally. Do you two *comprendo?*"

"Sure, Frank. We understand," Lester mumbled.

Chester remained silent through the entire meeting.

"Now get out of here, and go out that door," he said in a softer tone. He pointed to the back of the chambers.

Judge Franklin Z. Maurer heard Lester's assurance, but doubted his sincerity. *A couple of real tools,* he thought to himself, as he considered the day's events.

Chapter 37

I drove back to Molalla, still stuffed from my lunch at Mike's, but really thirsty. I stopped at the Mulino store and went in to get something cold. It couldn't be a beer because I was still on duty, but that's what really sounded good. That would have to come later. I decided on a sixteen-ounce Dr. Pepper, in the bottle and not from the fountain. It was much better in the bottle.

I got back in the cruiser and back out on Highway 213. I passed Publishers lumber mill and thought again about Steve Carlson. It wasn't the same mill, but it still reminded me of him. I took the cutoff at the Elbow Room Tavern, the place to be after a shift at the mill, and drove back to the station.

Mikey was still here. I knew he would be because he wanted to know everything that went on. I parked in my spot and entered through the back. He was at our part-time secretary's desk, which was not being used at the time. He was writing up his report for the day. I braced myself for the questions that would surely come, and they did. I answered all three of his questions, and then told him all about the trial.

"So you think he'll get off?"

"I can't be sure, but it really looks like it."

"So your testimony, you really think that's what ruined the case for the D.A.?"

"Again, I can't say for sure, but yeah, I think so."

"So how much longer do you think the trial will last, a couple more days?"

"If that—when you don't have a body, and you don't have any witnesses to the crime, it goes pretty fast. I'm not even sure why the D.A. thought he could try this case, let alone win it. I suppose he thought he could make a name for himself with a conviction in a high profile case like this. I think it blew up in his face today."

"Just one last question, Chief—it's one I asked you before the trial began. Do you think he's guilty?"

"No, I don't think he's guilty. I never have. Now I'm sure of it."

"So then, who did do it? Who set him up?"

"That's two more questions."

"You're right. So who do you think did it?"

"No idea."

"Fine. I'm gonna take off. I gotta softball game tonight. Maybe you should come out and watch it. It's over at the high school, starts at seven."

"No, don't think so, not tonight."

All I wanted was that cold beer and to kick back and watch the All-Star game. It should be a great game with Phil Niekro and Dan Quisenberry pitching for the American League, and Dwight Gooden and Fernando Valenzuela for the Nationals.

"Okay, then. I'll see ya tomorrow. Have a good evening," Mikey said, as he walked out the door.

I looked at the day's mail and took care of the most urgent, then decided the rest could wait. I headed home.

Chapter 38

The cell door clanged shut and Steve sat down on the cot. He was getting used to that sound, the door slamming shut. He had just eaten his dinner—a dried out fried hamburger on a stale bun with some ketchup and mayo to hide the taste. The fries weren't of the curly variety, but of the cold variety, greasy cold, which was the worst. He tried not to think of his mom's home cooking. Even Marine food was better than the food in this place.

Steve was alone in his cell. His cellie was probably working somewhere in the facility after eating his dinner, and Steve was glad to be alone. The day in court had gone better than he expected, much better in fact. For the first time in months, he thought that there might be a chance that he would get out of this mess, and this place. He was pleased with the way that Bill Baker was arguing his case. It was Steve's opinion that if the jury would deliver their verdict today, he would be a free man. He certainly hoped so, and even threw up a prayer every now and then. *Who knows? It couldn't hurt,* he thought.

He didn't like to look too far ahead. It wasn't over yet. But if he did get out of this, what would he do? He still didn't know what had happened. That would be the first thing, to try and figure things out. He wondered if Wes even knew what happened. It sure didn't work out as they had planned, and Steve hadn't talked to him since he'd been in jail. There was no way to talk about it since visitations were monitored, and any correspondence by mail was read first by the guards.

On the second meeting with his attorney, Steve shared what he knew about the situation, and what the plan had been, but when he heard that Sandi had been shot, and maybe killed, his blood ran cold.

And his arrest?—he knew he'd been set up, and told his lawyer that too. And Baker believed him. He was working his butt off to clear Steve of the charges. And it just might happen. But then what? Just go back to the mill? He lay down on his cot and closed his eyes, though his mind was still whirling at a thousand board feet per minute.

Chapter 39

Nicole was working her tail off back on the sixteen-footers where the two-by-fours were coming at a thousand board feet per minute. Eight thirty—lunch time—wouldn't come soon enough. The chain-crew would rotate after lunch and she would be on the eighteen and twenty-footers, which didn't come near as fast. She thought to herself that she was really getting good at this, and the guys were respecting her. It felt good to be at work. She could forget about her problems, get a good workout, and get paid for it too. It was good therapy, and she needed it.

She thought back to earlier in the day. Her grandma had been a great encouragement to her, and Nicole knew that she would soon have an answer. Grams would say that Jesus gave her the answer, but Nicole just thought that her grandma was really wise from living a long life. Whichever it was, Nicole would call Grams tomorrow.

"Hey, get your butt back here and give me a hand!" Nicole screamed at Tony, who was sitting down on the load of fourteen-footers that were in front of him. He got up and came back to help out. *Yeah, I'm just one of the guys,* she thought.

Chapter 40

Wednesday, July 11
Day 3 of the Trial

The sun shone through the curtains in my bedroom. I left the window open during the night to try to get it cooled down in the warm, stuffy house. It had been a good stretch with no rain, and I was glad for that. Too many years in L.A. had spoiled me and, even though I'd been back in the Northwest a couple of years, I still had a hard time adjusting to the rain, showers, and drizzle—one has to be from the Northwest to know the difference between the three.

I stayed in bed a few more minutes and thought about yesterday's events. Each day of the trial seemed to bring more questions and fewer answers. What appeared to be a slam-dunk for the prosecution was turning out to be a brick shot from 3-point land.

I rolled over and pushed myself up with my arms and put my feet on the floor. When you get to be my age, that's the way you have to do it, or you could end up with a bum back for weeks, or even months. A guy learns these things, usually the hard way.

I had a quick breakfast of cereal and toast and washed it down with yesterday's leftover coffee, took a shower, and got dressed. I went down to the station and did office duties for an hour and a half before heading back to Oregon City.

Would the trial be wrapping up today? Maybe, I thought, but I didn't know how many more witnesses the prosecution might bring to the witness stand. Whatever happened, I couldn't imagine it being more dramatic than it had been yesterday. Judging from the number of witnesses in the waiting room that first day, I assumed that there would be a few more to testify. The mental health folks would say that Steve Carlson has anger issues—a bad temper—and others who would say that he suffered from Post-Traumatic Stress Disorder. Eric Holton would try to salvage the case that had taken a nosedive yesterday, but I didn't think he would be able to pull out of it—the case would crash and burn. That's what I sensed.

There was tension in the air when I arrived at the courthouse. Maybe it was just me, but I've learned to trust my feelings over the years, even the quirky ones like this one. I walked into the courtroom about ten minutes of nine and found a good seat. Robert Payne hadn't shown up yet, maybe he wouldn't, but I saved the spot for him anyway. Good thing—he came in a few minutes later. At a few minutes after nine, we went through the "Please rise" ritual, which I had abandoned on Monday. The judge entered, and then the jury, all of them wearing their solemn faces.

Chapter 41

Nicole awoke from a deep sleep, rolled over and looked at her alarm clock on the night stand—10:07. She decided to get another thirty or so minutes of sleep and turned back over. It was ten forty-six when she finally rolled out of bed, chose some clothes from her closet, and went downstairs for a shower. Her mom asked if she wanted some breakfast, and she said that she did, that it sounded really good.

She planned to call her grandma to see if she had received an "answer from the Lord". Nicole didn't really care where the answer came from, just as long as she got an answer.

After getting out of the shower, drying off, and getting dressed, Nicole went into the kitchen and sat down to a breakfast of scrambled eggs, bacon, hash browns, and toast. Working at the saw mill gave her a hearty appetite. She didn't worry about gaining any weight, though. She easily worked it off during her shift on the planer chain.

She and her mother talked while she ate, her mother sitting opposite her at the kitchen table. Nicole realized that it was nearly noon and she really needed to talk to her grandma, but before she did, she wanted to call Sherry to get the latest on the trial.

"Thanks, Mom. That was delicious," she said, really meaning it.

"Oh, you're welcome, honey. What do you have planned today?"

There was a time not too long ago that the question would have really irritated Nicole, but she was growing up. She appreciated her mother more now than she ever had before.

"I thought I'd call and see if Sherry's home and go see her. I haven't seen her all week."

She took her dishes to the sink, rinsed them off, and put them in the portable dishwasher, another thing that was new. She went to the living room, picked up the phone and punched in Sherry's number.

"Hello?" Sherry answered.

"Hey, kiddo, what's up?"

"Kiddo—really, Nicole? Anyway, not much, I'm just layin' around watchin' T.V. How about you?"

"Just got up a while ago—I thought I might come over and get caught up on the news, if you know what I mean."

"Sure, come on over. When will you be here?"

"I'll be there in fifteen or so."

"Okay. See ya then."

Nicole hung up and went back in the kitchen where her mom was finishing cleaning up the kitchen.

"Mom, is it all right if I go over to Sherry's for a while?" she asked. "Please?"

"That's fine, honey. The keys are hanging up."

"Great! Thanks, Mom. Love ya," she said while grabbing the keys off the hook and heading out the door.

"Love you too, Nicole," her mother said.

Ten minutes later, Nicole drove into the Johnson's driveway

and parked the car, got out and walked to the front door. She rang the doorbell and was immediately greeted by Sherry's dogs. Sherry was at the door, pushing the dogs out of the way and yelling at them to shut up as she opened the door for Nicole. She followed Sherry into the living room where *The Price is Right* was playing on the T.V., and Bob Barker was wheeling and dealing with the contestants. Sherry sat down cross-legged on the worn but comfy couch, and Nicole sat in Mrs. Johnson's favorite chair.

"So, tell me what's going on. By the way, why didn't you go in today?

Chapter 42

The morning passed quickly. The first recess was at ten thirty, and then the lunch recess came at twelve thirty. Only an hour would be allowed for lunch today. I think Judge Maurer wanted the prosecution to wrap up their case today.

Robert and I went to lunch at The Verdict, a café across the street from the courthouse. We talked about the trial, but also touched on our summer plans and other small talk. With the shortened lunch break in mind, we stood, walked to the cashier and paid our tabs. We wanted to make sure that we got good seats again.

We went out the door and stood on the sidewalk. I stepped off the curb and started across, but Robert hesitated. I looked back, wondering what he was waiting for, and then realized that there was no crosswalk. We both laughed and walked across the street, the crosswalk fifty feet or so away.

We found our seats, and a few minutes later, court was back in session. Bill Baker cross-examined the witnesses, except for the short, pudgy psychiatrist who gave a lengthy, detailed description of PTSD. All in all, it was a pretty standard day with no fireworks display in the courtroom, which was too bad, because I like fireworks.

At two fifty-four, Eric Holton said with finality, "The prosecution rests."

So that was it, at least as far as the D.A.'s case was concerned. I assumed that Bill Baker would have witnesses who would testify to Steve's location at the time of the crime, and his whereabouts in the days following. I also figured that Baker would ask Steve's co-workers and bosses, even his mother, Mrs. Carlson—who wanted me to call her Jennie—about his behavior in the days before his arrest. Baker might even make a crack about the magic act again. I believed that he, Baker, had a promising career ahead of him. He had that flair, that "something special", that people who were excellent in their field possessed.

Judge Maurer declared that court was adjourned for the day and that it would again be in session at nine tomorrow morning. I drove back to the station and spent some time talking to Mikey, who was always interested in talking about the day's events. Molalla, as usual, had been a hotbed of inactivity, so the conversation quickly turned to the trial. After a half-hour or so, I decided to leave and have dinner at the Y, then head home to spend a quiet evening, maybe even read a book.

"I thought you were going to call the same time as yesterday."

"Sorry, but the judge gave us a short lunch, and I didn't have time to get to a safe place to call."

"Okay. So what happened today?"

"I think it's looking good. The prosecution finished with all his witnesses and is done presenting his case."

"So tell me..."

Chapter 43

The five-minute warning whistle blew at Publishers. Nicole always got to the plant early, at least fifteen minutes, so that she would be ready when the start whistle blew. Plus, the antsy and brown-nosing planer-man always started running a few minutes early so the production numbers would look better—every minute counts because every minute means money. Nicole stood in front of the "shorts" waiting for the first boards to reach her.

She reflected on her conversation with Grams earlier in the day. After spending a few hours over at Sherry's and getting all the details of the trial, Nicole went back home to call her grandma, to see if she had a plan, or at least some wisdom to give her only granddaughter. Janice Parker had gone into town to do some grocery shopping, which was a good thing. Nicole didn't want her getting suspicious.

"Hello?"

"Hi Grams—it's Nicole. I was wondering if you came up with anything. I talked to my friend, Sherry, who's been at the trial. She let me know how it's going."

"And, how is it going?"

"She thinks Steve might get off. His lawyer is a young guy and really good. But if it's rigged like that girl, Kim Williams, said it was, he's still gonna be convicted."

"I've been thinking and praying about it, and I believe you need to tell somebody in authority what you know, regardless if that young man is convicted or not. Somebody is guilty, and you have information that can help catch the real killer."

Grams is an avid *Perry Mason* fan, and imagines herself as being Della Street or the female version of Paul Drake.

"But, Grandma, I could be killed and even Mom and Dad, too!" Tears started falling down her cheeks.

"Nicole, everyone can't be crooked. They're just telling you that so you'll not say anything. We just need to figure out who that person is. Then we let that person know, but like an anonymous tipster."

Nicole thought to herself that her grandmother was having too much fun with this.

"Grams, this is real, not some TV show."

Grams sounded more like the teenager.

"I know, honey. I know it's serious, and I believe what I'm saying, too. Not everyone is a villain."

"So how do we find out who the good guys are and who the bad guys are? And even then, if somebody starts looking around, they'll know it's me that told 'em."

"I read in the *Pioneer* a year or so ago that Molalla has a new chief of police—came from L.A., had a long career there."

Grams took both local newspapers, the *Molalla Pioneer* and the *Canby Herald*, keeping up with the gossip of both places.

"I think he might be one we can trust."

"I don't know..." Nicole's voice faded with uncertainty.

"You have to do something, and I have some ideas on how to go about it."

"Fine Grams, I'm listening."

"This is going to be fun, dear. Here's what we'll do," she said, then proceeded to describe her plan in detail.

"Oh Grams, that will never work! Nobody will figure it out."

"Perry would figure it out."

"This isn't a TV show, Grams, it's real life!"

"Just trust me, dear."

They talked for another twenty minutes before hanging up. They had a plan. Not a good one, but they had a plan.

Nicole came back to reality. She had been missing her boards and the guy behind her threw them at her feet. When she first started, the guys were more than happy to back her up and throw the lumber that she missed on her load, but not anymore. *I'm just one of the guys*, she thought, and picked up the boards and stacked them. She thought again about the plan that she and her grandmother had laid out. She still doubted that it would work, and she was still scared to death.

It seemed to her that the shift would never end, but the whistle finally sounded—it was one o'clock in the morning. She took off the leather apron and rolled it up with her nearly worn out gloves rolled inside, and carried it under her arm. She grabbed her lunch bucket and thermos, and walked briskly to the parking lot, and got into her car.

Chapter 44

Thursday, July 12
Day 4 of the Trial

The sun shone through the curtains in my bedroom and it was *déjà vu* all over again, as the famous philosopher, Yogi Berra, once said. He also said "It ain't over 'til it's over," and I thought those words of wisdom were apropos to the trial. *Today would be the same routine, just a different day,* I thought as I rolled out of bed, old-guy style to save the back. All this week I had done the same thing every morning and planned to do so again today—eat breakfast, shower, get dressed, go out the back door, and drive to the station. I would get a little work done there before heading back for the fourth day of the trial.

The defense attorney, Bill Baker, would be calling his witnesses today. I thought there may be a possibility that I would be called back on the stand. Closing arguments may be heard today as well. If not today, then tomorrow. It would depend on the number of witnesses who would testify on behalf of the defense.

I grabbed my cup of coffee and walked out the door and got

into the cruiser that was parked on the east side of the house. I backed out the gravel driveway and on to Toliver Avenue, which was still free from traffic at this time of day. Actually, it's free of traffic any time of day.

I arrived at the station after just a few minutes and parked in my spot. I saw something at the back door—a piece of paper had been folded and stuck between the door handle and the jamb. I got out of the cruiser and went to the door. I removed the paper, unfolded it, and glanced at it while unlocking the dead bolt.

Once inside, I went to my desk to take a closer look at the paper and its message. It didn't make any sense, at least not to me. It was written with a blue, ball-point pen. On the paper, a short sequence of numbers was written—*5.34.6*. Following the numbers was a cryptic handwritten message—*Things are not as they seem. I know where it is.*

I sat down and looked at it for a minute or two, trying to discern the meaning. *Where what is?* I had no luck at all, not even any hunches, and hunches are what I do best. I set it aside and reached for the stack of yesterday's mail. I read through it, most of it landing in the circular file. Ten minutes later, Mikey walked in the back door, ready for another day in the salt mines, although *sawmills* would be more appropriate for Molalla.

"Hey ya, Chief."

"Hey, Mikey. How you doin' this morning?"

"Doin' good. I was just thinkin' on the way here how lucky I am to be working here. I just wanted to say thanks again for goin' to bat for me with the city council."

"You're welcome, and I did need another body around here. I'm glad they finally came around to my way of thinking. I'm happy you're here." I meant it, too.

"So what's new, anything?"

"Not much, just headin' in for the trial. I'm anxious to see what the defense attorney, Baker, might have up his sleeve today. Ya know, I have a gut feeling that Steve Carlson just might get off. Course, if he really is innocent, it means someone set him up."

"Sure looks that way." Mikey agreed.

"We'll see what happens today. Oh—there is something. This piece of paper was on the door when I got here this morning."

I picked it up and handed it to him across the desk.

"That's weird. Any idea what it means?"

"Nope, not a clue."

"Maybe a combination to something?"

"Could be, but to what? Well, anyway, there's a puzzle that you can work on today. Go ahead and hang on to it. I have to get goin' so I can get a front row seat. I'll talk to ya later," I said as I headed out the door.

I pulled into the parking lot at eight forty, and walked into the courtroom at eight forty-five. I snagged a good seat, although it wasn't in the front row. We went through the same routine when Judge Maurer entered, after which, the jury entered.

"Mr. Baker, do you have witnesses to call to the stand?"

"Yes, Your Honor, I do."

"Very well. Proceed."

And he did proceed. He proceeded to call witnesses that brought into question every witness and every piece of evidence that the prosecution had presented. Ken Pfeiffer testified that Steve Carlson had indeed shown up for work on the day of the crime, and was there for the entire shift. Two coworkers testified that they were in the break room with him during their thirty-minute lunch, proving that it was impossible that Steve Carlson could have committed the crime when the prosecution said it happened.

As to the evidence in the truck—the blood, the clothing—Baker again reminded the jury of the time that had elapsed from the alleged crime to the discoveries. He also reminded the jury of my earlier testimony concerning Steve's truck. He did the same thing with the evidence at Sandi Riggs' house—the tire tracks, the trashed house, the broken picture, the clock radio, Steve's Leatherman Tool complete with blood. He again reminded the jury that on the day after the crime, that I, a seasoned homicide detective, had found none of this evidence at Sandi's house.

The prosecutor, Holton, sat there quietly, having no questions for the witnesses. He objected once when Baker was "leading the witness," which was sustained, and Baker continued without batting an eye. He had the jury eating out of the palm of his hand, again. The defense took the entire morning session, which was interrupted by only one twenty-minute recess. The time flew by.

At eleven forty-five, Bill Baker stated, "I have no further witnesses, Your Honor. The defense rests."

There were murmurs throughout the courtroom. Most of us—well, I was—anticipating that Baker would call his client to testify, and I was disappointed when he didn't. I wanted to hear him speak, but I would just have to be satisfied with hearing the character witnesses' testimonies, presented expertly by Baker. The testimonies portrayed Steve Carlson as a good young man, one who had served his country, and was now a hard worker back in the town he grew up in. But they didn't go overboard in portraying him as the perfect man—he wasn't a saint—that wouldn't be realistic. Steve Carlson was just an ordinary, average guy.

Judge Maurer used his gavel to get our attention and quiet things down.

"The prosecution has presented their case in this trial of Mr.

Steve Carlson, and the defense has, in turn, responded. I'm going to adjourn this court for today and closing arguments will be held tomorrow morning at nine o'clock. I again remind the jury not to talk about this case to anyone, and if anyone does approach you concerning this case, you are to notify the court immediately. After the closing arguments, the jury will be sequestered until a verdict is reached in this case. Court is adjourned."

I left the courthouse and drove back to Molalla, stopped for lunch at The Hitching Post, and then back to the station. Mikey wasn't there—he was probably eating lunch somewhere. I decided to take the rest of the day to make my presence known around town, since I had been at the trial all week. I stopped by Jackson Chevrolet and talked to Howard, for a time, to see how business was going. Of course, I had to give equal time to the local Ford dealership, so I stopped there, too, and talked to the general manager, Sam Cook.

I drove out to Brazier Forest Products to see Luther Heinrichson. I really like the guy, but he keeps inviting me to church, the same church that Mikey goes to, and I keep declining the invitation. Maybe I would someday. We talked about topics that ranged from old-growth timber and the Spotted Owl to "The War" and to the Ducks' upcoming football season. He recounted 1983's Civil War game between the Ducks and the Beavers that ended in a 0-0 tie, the last tie in college football. That game had already been dubbed the *Toilet Bowl* because it was a rain-drenched exercise in futility. Luther had witnessed it first-hand with his son-in-law, an avid Beaver fan. There were eleven fumbles, five interceptions, and four missed field goals.

I chuckled as he talked. I had heard many of his stories before, but enjoyed hearing them again anyway. One of his favorite stories went back to his young adult years when he challenged a guy to a contest. Luther said to this arrogant guy who was also known for his fighting.

"I bet you can't touch that spot on the wall with your knee."

"I can, too," he responded with his cocky attitude.

"Okay, so do it then," and the guy did it.

Luther grinned as he continued.

"Now, if you get down on your hands and knees, you won't be able to do it."

Without thinking or maybe because he was just that dumb, the guy got down into position and promptly lifted his leg to touch the spot with his knee.

"NOW BARK LIKE A DOG!" he yelled and laughed at the guy.

And then Luther took off running because he wasn't a fighter. Those who watched the incident howled with laughter! I laughed again, too, even though it was the third time he had told me the story.

Luther and I had been talking for an hour before I realized the time and said I should get going. I told him goodbye and that I'd stop by again someday.

"Maybe this Sunday I'll see ya in church," Luther said smiling as I went out the door.

I ignored it. The secretary, LeAnne, asked me if I'd been going to the trial. I said that I had, and we talked for the next fifteen minutes.

"I sure hope he's innocent. He's such a nice guy," she said.

"That's what I keep hearing. Whatever happens, we should find out tomorrow unless the jury has a hard time coming back with a verdict."

I said that I had to get going and drove back to the station. Mikey was there this time, so we talked about the day, what was happening around town, but mostly about the trial. The more we talked, the more convinced I was—Steve Carlson was innocent.

If that was true, and he was found innocent, then who did do it? The town would be buzzing again. I asked Mikey if he had any luck on the mysterious note. He hadn't.

I left to go home right at six o'clock. When I got home, I threw a couple of hot dogs into a boiling pot of water and took a cold Coors out of the fridge. I looked in the pantry and discovered an unopened Fritos bag. Now that I had dinner figured out, the rest of the evening would take care of itself. Tomorrow would be a big day.

Chapter 45

Friday, July 13
Day 5 of the Trial

Friday the 13th: The Final Chapter was opening in theatres tonight, and I thought it was appropriate. Was this an omen? Not that I'm superstitious or anything. It's just, well, appropriate.

I sat in anticipation, waiting for the judge to appear and get the show on the road. This morning, I stopped by the station and told Mikey that he could come in today. I thought that Molalla would survive without us, but we came in separate vehicles, just in case. The courtroom was already full and electricity was in the air—the anticipation was palpable.

Robert Payne was sitting on the opposite side from me, behind the assistant D.A. Chester and Lester were in their usual spots that they had occupied all week. Sitting by them was one of their daughters-in-law, but I didn't know which one she belonged to. She was a bus driver, too, and probably a friend of Sandi's. There were more familiar faces today than I had seen the previous days. Wes Strohmeier was seated next to Robert. He was here on the day he testified, but I hadn't seen him the other days. There were some high school students that I recognized, but didn't know their names. Mrs. Riggs, Sandi's mother, was seated three rows behind the prosecutor's table with a younger woman who may have been Sandi's sister. Jennie Carlson sat in the row behind her son. The trial had taken a toll on her and her face showed it.

The scene was set. All the props were in place, and the audience was ready. The "actors" were ready, and then, the "director" entered the courtroom. I actually made it all the way to vertical this time, as Judge Maurer allowed for a dramatic pause, then said in his booming baritone that we should be seated.

The door to the jury room opened, and the six men and six women entered, filing into the two rows to the right of the prosecutor's table. The tension they were feeling was evident by the expressions on their faces. They knew they would be deciding a man's innocence or guilt, and thereby deciding his future, either freedom or prison.

I think most of the spectators, myself included, had already formed their opinions. Perhaps the jury had as well, at least some of them. But the final arguments by Eric Holton and Bill Baker would definitely affect the jury's final decision, one way or the other.

Judge Maurer spoke in his best baritone voice, "Is the prosecution ready to give their closing argument?" he said, authoritatively.

"The prosecution is ready, Your Honor."

This would be the speech of a life time for both young attorneys.

"Very well, Mr. Holton. You may proceed."

Holton stood at the table and spoke in a firm and controlled voice, "Thank you, Judge Maurer." He walked from behind the table and planted his feet firmly, as if bracing himself against a strong current. He stood at the podium and began.

"Ladies and gentlemen of the jury, I commend you this morning for the service that you have rendered this past week. There were many others who were summoned for jury duty, for this case, but for various reasons, you are the special ones that made the cut. And because of that, you now realize that it is your civic duty to perform this service. Our 16th President, Abraham Lincoln, had this to say about "duty": *'Let us have faith that right makes right, and in that faith, let us to the end dare do our duty as we understand it.'* What is your duty today, at this time in history? Your duty, as citizens of this country and of this county, is to determine the guilt, or innocence, of the man sitting before you, Steve Carlson. It is a solemn duty, and it is obvious that you understand that. You are not taking this lightly."

"This morning I will remind you of the facts of this case. It has been said that facts are stubborn things. They just won't go away. The defense would love for the facts to go away, but they won't. Mr. Baker performed all kinds of verbal gymnastics, trying to twist and turn the facts to confuse you, the jury. But ladies and gentlemen, you did not fall for it. Why?—because you saw the evidence—the photos of Sandi Riggs' blood on the floor of the bus garage, the blood that was in Steve Carlson's truck, and that the blood there matched the blood in the garage. You saw in Steve Carlson's truck items of clothing that belonged to the victim. These are facts, ladies and gentlemen, facts that point to the guilt of the defendant."

"You also heard testimony and saw photos of the victim's home, inside and out. In the driveway there were two sets of tracks. One of course was that of Sandi Riggs' '77 Ford pickup. The other set was clearly different—different tread, different width, deeper depth into the mud. And, lo and behold, that second set of tracks came from Steve Carlson's truck, a '64 Chevy, placing the defendant at the victim's home.

"And what proof was found in the house? You saw the photos—the carnage that was wrought by the defendant. Furniture was broken and overturned. Glass was broken from the kitchen window, and also the mirror on the victim's vanity.

"Let me remind you that there is no evidence of anyone else being at the house, only Steve Carlson. His Leatherman Tool was there. We know it was his because his initials were clearly engraved on it. And amazingly enough, there was blood on the knife blade that matched the blood at the bus garage and the blood in his truck. Oh, it is so true that facts are stubborn things."

"Perhaps the most damning evidence that Steve Carlson brutally murdered Sandi Riggs, is the broken and smashed frame that once held the picture of a happy, smiling couple. It was a picture of a better, much happier time. But that was long ago, and that couple was no longer together. In fact, that relationship had ended some four months earlier, when Sandi Riggs was admitted to the hospital with a cracked cheekbone and a deep gash that required no less than twenty stitches.

"It was a relationship that Steve Carlson did not want to end, but it did end. Months went by, and the anger of a jilted lover grew hotter and hotter. And finally, it erupted on that cold, January night. Sandi Riggs was the casualty of that eruption, the victim of the rage that had finally boiled over. And then, it was over. It was over for Sandi. It was over for her mother, Dorothy. It was over for her sister, Kari. And here we are today. I am confident that you, the jury, will say to Steve Carlson, 'It's over for you, too. You ended her life.'"

"At the beginning, I talked about your duty as jurists, and that it would be your responsibility to deliver a judgment, one way or the other, in this case. The evidence shows that Steve Carlson is guilty of murder. Today, Friday, the 13th of July, this whole tragic affair needs to be over, finished. You, ladies and gentlemen, are responsible for turning out the lights, because it's over. It's over for Steve Carlson, because he is guilty. And you, because of your duty to justice and to the facts, must deliver the verdict, 'guilty of murder in the 1st degree'. Thank you."

There was a moment of silence before Judge Maurer spoke.

"The court will take a recess and resume in twenty minutes," he said, then stood and went to his chambers.

I suddenly remembered, as the judge was leaving, that Mikey was sitting next to me.

"Well, what did you think of that?" I asked.

"That D.A. sounded pretty convincing, but the whole timing thing really bugs me, y'know? Why wasn't there any blood on his truck when we went out to the mill? Or why wasn't the house a mess when you were there?"

These things I had been wondering myself.

"I'm pretty sure that Baker will be asking those same things. We'll see soon enough."

There was a lot of talking going on out in the vestibule while we waited for the second half to begin. People started filing back into the courtroom with at least five minutes left of the break. People were waiting with anticipation.

"All rise," the clerk called out.

And we did, as Judge Maurer entered courtroom.

"Be seated."

We were, and Judge Maurer invited Mr. Baker to make his closing argument. He stood from his seat next to Steve Carlson's.

"Thank you, Your Honor. And thank you, ladies and gentlemen of the jury, for taking so seriously your decision in this case. You will soon be called on to make this very important decision, and I will do my best to convince you that Steve Carlson did not murder Sandi Riggs."

He stepped from Steve's side and moved to the podium.

"Ladies and gentlemen, I present to you Steve Carlson, magician extraordinaire!"

Baker said this as if he were in a Vegas showroom. And then he shocked us all by pulling out a magician's wand, putting a black top hat on his head, and a black cape around his shoulders. If he was going for an attention-getter, he got it!

"You are about to hear of some truly amazing feats, ladies and gentlemen, performed by our own defendant and Master Magician, Steve Carlson. Now unfortunately, Mr. Carlson will not be able to perform for you because he has been wrongfully accused of committing a heinous crime. Therefore, he has to remain seated at the defense table. So I asked my client if he could teach me some of his tricks to perform before you today, and he told me he would do his best to teach me. But then I realized something. I realized that I couldn't do amazing, sleight-of-hand tricks and illusions without having years of practice and experience."

As he spoke, he removed his cape, folded it, and placed it on the defense table. He placed the wand on top of the cape, and then put the hat on top of both.

"In fact, I realized that Steve Carlson could not do these either, not without years of practice. So how did he do the things that the prosecution would like you to believe? I am asking you to consider the facts of this case, ladies and gentlemen—no magic, no bluff, 'Just the facts, ma'am,' as detective Joe Friday would say."

Baker knew his jury. He himself was too young to remember the T.V. show, *Dragnet,* except from reruns, but he knew the jury would recognize the catch phrase. Once again, Bill Baker had the jury eating out of his hand.

"The state has presented their evidence. So, let's look at the facts as they are."

"One, there was a crime committed. You would not have been here all week if there wasn't a crime."

"Two, there was an awful lot of blood at the crime scene, so much that whoever it came from could not have survived the attack."

"Three, there was a lot of blood—the same type—inside Steve Carlson's truck."

"Four, there was clothing that belonged to Sandi Riggs that was found inside the defendant's truck."

"Five, there was evidence of a struggle at Sandi Riggs' residence up past Dickey Prairie, and that Steve Carlson's truck had been in her driveway.

"Six, there was a Leatherman Tool with the initials SLC, obviously standing for Steven Lane Carlson."

"And there you have it. Those are the facts that were presented. These are the facts that the state is hoping will convince you that Steve Carlson is guilty."

"A man by the name of Claude Bernard was a 19th century French physiologist. He had this to say about facts: *'A fact in itself is nothing. It is valuable only for the idea attached to it, or for the proof which it furnishes.'* Let's consider that statement for a moment. A fact in itself is nothing. That is true. The facts that the state presented don't mean a thing when they stand by themselves. They become valuable or worthwhile when true ideas are attached to the facts, and if the ideas are true, they then become proof. But this is only the case if the ideas, the interpretation of those facts, are true. Let's take a realistic look at the ideas, or the assumptions presented about these facts."

"Facts 1 and 2: There was a crime and the amount of blood suggests that the victim, whoever it was, did not survive the attack. The state is assuming that it was my client who committed this crime. Do the rest of the facts back up this assumption?"

"Fact 3: There was a whole mess of blood inside Steve Carlson's truck. The assumption is that the blood got there as a result of the crime. That seems to be a fair assumption, except for one thing. Please recall the testimony of the Molalla Chief of Police, Frank Thomas. On the late afternoon of January 23, the day after the murder, the chief and his deputy paid a visit to Steve Carlson, and, at that time, also inspected the defendant's truck. Don't forget the fact that Chief Thomas was a homicide detective for the L.A.P.D. for thirty years—he knows what he's doing.

"Upon inspection of the truck, Chief Thomas and his deputy found nothing out of the ordinary, and, most importantly, saw no blood. Now ask yourselves, ladies and gentlemen, does that make any sense, especially in the given time frame? The blood must have been placed there later. In fact, no blood was seen on that truck until the following Saturday morning, when Mr. Carlson was arrested. Then why, three days later, would the defendant have left his truck in his mother's driveway caked with blood? And why did it take the investigation three days to check his truck? Either Mr. Carlson is a total idiot, or, the more plausible explanation—he didn't put it there. Someone else had to have put the blood there."

"Okay. Fact 4: There was bloody clothing that belonged to Sandi Riggs found in that same truck. The assumption must be that Steve Carlson left her clothes in his truck, the same way as the blood. Is that a fair assumption? Of course not! Not when you consider that Chief Thomas had already inspected the truck, and it was free of blood, and free of clothing."

"Fact 5: There was evidence of a struggle at Sandi Riggs'

place. The assumption is that they fought. When would that have been? They fought and then he killed her later at the bus garage? That doesn't make sense. Chief Thomas was at the house on the morning after the murder, and saw no indication of a struggle, none whatsoever. Well, then, the state must assume that after the attack at the bus garage, Mr. Carlson then took Miss Riggs back to her house, sometime after Chief Thomas was there, and somehow she had enough life left in her to put up a fight—all without bleeding in the house! What?—she didn't want to make a mess in her house? Does that make any sense at all? Doesn't it seem logical that someone other than Steve Carlson caused the mess in her house, destroying the picture of them from happier times?"

"Fact number 6: A Leatherman Tool with the defendant's initials on it, a tool received from the company he worked for, was found at the house. The assumption is that after finishing off the victim, if indeed she was miraculously still alive, the defendant then trashed the house and accidentally dropped his tool onto the carpet.

Stifled snickers were heard around the courtroom, mainly from the males in attendance. It was not an accident that Baker used that term. I think I even saw the corner of Judge Maurer's mouth raise in a mostly imperceptible smile. Baker used his "incredulous smile" at this point, to emphasize the absurdity of the state's case, and I have to admit that it did sound absurd.

"Might it be more plausible that the same person, the one who put the blood in Steve's truck, also, at the same time, took the Leatherman out of the glove compartment where he kept it? Why yes it does, much more likely."

"So that's the state's case, ladies and gentlemen. The ideas that the state has attached to the facts are ludicrous. If the facts furnish any proof at all, it is that Steve Carlson is innocent. Nothing else makes any sense. The fact that Steve Carlson's foreman at Brazier claims that Steve was at work the entire time, along with his work buddies saying the same thing, prove that he couldn't have committed this crime.

Those closest to Steve saw no change in his behavior other than concern that Sandi Riggs had gone missing and was assumed to be the victim of a brutal murder."

"Ladies and gentlemen, it is now up to you to decide the guilt or innocence of Steve Carlson. The case that the prosecution presented has more holes in it than Swiss cheese, and does not offer any proof that Steve committed this crime. Add up all the facts and the testimonies, all the evidence, and the only logical conclusion is that someone else committed the crime, and then framed Steve Carlson. I ask you, please, give this innocent man his freedom, freedom that he deserves, and even fought for while serving in the United States Marine Corps. I ask you for a verdict of acquittal. The defense rests, Your Honor."

Judge Maurer gave instructions to the jury and then dismissed them to the jury room. He struck his gavel and said that court was adjourned until the jury reached its verdict. We stood as he exited and then the courtroom emptied quickly.

Mikey and I decided that we should go to Mike's Drive-in, the second time this week for me. I got the *Mike's Special* again and Mikey ordered the same. We sat and waited for our order. There were others from the courtroom who had the same idea to come here. It appeared that all were in deep discussion about the case and what the verdict might be. It was no different for Mikey and me.

"So boss, what's the verdict?" he asked.

"I have to say that if the jury convicts him, there is something seriously wrong with the justice system, at least in Clackamas County. I think he's innocent, always have, really. I don't think we'll have to wait too long for the verdict. It will be today for sure. No jury is going to want to sit on this one for the weekend."

Mikey agreed, "How could a jury come to any other conclusion? But what if they do?"

"Do what?" I asked.

"Come to another conclusion."

"We'll just burn that bridge when we get there," I responded, smiling.

Mikey was too young to realize that I misquoted the phrase.

Our specials were brought to our table, and the sight and the aroma made me realize how hungry I was. Mikey must have been, too, because he wolfed it down like a, well, like a wolf. We ate it all, down to the last fry. We slurped down the last of our shakes—mine was chocolate, his was blackberry.

We got up from the table and I went to pay for our lunches. We had some time before the jury would return with a verdict, so we drove back to Molalla just to see what was happening there, but mainly just to kill some time.

We continued to discuss the case—the million dollar question?—"Who dunnit?" We didn't have a clue. But, as it turns out, we did have a clue. We just didn't realize it. But the verdict wasn't yet in. So we waited.

Part III

Chapter 46

Sunday, July 15, 1985

Most people assumed that when the trial was over, things would get back to normal in Molalla. But that was also assuming that Steve Carlson would be convicted of murdering Sandi Riggs, which he was not. Why the D.A. thought that he had a solid case, I don't know, but Carlson's young, upstart attorney chewed up his advocate and spit him out. The jury was in deliberation for four hours, and I'm not sure why it took that long. There must have been one or two that believed Carlson was guilty, or at least had doubts about his innocence. But eventually, the verdict was delivered by the jury's foreman. The courtroom erupted as Judge Maurer repeatedly pounded his gavel and tried to restore order to the courtroom. There were tears all over the room—the most, I believe, came from Jennie Carlson, Steve's mother. She clung to her son, and he gave a genuine and heartfelt hug back to her. He was a free man.

Most everyone in Molalla believed that the murderer was be-hind bars before the trial and would continue to be after conviction.

But now, the town folk were divided. Some believed that the jury got it wrong, that Steve Carlson was indeed guilty, but most believed that the jury got it right. Either way, it meant that there was still a murderer running around free, maybe even someone in their own town. People asked me, publicly and privately, what was being done to catch the killer. I responded with my pat answer—law enforcement investigators are pouring over the evidence again in order to identify potential suspects. I didn't tell them that Mikey and I were conducting an investigation of our own. It was only since Friday that Steve Carlson was found innocent, so we hadn't had a lot of time, but there was an interesting development earlier today.

I was taking it easy on the couch just after lunch, watching an old John Wayne movie— *McLintock*—when the phone rang. I stretched to reach it and couldn't quite get to it. I sat up and scooted closer to the phone and managed to reach it, but not before I knocked my Coors over and spilled it all over the carpet. I answered the phone.

"Dammit," I spoke into the mouthpiece.

"Jeez, Chief, you need to go to phone-answering etiquette school. Didn't your mama ever teach you phone skills?"

"Oh, Mikey, it's you. I just spilled my beer all over when I reached for the phone. Anyway, what's on your mind? I hope it's important."

I was pretty sure he could tell that I was annoyed that he called me.

"Church just got out and I had to call and tell you what Pastor Chuck spoke about today," he said excitedly.

He was excited. I was annoyed.

"Are you serious, Mikey? I told you I might go to church with you some day, but I don't need a play-by-play before that day. Just cut to the chase and tell me why you called."

I spilled my beer over this? I thought.

"I'm trying. Just listen. I know what that note means, the one you got last week. I know what it means!"

"What? How? Tell me."

"Can I come over? I have to show you. I can be there in five minutes."

"Do I have a choice? See ya in a few minutes."

Mikey knocked on the door about the same time I finished cleaning up the spilt beer. I hollered for him to come in. I was still irritated about the beer, but my curiosity was piqued. He walked in, said hello, and asked if we could sit at the kitchen table.

"Yeah," I answered.

I walked to the fridge and retrieved another beer, then sat down at the table.

"What do you have that's worth me spilling my beer all over the carpet?"

"Sorry about that, Chief, but hear me out. I have to start with the passage that Pastor Chuck mentioned today. It was Deuteronomy 34:6."

"And that's supposed to mean something to me?"

"No, and it didn't to me either, not at first, but let me read to you what it says."

"Fire away." I really wasn't in the mood for Deuteronomous or whatever it was, but Mikey was adamant.

"Here's what it says... *And He buried him in the valley in the land of Moab, opposite Beth-peor; but no man knows his burial place to this day.'*"

"Whose burial place?"

"Moses, but that doesn't matter. Listen to the reference, where this verse is found. Remember the note?"

"Yeah, *5.34.6*—then it said, *'Things are not as they seem. I know where it is.'* I memorized it. I don't know why, but I did."

"I did too. I guess I'm learning from the best," he said, trying to get back on my good side.

"Flattery will get you everywhere," I smiled, my annoyance starting to dissipate.

"Okay. So when the pastor read the part about no one knowing where Moses' burial place was, I thought how ironic that was. I mean, not knowing where Sandi Riggs' burial place is. And then 34.6, the chapter and verse, the same as the note."

I was getting a bit more interested. I scooted my chair a little closer to Mikey.

"So you're saying that the note is referring to this verse in Deuteronomous?"

"Deuteronomy, and yes, that's what I'm saying."

"What about the five? It was 5.34.6."

"Right—Deuteronomy, it's the fifth book of the Bible. The reference for this verse is 5.34.6. Chief, I don't know about you, but I don't believe in coincidences. Whoever wrote that note knows where Sandi Riggs is buried."

It made sense. I didn't believe in coincidences either, although not for the same reasons as Mikey. I had seen many so-called coincidences while on the L.A.P.D. I can't explain them, but there seems to be some cosmic force or something. But I didn't want to philosophize about that now.

"Mikey, it looks like you may have something here. That's a good piece of detective work." I had almost forgotten about the beer.

That was earlier today. I went down to the station after Mikey left and now I'm just sitting at my desk, pondering what it all means. The more I think about the note, the numbers, and the verse that Mikey read—it really does seem that this person could have information. Maybe he or she does, but why so cryptic?

Leaving a note, a series of numbers, why not just come and talk? We still wouldn't know what it means if it wasn't for Mikey going to church yesterday and hearing that verse. Coincidence? And why would anyone in their right mind think that someone could decipher that code? And yet, Mikey did. Go figure. Now all we could do is wait and hope that we got some more notes, preferably of the non-cryptic variety. I started on some of my neglected duties from last week, but *5.34.6* wasn't too far away from my thoughts.

Chapter 47

"Hey Mom, I'm gonna stay the night over at Nicole's if you're okay with that," Sherry asked.

"That's fine. Do you need a ride up to her place?"

"I was wondering if I could use the car. Nicole always drives, and I thought I would drive for a change. We might go to a drive-in tonight."

"I guess it's all right," she said, not feeling quite right about it. Mrs. Johnson knew she would have to let go some day—just not today.

"Thanks, Mom. I love you."

"I love you, too, honey. The keys are in my purse."

Sherry didn't like lying to her mother, but she really wanted to hook up with Chris. She had met him at a party right after graduation and had been seeing him ever since. Her mom knew about him, had met him once, but didn't have a clue that she had been sleeping with him. She told Nicole, but no one else.

He was twenty-one and shared an apartment with a friend of his in Clackamas, right by the mall. His friend wouldn't be there tonight, so he called and invited Sherry to come over for the night. She didn't hesitate to accept the invitation. She got goose bumps all over whenever she thought of him. *He's really hot, too,* she thought, as she drove towards town, not up the road towards the Parker's. Sherry's mother couldn't see the end of the driveway, so she couldn't know which direction Sherry had gone. The car radio was playing their song, the one that was playing when she and Chris first met...

I am so into you
I can't think of nothing else...

Sherry didn't believe in coincidences. This was their song and the goose bumps came again, running up and down her spine. She navigated the turns on the crooked, windy road to Molalla. When she looked in her rearview mirror, she saw a dark-colored truck that was gaining on her, so she sped up a bit. She hated tailgaters and usually drove fast enough that it wasn't a problem, especially on these country roads. She looked again in her mirror and saw that the rig was drawing closer—too close. She sped up as much as she dared, but the truck continued to gain on her. It loomed large in the rearview mirror. She started thinking that it was going to hit her.

"Redneck prick!" she cursed at the mirror that held the image of the truck.

Sherry sped up even more and was terrified to be going as fast as she was, nearly hitting seventy miles per hour. The tires on her mom's Firebird squealed as she went around the corners. The truck now filled the entire mirror.

"What the hell? Shit!"

The truck rammed her and the right-side tires went on to the gravel shoulder and dangerously close to the ditch. She brought the car back onto the pavement, almost over-steering into the ditch on the opposite side. It was all Sherry could do to keep it on the road, and the truck was still just a few feet behind her.

Tears started to burn her eyes. It was nearly dark outside and she could barely see the road ahead of her. The truck's lights were on high beam and were blinding her, too. She wiped the tears from her eyes in time to see the sign—twenty-five mph curves ahead. The Firebird had just topped seventy-five. She slammed on her brakes in time to make the corners at fifty when the truck from hell hit her again. The car went into a spin and Sherry lost all control. She saw that she wouldn't make the corner and braced herself for the impact, milliseconds away.

The red Firebird left the road—airborne—and then crashed down the steep hillside, flipping once. It came to rest, lying on its top, in a small creek that ran through the bottom of the ravine. The car rested on its backside, like the Challenger space shuttle ready for takeoff, propped up by a large Douglas Fir.

Water came in through the shattered back windows. Sherry was unconscious. Her seat belt and shoulder harness held her in the driver's seat, but she had hit her head violently on the steering wheel in the crash. If she could open her eyes, she would be looking through the branches of the tall fir trees at a few stars that dotted the dark sky. The water rose inside the car, now almost to the back of the driver's seat that held Sherry.

The black truck came to a stop. There were two men inside.

"I'm going down to make sure she's dead. You drive down the road and come back in fifteen minutes or so. I'll be up the road a ways when you come back. Pick me up."

He jumped out of the truck and started down the ravine when he heard the urgent honking coming from the truck. He scurried back up to see what was going on.

"Get in. There's someone coming, about a mile down the road. I saw the headlights. We gotta get outta here!"

He jumped back in the truck as they turned around, heading back in the direction they had come.

"She's dead. She has to be. Understand?"

"Yeah. I got it."

Chapter 48

Fred Thompson pulled out of the church parking lot. The Sunday evening service was over and it was time to go home. He had stayed and talked with the pastor for a while after the service. It helped some, but still, he dreaded going home to a quiet, empty house.

Fred was a fifty-five-year-old logger, a job he started right out of high school. That summer, he married his high school sweetheart. They had enjoyed a good life together, until last year, when Dorothy—most people called her Dottie—was diagnosed with colon cancer. She *fought the good fight*, as the Bible says, but the disease finally got the best of her, and on the last day of September, she slipped quietly away. Fred drove south of town to the quiet house, reminiscing along the way.

It was mostly dark out. There was still a little pink in the sky, but that was to the west, and he was headed south and east. He was going uphill and approaching a series of sharp curves. He saw a single light, shining up through the Douglas fir trees, like one of those spotlights at the grand opening of a new shopping mall. He braked to a stop, grabbed a flashlight out of the glove compartment, and got out of the truck. He walked to the edge of the road. Down at the bottom of the steep ravine was a car, its lone headlight shining toward the sky.

Fred was used to this kind of terrain. He went over the edge and got to the car as fast as any twenty-year-old. He reached the passenger side and peered in the front window, using the flashlight. He saw the girl, unconscious, he hoped, not dead. A wicked gash spread across her forehead and disappeared into her mangled hair. He was standing in three feet of water that was running swiftly. He needed to get to the other side, fast, to get her out. He prayed one of those quick, urgent prayers.

The black rotary-dial phone rang three times before it was answered.

"Yeah."

"It's done."

"You're sure she's dead?"

"She's dead."

"And you're sure that no one saw you?"

"No one saw us."

"Good." He hung up the phone.

Chapter 49

It wasn't easy but Fred managed to get to the driver's side window. The water was at the back of her head. It was deeper on this side and the current was stronger. The car could shift at any time and submerge the entire vehicle.

He tried to open the door with no luck, but Sherry had partially rolled down the window when she left the house. Fred was able to put his arm through the opening, but couldn't quite reach the handle to roll down the window. He needed to be a little taller. He shifted his feet, hoping to find a rock or submerged tree limb, something that would give him another six inches of height. His right foot hit against something that felt pretty solid. He stepped on to the rock and tried reaching the window handle. He almost had it when his foot slipped off the rock, wrenching his arm and shoulder in the window. He winced in pain and tried again to stand on the rock. The pain that shot through his arm and shoulder would have been unbearable under normal circumstances, but the adrenaline was flowing strong and hard. His right foot once again was on the rock, his left foot on nothing and being pulled downstream by the current. He strained to reach the handle. He had it. It was in the down position and he was able to make a half turn, moving the window down a couple of inches. He needed it down more. He pushed the handle back, counter-clockwise, to the down position, and the window moved two more inches. He continued the process until the window was all the way down, praying that the car would stay where it was.

Now what? He reached into the car, putting two fingers to her neck to check for a pulse. He couldn't feel one, but the conditions made it difficult to detect. He reached down, trying to find the button to release the seat belt and shoulder harness. He found it and pushed it. It released. He put his hands under the girl's armpits and pulled with all the strength he had. Her upper body moved, but her legs were pinned down by the steering wheel. He would have to pull himself through the window, get in the passenger side and pull her legs free, straightening them.

Fred Thompson wasn't a huge man, but it still was a relatively small space inside the mid-sized car. He pushed and pulled his way inside and was able to move across the still unresponsive girl. He was no contortionist, but he managed to get into the passenger seat. He was on his knees on the back portion of the seat, facing the girl. He reached down and grabbed both of her knees and pulled. They moved a little bit. He tried again, and this time they moved more, but the shift handle stopped the progress. Lifting her right leg, then her left over the shifter, he was able to straighten her. Her back now rested on the driver's door. He would have to get out on the passenger side and go back to the driver's side to pull her out. It was a good thing that Fred was in relatively good shape for his age.

The passenger side window rolled down easily. He pulled himself through the window, backwards, and then rolled over to get out the rest of the way. He literally swam out of the car. Once he was out, the current pulled him downstream twenty feet past the car. He got his feet under himself and slowly worked his way back to the driver's side window, fighting the current all the way.

Fred had better luck this time as he pulled Sherry, still unconscious, from the car. The water actually helped the process this time because the water in the car had reached a level that gave the body buoyancy. Fred braced against the current, knowing that as soon as the girl's body was out the window, he would have to fight the current for both of them. She came free from the car. Fred held her securely under both arms as the current grabbed the lower half of her body.

Slowly and straining, he was able to reach the side of the swollen creek and pull her to safety. Once on dry ground, he checked her airway for any blockage, and then checked her breathing. Lying on her back he was able to see her chest was rising and falling with each inhalation and exhalation. The movement was nearly imperceptible, but she was breathing. Fred breathed a prayer of thanks to God, and asked again for help and strength. He would have to carry, pull, or whatever it took to get her up the steep ravine and to the road.

He picked her up, cradling her in his arms, and carried her as far as he could until it was too steep. He would have to pull her the rest of the way. He scooted on his hind side and pulled, moving inches at a time. He wondered if he would have enough strength for the task. He thought to himself, *just one butt cheek ahead of the other*, trying not to think past each small "step".

It seemed like an hour, but really, only twenty minutes had passed. Every few feet he would check for breathing—so far so good. He looked behind him and up. They were almost to the top, only a few feet to go. Fred dug in with renewed energy. One last tug and they were on the edge of the road. He laid a few moments on his back, catching his breath, and hopefully, get a new surge of power in his muscles.

As he lay there, he looked at the top of the trees. The lone headlight continued to shine like a beacon—this time, though, it was a beacon of hope. Then the light moved, and he heard a loud crack from below. The pressure from the car and the current had snapped the tree that was holding it upright. He could barely see it, but the car ended upside down in the middle of the creek, fully submerged. And once again he thanked God.

He got himself upright and then managed to pull the young girl to his pickup, her feet dragging on the pavement. It wasn't easy—none of it had been easy—but he got her into the truck, leaned her against the passenger door, and then got in himself on the driver's side. He turned the truck around and headed back down the hill to the first house he saw that had lights on. He pulled in the driveway, got out and ran to the front door, knocking urgently. A middle-aged man answered the door.

"I need help. It's an emergency. There was a wreck up the road a ways. She needs an ambulance."

Chapter 50

Monday, July 16

It was around ten thirty last night when I received a call from the 9-1-1 dispatcher telling me that there had been a single-car accident up on Wildcat road. Fred Thompson, a local guy, had rescued a young female from the car at the bottom of a ravine. He was able to get her up the steep incline and into his car. He drove her to a nearby house and called 9-1-1. The girl was unresponsive when the paramedics arrived at the house. Ten minutes later, they pronounced her dead. That's when I got the call. A driver's license was found in her back pocket, a gal by the name of Sherry Johnson who lived just a few miles up the road from the accident. She was barely eighteen years old, just graduated from high school, I guessed.

I got out of bed, pulled on a clean pair of pants and a shirt, and grabbed my badge off the dresser. I walked out to the kitchen and put on my socks and shoes. I had to drive to the girl's home and let her parents know. This was the worst part of my job.

I got in the cruiser and drove up Wildcat Road, past the scene of the accident. An investigation of the crash wouldn't happen until tomorrow morning, in the daylight. The mailbox with 12679 stenciled on it was on the opposite side of the road, next to the driveway. I couldn't see the house from the road, but I turned in and came to it a few hundred feet off the road.

I walked to the front door and rang the doorbell. It was as though I had set off a dog alarm. I didn't know how many there were, but they greeted me from the other side of the door, thankfully. It took a while for any human response to the alarm, and then I heard a female voice. She was yelling at the dogs.

The door opened a crack and Mrs. Johnson, I assumed, peered at me through it, shielding me from the still-barking dogs. The questioning look on her face turned to terror when she saw the badge.

"Hello, Ma'am. I'm Police Chief Frank Thomas." I said it loud enough to be heard over the barking. "Are you Mrs. Johnson?"

"Just a minute," she said to me, and then yelled at the dogs again, "Get back! Shut up! GET BACK!"

She stepped outside, quickly closed the door, and answered my question, "Yes, I'm Mrs. Johnson. What happened? Is it Sherry?" Her voice matched the terror on her face.

"Sherry was in an accident." I paused. I'm sorry, Mrs. Johnson, but…" my voice got stuck in my throat. "I'm sorry. Your daughter didn't survive the crash."

A few seconds passed, her mind trying to comprehend what she had just heard. Then she fell into me and wailed—it was the most pitiful, sorrowful sound I have ever heard. The wailing turned to uncontrollable sobbing as she clung to me. All I could do was wrap my arms around her.

I hated my job, at least right now, at this moment. When I was in L.A., there was a host of other professionals who would deal with a victim's family members—psychiatrists, counselors, victim's advocate groups, and others. Not so in Molalla. I was it.

Several minutes passed and I asked her if I could drive her to where her daughter was so she could see her. She accepted the offer. I knew this would be another heart-wrenching scene and prepared myself as best I could on the way down to town.

After the viewing, and allowing Mrs. Johnson some time alone with her daughter's body, I offered to take her over to her pastor's house. I hoped that he or his wife might be able to be with her, and pray with her. The pastor lived in the parsonage right next to the church. I escorted her up to the door and rang the doorbell. We waited a few moments and rang the bell again. A minute later, the pastor answered the door, his wife looking over his shoulder.

"Pastor, I'm Chief Thomas. I'm afraid there's been a tragic accident."

I briefly shared what had happened. His wife, stepped around her husband and put her arms around Mrs. Johnson, then led her to the couch and sat down next to her. I asked if I could help with anything. Pastor Stafford said thank you for all I had done and that he and his wife would take care of her. That's another job that has to be tough—comforting grieving people like Mrs. Johnson.

That was last night. I drove up to the crash site this morning and called Mikey to meet me here at ten o'clock. A tow truck should be here by that time to winch the vehicle up the steep ravine and onto the road. From the road, it looked to be some kind of sports car, but it was so mangled that it was hard to tell what it was.

Mikey arrived five minutes after I did, the same time as the tow truck. After introductions, the three of us walked to the point where the vehicle had left the road. A couple hundred feet up the road, skid marks appeared, and then ended abruptly. There were no marks where the car went over the edge. There was a broken tree limb about fifteen feet up the tree. The driver of this car must have been flying, literally. Speed was definitely a factor in this crash.

Traffic was light. In fact, there was no traffic, not a single car, which wasn't unusual, especially this far up in the foothills. We continued to look around for other clues that might tell us what happened. Mikey followed the skid marks up to where they started. He let out a whistle and motioned for me. The driver, Denny, began the process to winch the vehicle.

"Wuddaya got, Mikey?"

"Look here," he said, pointing down to where the skid started. "Then come down here and take a look. See what happens to skid marks right here? They were in a straight line and then, right here, they take off in another direction, to the left."

"Okay, that does seem unusual. She must have started into a spin right here."

"That's what I'm thinking. Now look back here," he said, pointing down again. "It looks like another set of skid marks, but these tread marks are much wider than the others. They're relatively short in distance, but it looks like there may have been another vehicle involved. Maybe a couple of kids racing down the hill that went way wrong."

I was becoming more impressed with the kid all the time. He was making sense.

Chapter 51

Nicole looked at her alarm clock—10:08—and decided it was time to get up. Work would come all too soon, and Nicole had a lot to do. She would go over to Sherry's and talk about the trial and see if she'd heard anything else. She needed to call her grandma too, even though she didn't think it mattered anymore. Steve was off the hook and she had no desire to tell anyone what she knew. It was safer that way.

She took a shower, got dressed, and went downstairs to find something to eat. Her mom was doing dishes in the kitchen. Mrs. Parker offered to make her a meal, which Nicole gratefully accepted. She soon had a great country breakfast in front of her. A pork chop, leftover from last night's dinner, two scrambled eggs, some hash browns and a cup of coffee. Nicole never drank coffee before she started working at the mill, but now, it was part of her daily diet. Her appetite had also increased dramatically since starting at the mill.

Nicole and her mother had a pleasant conversation while Nicole ate and her mother sipped a cup of tea. Nicole finished the meal and said thank you to her mom. She took her dishes to the sink, rinsed them off and put them in the dishwasher.

"I'm going over to see Sherry, if it's okay. Can I borrow the car?"

"That's fine, honey. I'm not going anywhere today."

Nicole took the keys from the rack on the side of the cupboard and gave her mom a hug. "Thanks, Mom. I love you."

"I love you too, honey."

She went out through the back screen door and noticed a slip of paper under the wiper blade, not unlike the note she had left at the police station. She unfolded it and read it, instantly turning pale, her knees nearly buckling underneath her.

Let this be a warning. Keep your mouth shut or you'll be next.

She felt nauseated, but she couldn't go back inside—her mom would ask her all kinds of questions. She decided to go over to Sherry's anyway. Maybe she had received a similar note. Nicole forced herself not to think about what the warning might be.

She drove down the long driveway. It was only a few miles to Sherry's place but it seemed much longer this morning. She pulled into the long driveway and parked the car in front of the house. She walked up the steps to the front door and rang the doorbell, expecting the dogs to greet her, and then to hear the sound of Sherry's feet coming down the stairs to open the door.

The dogs came, but Sherry didn't. No one did. Inside, the chiming stopped, but the barking didn't. She tried the doorbell again with the same results. She tried the door. It was locked. It was unusual that no one was home. She walked around the right side of the house and looked in the double-car garage, through the side door window. There was no car, only the 4-wheelers that she and Sherry would take out in the woods on occasion, and sometimes out to Sand Lake.

Nicole walked back to her car. Sherry rarely went anywhere

before noon—her mother either. *Maybe she or her mother had a doctor's appointment or something.* She could only hope.

She reached into her jean pocket and pulled out the note, reading it again. A wave of dread washed over Nicole as she got back in the driver's seat. Something had happened—she could feel it. She pulled out onto the road and headed towards town. Five or six miles down the road, there were two police cars, their lights flashing, and a tow truck backing to the edge of the road. There had been an accident. Nicole brought her car to a stop, recognizing Molalla's chief of police as he approached her car.

Chapter 52

We heard a car coming from up the road. It hadn't rounded the corner yet, and then it came into view. The driver slowed to a stop, a young gal, looked to be about the same age as the crash victim. I recognized her, but didn't know her name. I walked up to the car and spoke to her through the open window.

"There's been an accident," I told her. "A car went over the edge of the road last night."

"Is the driver okay?" she asked.

She seemed a little shaken—probably the first time she'd been at the scene of an accident. "No, I'm afraid the driver didn't survive."

"Who was it? Who's the victim?"

She grew pale and I realized that there was a strong possibility that they knew each other. I should have figured it out before.

"Her name is Sherry Johnson. Do you know her?"

Tears filled her eyes, then the tears turned to sobs. "No! It's not true. It can't be," she screamed through her sobbing.

My heart ached for this young lady. I gently placed my hand on her shoulder.

"I'm sorry. What's your name?"

"Nicole Parker," the sobbing starting to subside. "I live up the road a few miles past Sherry's place. She's been my best friend forever."

"I'm sorry, Nicole. Can I help you get somewhere?"

"No, I want to go to my grandma's," she cried.

"I can have Mike over there follow you if you want—just to make sure you get over there safely."

She looked in Mikey's direction and thought about it.

"No. I'll be okay. Thanks."

"Be careful then."

I watched her drive away and thought how cruel, and painful, life can be.

Chapter 53

Tears filled Nicole's eyes, blurring her vision, as she drove down to Molalla and then to her grandma's place in Canby. She wasn't sure how, but thirty minutes later, she arrived at her grandma's. She was scared, terrified really, her heart broken. She didn't know what she would do. She drove into Gram's driveway, got out, and walked around the back where she thought she would find her.

"Grams." Nicole started sobbing again, and her grandmother, startled at first, got up and put her arms around her granddaughter.

"What's wrong, sweetheart? What happened?"

It took Nicole a while, but she finally told Grams about Sherry. Grams knew that there were no words to help, so she continued to hold her only grandchild.

We watched the car being pulled slowly from the bottom of the ravine, and eventually all the way up to the road. It was upside down, but Denny said he would get the car turned right-side-up shortly.

He stretched the cable across the undercarriage of the car and attached the four inch hook to the top of the door frame, which was at the bottom now. He got in the tow truck and stretched the cable until it was taut, then started the winch. The hoist was at a forty-five degree angle which was enough to slowly bring the car to rest on what would have been its four wheels, but two were sheared off. The red Firebird was barely recognizable, as mangled as it was. How Fred Thompson got her out of that mess was beyond me.

"Mikey, I'm going to go check out the Johnson place again. I'll be back in a little while. While I'm gone, get some measurements, skid marks, distance from the road to where the car came to rest. Let's try to figure out how fast she was going when she bit it. Check out the car before Denny takes it."

"Okay, but what am I looking for on the car?"

"Don't know. If you see something that seems peculiar, write it down."

"Got it. What are you looking for up the road?"

"I don't know that either, just going to look. I'll know it when I see it."

"Detective work, right?

"That's right, Mikey, detective work. There might not be anything, but I have that gut feeling."

Chapter 54

After holding her for several minutes, they sat down at the table on the back patio, Gram's favorite place to visit when the weather permitted.

Nicole told her the whole story. She pulled the note from her pocket and showed it to her grandmother. The expression on Gram's face changed from compassion to one of alarm.

"There's got to be someone you can trust with this, Nicole; I mean someone in law enforcement. You can't live the rest of your life with this weighing you down."

"I know, but I'm scared. My best friend"—Nicole choked back a sob—"is dead. The note said it would happen again if I didn't keep my mouth shut."

"But you can't do that. We have to find someone. What about the note you left for the chief of police?"

"I don't think they figured it out, Grams. Not everyone knows the Bible like you. He probably gave up trying to figure it out."

"But do you think you can trust him? Do you think he's involved with this family?"

"I don't know; I don't think so. He's only been in Molalla a few years, if that. He seems to be okay from what I know about him."

"Well then, I suggest we write him another note, not so cryptic this time. We have to do something. The bad guys don't know that you know yet, but they will soon enough. But you have to show them, or at least make them think, that you won't say anything. Do you have any idea why they killed Sherry?"

"I think if Steve Carlson would have been convicted, nothing would have happened. But he wasn't, and the investigation will start up again, probably already has, Grams. I think they started worrying that I might say something."

"But why would they kill Sherry—why not you?"

"Because Sherry has a big mouth—they made sure she wouldn't talk to anyone and figured by threatening me again, well, that I'd stay quiet. But I don't want to. They killed her, Grams." The tears came again, rolling down her cheeks.

Grams was thinking. "That makes sense." She scooted her chair next to Nicole and put her arm around her. "Now listen. You need to go to work today just like nothing happened."

"No, I can't. I can't do it," Nicole responded incredulously.

"Yes you can. You have to. I'll write a note to the chief. You swing by after work and pick it up. I'll leave it under the doormat. Leave it at the police station, same as last time."

"Grams?" Nicole separated herself from the embrace and looked her in the eye. "I'm scared. Will you please pray for me? I don't think I can do it."

Grams pulled Nicole back to herself and hugged her again. "Of course I'll pray for you. And you can do it. God will give you a way.

"Thanks. I love you Grams."

The tears continued to run down her cheeks.

Chapter 55

I drove up the road to the Johnson place and looked around. There didn't seem to be anything out of the ordinary. I drove slowly on the way back, looking for anything that might help piece this thing together. About a mile above the wreck, there were tire marks in the loose gravel on the shoulder of the road. They came pretty close to going in the ditch, but the vehicle must have recovered, judging by the tracks coming out of the ditch. I got out to look around and found a piece of plastic from a tail light or brake light. I picked it up and stuck it in my pocket.

A few minutes later, I drove back down to the crash site. Denny had already left with the car. Mikey was just coming up from the ravine holding a tape measure in his hand. I pulled over and spoke through the open window.

"Are you ready for some lunch?"

"I'm famished, Chief."

"I'll meet you at the Y. What do you want? I'll order," I offered, and he accepted.

"I'll have a Y-Burger basket with onion rings." The Y-Burger consisted of a one pound patty the size of a dinner plate. The onion rings came on another dinner-sized plate.

"You must be really hungry, Mikey."

"Yessir, I am."

I got to the Y and Mikey came about five minutes later. We found an empty booth only because the lunch hour rush was mostly over with. We talked about the accident, making sure to keep our voices down. You never knew who might overhear our discussion.

"You find anything up there after I left?"

"Yeah, I think so, but maybe it's nothing."

I was listening and asked, "So, what is it?"

"Well, you saw what appeared to be another set of tracks. When I was inspecting the vehicle, I noticed something on the rear fender, passenger side, close to the tail light. Now, there's no way of telling if it was there before the crash, but there was a dent and some black paint there. The dent wasn't necessarily unusual, but the black paint? I thought that was unusual—looked like maybe another vehicle may have clipped her, sending her into a spin. But that's all speculation. That paint may have already been there."

I pulled the piece of broken tail light out of my pocket and laid it on the table in front of Mikey.

"Found this up the road a mile or so. Looked like a vehicle almost went in the ditch up there, fairly recently. We'll check this piece with the car's and see if it matches. I'll talk to Mrs. Johnson to see if that dent was already there."

"Can we do something before you go talk to her?"

"What's that?"

"Well, I don't know if it's protocol and all that, but I'd like to go see if Steve Carlson is around. Just to chat, ya know?"

"He probably doesn't feel much like chattin' right now, especially with a police officer," I suggested.

Today's events, with a possible hit-and-run, made me forget all about the renewed murder investigation.

"I know, but it couldn't hurt, just to see," Mikey persisted.

"All right, I'll go with you."

"Let's go then."

Mikey was already up and heading for the door. I laid a ten on the table, got Violet's attention and told her to keep the change. She smiled and said that she would see me next time. Sitting at the booth next to the door was Lester and Chester Williams, the bus garage owners.

"Hi ya, Chief." It was Lester, I think.

"Hi Lester... Chester." I looked at both as I said it. "How are you guys?"

"We're doin' fine," they answered simultaneously. "Is there any news on the murder investigation?"

"If there was, you know I couldn't tell you anyway."

"Or what—you'd have to kill us?" Lester laughed, and Chester choked on a fry, coughing into his napkin.

I laughed too, "That's a good one—sounds like a line from a movie."

Lester continued to talk, "We heard there was a wreck up Wildcat last night. What happened?"

News gets around fast in a small town.

"A car left the road. Young gal got killed."

Lester said, "Oh, sorry to hear that. I always hate to hear it when a young person dies like that. It's a darn shame."

I agreed, "Yes, it's terrible—a very sad thing."

"Who was it?" Lester asked. "We might know her; or her family anyway."

"Her name was Sherry Johnson. She just graduated this year—probably rode one of your busses," I answered, but not wanting to say anything more. "Well, I'll be seeing you guys."

Chester continued his coughing fit.

"Are you okay?" I asked, thinking I might have to apply the Heimlich maneuver.

Lester answered for his brother. "He'll be fine—happens all the time."

"Okay, then," not so sure that he would be fine. "I'll see you fellas."

I met Mikey back at the station to drop off his car. It was across town to the Carlson residence, but, in Molalla, that wasn't too far. Besides, I was kind of looking forward to seeing Jennie Carlson again, but I didn't say that to Mikey.

We arrived at the house. There was no car in the driveway, and it didn't look like anyone was home. We went to the front door and I rang the doorbell. We laughed when the bell's rendition of *Yankee Doodle Dandy* could be clearly heard out here on the porch. Unfortunately, the melody didn't bring anyone to the door. We were somewhat disappointed, although for different reasons.

"Nobody's home there."

We turned to see a man in his forties walking across the driveway, a black lab at his side. He wore black-rimmed glasses with thick lenses, but not quite Coke-bottle thick. Mikey and I stepped off the porch and met him at the sidewalk.

"I'm Jennie's neighbor, Brian Adams," he said, sticking out a greasy hand as the lab sniffed my crotch. "Excuse the grease. I was just workin' on my lawnmower—Brandy, knock it off, ya dang dog!"

Brandy stopped sniffing, but continued to smile a dog smile at me. I shook Brian's greasy hand and said, "Hi. Frank Thomas. This is Mike Benson." Mikey shook hands too. "So, do you know where Steve or his mom might be?"

He shook his head, "Not sure where they went, but Jennie told me that her and Steve were getting away for a while. Can't say as I blame 'em—I'd want to get away, too."

I agreed. "Yeah, I'm sure I would too. Well, if you see them when they come back, will you give me a call?" I handed him my card.

He took it, looked at it, and said "Sure. No problem."

We turned and walked back to the cruiser with Brandy escorting us.

"I think they'll be gone for a while, like maybe a long while."

We both turned around together, kind of like we practiced the move, like synchronized swimming or something.

"What makes you say that?"

Brian was smiling at Mikey and me, and said, "You two looked like Fred and Ginger right there."

Mikey was clueless, but I knew who he was referring too. I laughed—I liked this guy.

"So what makes ya say that?" I asked.

"Well, they had four suitcases, big ones, not the 'just for one night' kind. Jennie asked if I would watch the place for a while, mow the grass, water her flowers, ya know."

"You're right, it doesn't sound like an over-nighter. Okay, thanks again."

We turned again to leave, and Brian called after us one more time.

"Have any idea who dunnit, who killed that Riggs girl?"

"Not a clue," which wasn't quite true.

We finally escaped the inquisitive neighbor and the crotch-sniffer named Brandy. Mikey went home when we got back to the station, but I stayed for a couple hours, doing paperwork that had been stacking up. Then I went home—threw a couple of patties on the grill. All in all, this day sucked, as Mikey and his generation would say.

Chapter 56

It was one-thirty in the morning when Nicole walked out to the car. She was exhausted, not only from the physical labor, but even more so from the emotional hell that she had been through that day. Nicole wasn't sure how she made it through the shift. She wouldn't have if it wasn't for a few of the guys who were helping her out. They'd heard about Sherry and knew that they were close friends.

By the time she got to Canby to get the note from her grandma, it was two o'clock. She got into town, parked in front of the White Horse, and walked to the police station to leave the note. She got home at three o'clock. Nicole climbed into bed and cried herself to sleep, surprised that she had any tears left in her eyes.

I pulled into my reserved parking spot and could see that there was a piece of paper left at the same place as before. It looked like our reluctant informant might be giving us more clues. I took the note off the glass, unlocked the door, and went to my desk to read it. There was nothing cryptic about this one. I got up and was heading out the door when Mikey drove in and parked next to me.

He didn't waste any time with a greeting. "Where're you headin' this early?" he asked.

I tossed him the note and gave him a minute to read it.

"I'm going to see her, but I don't want to drive the cruiser over there. Can I use your rig?"

"No problem—here ya go," and he tossed me the keys.

"I'll fill you in when I get back."

"All right boss. Later."

My head was spinning the entire twenty-minute drive to Canby. The contents of the note were disturbing, to say the least. There was an address and a first name—Gloria. She said to come to the address and make sure that no one saw me leaving town, and, for goodness sakes, don't drive a cop car. Those were her words.

Mikey was right about the first note. It was from the Bible and he had interpreted it correctly. The second note strongly suggested that this person knew the location of Sandi Riggs' body. The note also indicated that the body's location would go a long way toward naming the killers, plural.

I parked Mikey's car around the block from the address, as instructed in the note. I walked across a vacant lot, also as instructed, and came to the weathered cedar fence. There was a gate at the left end of the fence—it opened.

"Chief Thomas. Come in over here."

I turned to face a lady who looked to be around seventy or so. I walked to the gate, neither of us saying anything until we were within the confines of the fence in what I assumed was her back yard.

"My name is Gloria Parker. Thank you for coming on such

short notice," she said, concern showing in her eyes, mixed with fear.

"Hello, Gloria. You can call me Frank," I extended my hand, which she shook, "it seemed like I needed to come right away."

We sat on her back patio that had a little flower garden in the middle of it. Little pop-up sprinklers were watering the colorful array of annuals. The umbrella shaded the table where we sat and I settled in to hear the story that Mrs. Parker had to tell.

It was an hour later when I stood to leave. I thanked her, and went out the same way I had come in. I drove back to Molalla, taking the back roads, being careful to avoid anyone who might recognize me and wonder why I was driving my deputy's car. I parked Mikey's car and went in to the station. He was sitting at his desk, looking up at me expectantly when I entered.

I returned his look, "You won't believe this, Mikey."

"What's going on? What'd she say? You know who the killer is?"

He fired his volley of three questions at me, which I was getting used to by now, and only answered the last one. "We're talking killers—there's more than one."

His eyes widened, and his voice took on that higher pitch that it does when he gets excited. "So who is it? Tell me."

I went over and poured myself a cup of coffee that he had made and sat down at my desk. I recounted the story that Mrs. Parker had told me.

"Wow. I mean...wow! So what do we do now?" He was chompin' at the bit to go catch the bad guys.

"Hold on there, cowboy. There's a lot we don't know, first of all, and secondly, we have to call this in to the state police."

"But, what about the girl? Won't that put her in danger if those detectives start snooping around up there? Don't you think we should go check it out, drive up there, you and me? If it's true like she said, we don't know who all is involved."

Mikey was making good sense, but I wasn't thrilled about stirring up a deadly hornet's nest that could get us killed. There was already one person dead, and if Mrs. Parker's story was true, the Johnson girl was a victim of foul play too.

"C'mon, Chief. You know I'm right. We gotta do this," he pleaded.

I thought about Dickey, my partner, and how we were back in the day. We would have taken the bull by the horns—a much more appropriate saying for Molalla than for L.A.—and we would have gone out and got the bad guys. I knew Mikey was right. I started to remember what it was like to be young again, except for the physical part—I don't think I'll ever remember that part. I came back to the present.

"You're right. I agree. But let's get a plan together. The only evidence that we have is hearsay. We can't just go up there and start digging up a driveway to find the body. Let's figure this out."

I was reminded again of how Dickey and I would go out after work for a beer and talk about things, plan things, and by golly, we would get it done. We caught a lot of bad guys over the years. I got a little misty-eyed just thinking about it, so I changed the topic to food.

"Wuddaya say we go get some food in our bellies? I always think better that way anyway. Where do you want to eat? I'll buy."

"The Y?"

"We just ate there yesterday."

"Your point?"

"Fine."

Chapter 57

I ordered the breaded veal cutlets, mashed potatoes and gravy, fresh corn on the cob smothered in butter, and a dinner roll with butter and boysenberry jam. Mikey had the Y-B*urger*, again, this time with spicy fries and a boat load of ketchup, and a thick chocolate shake to wash it all down. Neither of us talked much as we devoured the feast in front of us and waited for a plan to develop.

Mikey broke the silence between us, "Why do you suppose they killed Sherry Johnson, assuming the Parker girl's story is true?"

"I'll tell you what I think. From what her grandma told me, and what Nicole told her, the Johnson girl had a big mouth. She was a loose cannon in their eyes. After Steve Carlson was found innocent, the Williams family knew that the investigation would be ramping up, and they didn't want that girl talking—'loose lips sinks ships', as they say."

"Who says that?"

"Never mind."

"But why not Nicole Parker—it sounds like she knows more than the other one?"

"Okay. So they kill Sherry and make it look like an accident.

Nicole knows it's not an accident, though, and they make sure she knows it by leaving that note. Nicole's the quiet one, more likely to keep it to herself, especially when they threatened to kill her and her parents. She knows they would, too, since they've killed two people already. What they didn't consider was that Nicole is one tough cookie. I don't know Nicole's parents, but I got the idea that her grandma is a strong woman. She must have passed it on down to Nicole."

I could tell the wheels were turning in Mikey's brain.

"So what do we do now? Did those cutlets you ate give you any brilliant ideas?"

"I think it was the whole meal, right down to the roll and jam, but yeah, it inspired a plan."

"So tell me already."

"Fine, but let's get out of here. I don't want anyone eavesdropping on us."

The Y was starting to fill up with locals and, at this point, I didn't know the good guys from the bad guys. We left and drove over to my place and talked about it for a couple of hours while I downed a couple of beers and Mikey drank his Coke.

He got up to leave. "See you in the morning, Chief."

"Okay."

Chapter 58

Wednesday, July 18

Mikey and I met at the station and worked out a few more details of the plan. It was nine thirty when I headed out south of town, the opposite direction of Oregon City, up Wildcat Road. This route would take me past the crash site where Sherry Johnson went off the road. Farther on up Wildcat was the Johnson place. I heard that Mrs. Johnson, Corrine, was staying at her pastor's place for a while. The house would be empty. I decided to stop by the place, looking for any evidence that would suggest that the accident wasn't an accident, but the search didn't reveal any clues at all. I wasn't surprised, but it was worth a look. I continued up Wildcat, past the Parker home, and five miles beyond, I came to the place that I had come to see.

I had an address, and Mikey was familiar with the area. He was able to give me good enough directions to get me to the Williams' place. I saw the driveway—at least I thought it was the right one. There was a mailbox on the opposite side of the road. It had no name or number on it, just an old, gray, dented box with a faded red flag, sitting on a leaning and rotting six-by-six post.

The house wasn't visible from the road. I turned into the gravel driveway, rounded a corner and there stood the house, if you could call it that. It was more like a shack, but even that was a stretch of the imagination. It was gray with aged plywood siding that looked like it had never been painted. A porch was loosely attached to it, sagging badly, with a railing around it that was broken in three places. The roof was covered by at least four inches of moss, more in some places. A chimney that was missing more than a few bricks was sitting precariously on the ridge of the house, and out of it came some curling wisps of smoke. On either side of the house were a couple of wrecks, cars that may have run at one time, but certainly didn't now. The gravel and dried-mud driveway had given way to a concrete driveway that didn't look very old, at least compared to the rest of the place. It could easily have been put in six months ago.

I got out of the cruiser when, at about the same time, the front door opened, revealing a little girl, four or five years old, with her brown hair in braids. She was wearing a tattered summer dress, and no shoes or socks on her feet. I figured that this must be the little girl that innocently talked to her friends, Nicole and Sherry, on the morning after. She looked warily at me, and from inside I heard her mother yell, "Get your butt back in here, Kayleen." Then for emphasis, she added a loud, "NOW, dammit!"

Her body turned to go back in but she continued to watch me, not looking where she was going. I had to ask myself if I was really in Oregon, or if I'd been transplanted deep in the Ozarks. The yellow-stained commode sitting by the side of the porch and the outhouse a few feet away from it confirmed it. *I really am in the Ozarks*, I thought, taking it all in.

I walked up the two steps to the porch, not sure if they would support me or not. I knocked on the partially-open door through which Kayleen had disappeared. A woman's face peaked through the opening—our eyes met, but she didn't say a thing.

"Good morning, Ma'am. I'm Chief Thomas, with the Molalla police department. We've been getting reports of some poachers in the area. I've been asking folks around here if they've seen or heard anything suspicious, you know, like gunshots?"

"All the time—there's gunshots all the time 'round these parts. Nothin' unusual though, happens all the time."

At least she didn't slam the door in my face. She was probably starved for some adult conversation.

"Well, that's pretty much what most of the folks have been sayin'. If you hear of anything suspicious or unusual, would you give me a call?" I handed her my card but doubted she would ever use it to call me. "Goodbye, Ma'am."

She closed the door without saying goodbye. I turned and again was careful as I descended the steps and walked across the driveway to the cruiser, wondering if I was walking on Sandi Riggs concrete grave.

Chapter 59

It was decided that Mike would talk to Nicole Parker. Chief Thomas had called Nicole's grandmother before he left on his mission up at the Williams' place. He let her know that Mike would be contacting her, and that it was necessary to meet with Nicole and talk with her about the situation.

Mike was dressed in cut-off blue jeans, converse tennis shoes, and a tee shirt that said, *Here today; gone to Maui,* on the front and a surf scene on the back. He drove his car to Mulino, a small community surrounded by farms, with its own grade school, a country store, and the post office. There's a small airport, too, that is popular among plane enthusiasts. The Airport Café borders the airport and always has its share of "fly-in" customers when the weather was favorable for flying.

Mulino also has a small public golf course—Ranch Hills it's called—just a mile or so off Highway 213. That's where Mike would meet up with Nicole. No one would think it strange that he would be meeting her for a round of golf. They were close enough to the same age that anyone who saw them would think that they were a couple of kids out on a date, or just school friends enjoying each other's company.

He pulled into the gravel parking lot and saw the black Chevy Citation that Nicole's grandmother said she would be driving. He parked next to her and got out of his car, and a couple seconds later, Nicole opened her door and got out. He had seen her the morning after the wreck, but she was inside the car. He did the 'look-over' that most guys do when they meet a girl, struggling to remember that he was here on business. He figured, though, that he did have to act the part of a boyfriend. They were the only ones in the parking lot.

"Hi, you must be Nicole." He felt stupid for saying it—who else would she be?

"Hi, yeah, I'm Nicole, nice to meet you, Mike."

Instead of a handshake, she gave him a hug, giving the appearance that they were just good friends to anyone who might see them. Mike enjoyed the hug, and even felt his face flush a bit. He hoped that she wouldn't notice.

"Wuddaya say we go shoot a round of nine? We can talk as we go," Mike suggested.

"Sounds good—let's go."

Mike got his set of clubs out of the trunk that both of them would use. Ranch Hills was casual enough that you could share clubs, and wear cutoff jeans and tee shirts. They went into the clubhouse where he paid for both of them. The man behind the counter, who also was the owner, told them to have a good time and to please replace the divots.

"We will," Mike said, and they walked out the door to the first tee.

"Have you ever golfed before?" he asked.

She laughed. "Just putt-putt, if that counts. What's a divot, anyway?"

"You'll see soon enough. I'll go first, then, and show you how it's done," he said, rolling his eyes to let her know that he was no pro at this.

His shot off the tee went fairly straight, hooking just a bit but still on the fairway. Mike suggested that she start out using a five-iron. She took a few practice swings and stepped up to the ball. Her first attempt missed everything, and her second missed the ball, but carved out a large divot on her side of the ball.

"That is a divot," he said, laughing, pointing to the clump of sod five feet in front of the ball.

On her third attempt, she made contact, with the ball this time. It didn't go very far, but it went straight, and she was delighted. For a moment, she almost forgot why she was here with a guy she didn't even know. She rarely dated in high school, not because she didn't have the opportunity, she just wanted her life to be as uncomplicated as possible. And this couldn't be considered an official date.

She thought about her life now—complicated in ways she never imagined. And that triggered thoughts of Sherry, and the tears came again as they had so often. *Would they ever stop*, she wondered.

Mike replaced the divot and noticed that she had grown sullen and quiet as they walked together down the center of the fairway. He felt bad for her, with all she had been through. He waited until they were on the second hole before he brought up the subject that they had come to discuss. There was no one else on the course and that made it easy to talk.

By the time they reached the tee on the seventh hole, she had shared the whole story, from the night on the steps of the high school, to the present, not leaving out any detail. He was glad that she trusted him. He talked to her about the plan that he and the chief had come up with, a plan that would involve her and her family leaving town for a while, maybe a few weeks until it was all over. This was the second plan that Nicole didn't think would work, but she was proved wrong about her grandma's plan. Maybe she would be wrong about this too.

"You'll never convince my dad to leave, especially for that long. He won't do it. I guarantee it."

"What if Chief Thomas talks to him. They're both from the same generation, maybe your dad would listen to him. It would be the safest way for you and your parents. It might not even be a bad idea for your grandma to go with you all, a nice family vacation."

"If Chief Thomas is able to talk him into it, he'll be the first to talk him into anything," she replied, her doubt evident in the sound of her voice.

"When we get done out here, I'll talk with him. He'll pay a visit to your place. I'm assuming you'll be at work, right?"

"Yeah, but I don't want to be there. My grandma says that I need to, though, so the Williams family doesn't think I'm talking. I suppose she's right, and I'll do whatever it takes to see them get caught."

"Call home at your lunch break. Chief Thomas will talk to your dad before then," Mike suggested, then added, "Speaking of the Williams clan, do you have any idea which ones might be involved?"

"I don't really know. Connie Williams is Paul's wife. That's where Sandi's body is buried, up at their place. Then there's Kim. She's a niece, Paul's brother's daughter, the one that warned Sherry and me that morning. I think her dad's name is Tim. Beyond that, the judge may be involved, and even the D.A. According to Kim, there's a lotta them involved. That's why I was so scared. I didn't know who I could talk to. I hoped that it would all just go away. I guess that doesn't happen in real life, does it?"

"No, not usually—but this will work out. I have a lot of faith in the chief. More than that, I believe that God will work it out."

"You sound like Grams—she thinks God will work it all out too. I don't know about this god-thing. Why would a good God let any of this happen? How could he let Sherry die?"

"I wish I could give you a good reason, but honestly, I don't know why God lets bad stuff happen." He could have given some reasons, but didn't feel that it was a good time for a theological discussion.

"At least you're honest and aren't making up some phony answer."

He was glad he kept his mouth shut.

They had forgotten all about golfing and just walked and talked. They approached the ninth hole and decided to tee off, so that if anyone was watching, all they would see was cute young couple having a fun time together.

Chapter 60

No sooner was Chief Thomas out of the Williams' driveway that Connie Williams was on the phone, calling her husband, Paul, at work.

"A cop was here," she hissed into the mouthpiece—she was upset.

"When? Why?"

"He just left. He said he was looking for poachers up here."

"What did you tell him?"

"What the hell d'ya think I told him, that we're all dealing drugs up here, and that we're killing anyone we think might talk? You think I'm a fool?"

"No, I don't." he said, trying to calm her down. "What did you tell him though?"

"He asked if I'd heard any shootin' goin' on up here, and I told him, yeah, all the time—could very well be some poachin' goin' on."

"Did he ask any more questions?"

Calming down some, she answered, "Not really—just said that most people he's talked to are saying the same thing. He left his card for me to call him if I heard anything."

"Who was it?"

"Card says Frank Thomas, Chief of Police in Molalla."

The line went dead in Connie's ear. Paul hung up and immediately dialed another number.

We got problems. It's that cop, Chief Thomas. He was just out at the house. Connie just called to let me know."

"What was he doin' out there?"

"Some bullshit story about poachers, said he was wondering if Connie had heard or seen anything unusual. I think he suspects something. Wuddaya wanna do?"

"I'll take care of it. You gonna be around the phone for a while?"

"Yeah, I'll be right here."

"I'll call ya back."

Chapter 61

"**No!**" **Chester Williams'** voice boomed over the line to his brother's right ear. "Two people are already dead. Now you're talkin' about another one, this time a cop!"

Lester couldn't see Chester over the phone lines, but he could picture his twin's face, beet red, and his nose a shade darker. The small wisp of white hair, rising above the rest of his thinning hair, would be standing up in protest.

"He knows something. He's gonna keep snoopin'. We can't let him do it," Lester said.

"Let him snoop. He ain't gonna find nothin'. Don't do somethin' stupid, you old fool! Bryce took care of the Johnson girl so she won't talk. And you don't think that the chief has told anyone about his suspicions? You know damn well he has! He ends up dead—they'll be all over our asses."

Lester let him vent for a few more seconds and then tried to reason with him, "Listen, Chester, we'll get someone from down south to come handle it, professional like. There's no way they'll connect us with him."

Lester hadn't seen Chester this agitated about business matters before. But then, neither of them had been through something like this fiasco. This was uncharted territory.

"I'm tellin' you, Lester, if you waste that cop, I'm out! Are you hearing me, Les? I'm gone."

"Now just calm down. We'll get through this, Chester. It will work out. It always does."

Even though Lester was always more daring and more vocal than Chester, he depended on the calming, and more cautious, demeanor of his twin. The strengths of each had served them well over the years, but now, they were in danger of coming apart at the seams.

"Okay, Chester, I'll hold off, at least for a while, but if he keeps snoopin' around, we need to take measures."

There was silence on the other end of the line. Lester hung up, but he had no intention of holding off. He'd be damned if he would let the business be destroyed by some podunk cop from Molalla—damned if he would. He and Chester had given their lives for this business, their very souls. He picked up the receiver again and dialed.

"Get'r done."

"When?"

"Tonight."

"Consider it done."

"And the Parker girl?"

"Do it."

Chapter 62

After the trip out to the Williams' place, I drove back to town, stopping at the accident scene one more time to have a look. I stood where Sherry's car left the road and closed my eyes, trying to construct in my mind's eye what may have happened.

Speed was involved, no doubt about that. But why? Why did she feel the need for speed, so to speak? She knew the road, probably had driven it at least a hundred times in the couple years that she had her license. Alcohol wasn't a factor. The questions were recurring thoughts, and my inner voice kept whispering to my subconscious, *they wanted to kill her.*

I knew it was true, but I didn't have any concrete evidence to prove it. I drove back to the station. Mikey wasn't there. He was probably still on his "blind date" at the golf course with the Parker girl. I smiled and thought that he probably didn't mind that assignment at all.

The black paint on the rear fender of the Firebird prompted me to call DMV and do a check on vehicles that the Williams family might own. I started by checking out Paul Williams. There were two vehicles registered under his name, but neither of them was black. I checked out Paul's father, Lester Williams, and his twin brother, Chester, but again, neither of them owned a black vehicle. Frustrated and hungry, I realized it was already one o'clock and I hadn't eaten lunch yet. I drove to the Y, not only to satisfy my appetite, but I wanted to talk to Violet, too. I wanted to get a little more information on the Williams family, and I knew that she would be able to supply it.

The parking lot was still full despite the fact that it was well past the noon hour, already one twenty. I went inside and saddled up to the counter. Violet was busy cooking up orders when she looked up and saw me.

"Hey Chief, what'll it be today?"

"The special, please—what else?"

In five minutes, the steaming hot plate of fried chicken, mashed potatoes and chicken gravy, and corn on the cob, was set before me.

"Violet, I don't know how you do it. You're the best."

She smiled and acknowledged the compliment. She didn't have any more orders that she was cooking up, so she came over and asked me how things were going.

"I've just been working on the Riggs case again. Then there was that unfortunate accident up on Wildcat."

"That's sure too bad about the Johnson girl—such a nice girl. I hate to see stuff like that happen, especially to young people."

"Yeah, it's a tragedy, all right. I hate responding to calls like that. It's the worst part of my job," I responded, while pondering how to ask Violet about the Williams family, without her getting suspicious.

Right then she spoke up, "She and her mom live clear up Wildcat, don't they? Wasn't it just a few miles from her place where the accident happened?"

"Yeah, they live way up there, just a couple of other folks

above them. The Parkers live up past their place, and then just one more house up there—one of the Williams family. You know who they are?"

"Sure, I know that family—lived here almost as long as I have. Paul lives up there at that place."

I didn't even have to ask a question. She kept talking and gave me information about the whole family.

"Chester and Lester, the twins, own the bus company—have for years. Of course, you know that Sandi Riggs was one of their drivers. There's Paul, and then his brother, Tim, who lives out in Colton."

Violet kept talking, and before too long, she had rattled off the names of the twin's siblings, at least the living one, all their children, and several of the in-laws—a very large family. The list included a judge named Maurer and an Asst. DA named Holton. I almost choked on the chicken that caught in my throat but tried to look impassive while trying to remember names.

"Well, Violet, that meal was great as usual. It's a shame you're married?"

She chuckled. "Why, got something in mind?"

It was my turn to laugh. "I was just thinking that if we would have met fifty years ago we coulda made some beautiful music together."

She winked.

I paid the tab, left a tip on the counter and drove back to the station. Mikey was back by this time and I was greeted by the usual 'Hey Chief'. I asked how his "date" had gone and noticed tinges of red on his face. He gave me the details, at least those pertaining to the case. Looks like I would be making another trip up Wildcat, this time to have a talk with Pete Parker, Nicole's dad. Then I told Mikey what I had been up to.

"I want to run these names and see what shows up."

"Want me to do that for you?"

"Yeah, that would be great."

I handed him the list I had made out in the Y's parking lot and he promptly got in touch with DMV. While he was doing that, I sat and thought. I thought back to the morning I got the call from Robert Payne to come to the bus garage. I started going through all that had happened since. I was lost in my thoughts for a good twenty minutes.

"BINGO!" yelling it like he just won the game, startling me.

"What'd ya find?"

"Jeff Williams, son of Tim Williams, Lester's grandson. There's a brand new truck registered in his name—a black Chevy."

Even though it was not proof that this truck was involved with the crash, things were beginning to add up.

"What's the address?"

"It looks like he lives at his mom and dad's place, out in Colton."

"Wanna take a drive?" He was already out of his chair and heading toward the door.

The drive out Highway 211 to Colton took only fifteen minutes. We took Mikey's car so as not to attract any attention. The Williams' place was located just off the highway, on Deer Creek Lane. We did a drive-by looking for the house number, but we saw the truck before we saw the number.

"Go to the end of the lane and turn around, then park at the school, around the other side from the house," I instructed, trying not to make us look too conspicuous.

"Okay."

We drove by the truck again, but it was hard to tell if there was any damage on its left side. We turned back toward the school and parked.

"Why don't you let me go check it out, Chief? I can be *velly, velly* sneaky."

I laughed at the kid. "Fine, but if anyone sees you and asks what you're doing, you better have a good answer ready."

"I will," he said, his excitement obvious. He got out and doubled back to the Williams' place.

About fifteen minutes later, I saw him heading back to the car. The grin on his face told me that his mission had been successful, whether that meant not getting caught, or maybe it meant more. I would soon find out. He got in the car.

"I saw it, Chief. I saw the damage. It wasn't much, but it was there, right there on the left fender—just a slight ding and some scratches, and the paint was definitely scraped off."

"Good work, Mikey."

"Thanks, but I got more."

"More what?"

"I scraped off a little paint of my own and put it in this baggie here." He held it up proudly for me to see. "I figured we could compare it to the paint on the Firebird to see if it matches."

"All right, Mikey. We're gettin' somewhere now." Again I was impressed. He was going to be a good cop—shoot, he already was. "Let's get back."

This was going to be tricky. Many of the Williams family were more than likely involved, maybe even the judge and deputy district attorney. We arrived back at the station and went inside to talk about what to do next. I knew at some point soon I would need to let the county and state police know of our findings, and figured it would be best to contact Collins and Warren. I called them *Starsky and Hutch* when it was just Mikey and me around. It was doubtful that they were involved in any way with this family, but who knew for sure?

The questions kept spinning around in my mind—*who pulled the trigger? Do we try for a warrant, and for whom—Paul Williams for having a new driveway? Or maybe for Jeff Williams for hit and run, if the paint on his truck matched the paint on Corrine Johnson's Firebird?*

"Mikey, it's all adding up, but all we have is a whole lot of circumstantial evidence. And what judge are we going to get to issue a warrant? Certainly not Judge Maurer, but you know all those judges talk anyway. Maurer will find out one way or another."

We sat and talked for an hour proposing different ideas and strategies, but for every solution, there were ten reasons why it wouldn't work. We both decided that a good night's rest might be what we needed, and that, in the morning, we would meet again.

"I'm going to see Pete Parker before I go home. I'll be in at eight in the morning."

"All right, Chief, I'll see ya then."

Chapter 63

Another drive up Wildcat—it was the second trip up there today. Again, I passed the crash site and the Johnson place, and turned in the long driveway to Pete and Janice Parker's home. I decided that it would be best to talk to the couple together. To my knowledge, neither one of them had a clue that their daughter had been carrying such a huge burden, in addition to the fact that her best friend had been killed and, most likely, murdered.

Nicole was at work and the Parkers only other vehicle was parked in front of the house. *Good*, I thought, *Pete is home.* This was a first-time meeting, but according to Mikey, he's a good guy. I went to the door and rang the bell. Mrs. Parker came to the door, a look of alarm spread across her face when she saw me. I drove my personal vehicle up here, still dressed in civilian clothes, so as not to attract attention, but she recognized me anyway.

"May I help you?" she asked, visibly shaken.

I'm sure she was thinking about Sherry Johnson and the visit that I paid to Mrs. Johnson.

"Good afternoon, Ma'am. I'm Chief Thomas with the Molalla Police. Don't worry, there hasn't been an accident or anything. I just would like to talk to you and your husband about a situation that you need to be aware of."

She looked relieved, but at the same time showed concern. It's usually a traumatic experience for anyone when the police come for a visit. She invited me in and excused herself to go out back to get her husband. They walked in together from the back of the house. I could tell by his firm handshake that he was one of the good ones, and by his calloused hands that he was a hard worker.

"Please have a seat," Mrs. Parker offered.

"Thank you." I sat down in the overstuffed chair that was well-worn, but comfortable. Neither one of the Parkers was comfortable, though.

"So what brings you out here, Chief? I don't think it's a social visit." He said, friendly, but understandably guarded.

"You're right about that, Mr. Parker, it's not a social visit."

I launched into the whole story, beginning with that fateful January night. It took me a good half-hour to tell it. They mostly listened, but interjected with a few questions here and there. Mrs. Parker was alarmed and became more agitated the more she heard. Tears began to flow from her eyes. Mr. Parker received the story in a much more stoic fashion, although his eyes betrayed the concern that he was trying to cover.

"I'm afraid that your daughter is in grave danger, the both of you as well. What I am suggesting, no, urging you to do, is to take a vacation and get out of Dodge." Mrs. Parker looked confused for a moment, but Mr. Parker was familiar with the phrase.

"I can't do that. I can't just call up work and tell them I won't be in."

"I understand, but these are extraordinary circumstances that Nicole, through no fault of her own, has gotten involved in. You know that these people mean business and you don't know what they might do next."

Mrs. Parker spoke, "But why didn't she tell us? We would have listened."

I could tell that she was hurt that Nicole hadn't confided in her, but I certainly understood why.

"She's scared, Ma'am. She believed that you and Mr. Parker would be safe if she didn't say anything. When Sherry was killed, she knew that nobody was safe. You have a very brave daughter. And she is greatly concerned for the both of you, and her grandma too. That's why I'm urging you to do something that goes totally against your grain. I'm not being dramatic when I tell you that it's a life and death situation."

I stopped talking and let my last words hang in the air. The Parkers were both silent for several moments, except for the sniffles that came from Mrs. Parker.

Pete Parker spoke slow and measured, "I guess we don't have much choice, do we? I have a hard time believing that the Williams family is involved in all this. I've know them for years, went to school with some of them. And Lester and Chester?—I can't believe it."

"I'm sorry, Mr. Parker, but it is true. Can I count on you to be packed and ready to go when Nicole gets home from work? It's imperative that you leave as soon as possible. Here's the number to the police station, and my home, too. Call me when you get to where you're going."

I stood to leave, shaking Mr. Parker's hand, while Mrs. Parker started sobbing. I spent the drive back to town deep in thought. *Now what? What should the next step be?* Before I knew it, I was pulling into my driveway.

Chapter 64

Chester Williams was beside himself. He knew there was going to be more killing, and all he wanted was out of this mess. *After all*, he thought, *it was his fool brother who started all this killing business.* Chester sat in his over-stuffed chair, brooding over the sad state of affairs. *Things had gone so well for years. The business was more lucrative than either one of them could have ever imagined. And who was it hurting anyway? All that it did was give a buzz here and there to some kids. It didn't hurt anyone.*

He contemplated his next move. The best thing he could think of was to get out. Just leave. He decided that's what he would do—run. He had always been the coward, the one that was always scared. He got out of his chair and walked to his bedroom to start packing—the sooner he got out, the better. He had enough cash hidden away that he could go where no one would ever find him. He opened his top dresser and started removing his socks and underwear. He was startled when he heard a loud crash in the living room.

He walked back out to the living room and saw two men, muscular, probably in their early thirties, and Chester knew that this wasn't a friendly visit. His bladder emptied into his diaper.

"Hello, Chester. You know, you and your brother have made our bosses very unhappy. They say you guys really had a good thing goin' up here in the great Northwest. But now they say you guys are causing too much trouble. Wuddaya say to that, Chester?"

Chester didn't like the grin on the thug's face.

"I ain't done nothin'. It's all my fool brother's fault. He's the one that screwed everything up. Go talk to him!"

Chester's voice was rising in pitch, something that happened when he got scared, excited, or nervous. He was all three this time.

"Our boss seems to think it's the both of you that messed everything up, and they sent me and my partner up here to take care of it."

Before Chester had a chance to move, the silent partner came and bear-hugged him from behind.

"Our boss says that you are becoming quite despondent, you know, sorry for all the things that you've done. He said that you were even becoming suicidal. Ain't that something, Chester?"

Chester started shaking.

"C'mon. I just want to get outta here. I was just packin'. My damn brother's the one you want. He's the one that started all this killin'!"

The silent one continued to hold him tightly.

"Not much loyalty to family, huh Chester?—I thought twins were supposed to be close like that."

Chester pleaded, "Really, let's talk this out. Let's go see my brother. He'll straighten this whole deal out."

"That wouldn't make our boss happy, Chester." The speaker wrinkled his nose. "You mess your pants, Chester? You really stink."

Chester started crying as the speaker reached into a bag that was at his feet, and pulled out a rope. Chester recognized it from his own shop. He started to shake all over, and his crying turned to sobs.

"Now, calm down, Chester. You gotta write a note before we take care of you. You ready to write? I'll help you. I'll tell you just exactly what to write, Chester."

He wrote the note at the kitchen table using his own personal pen. Then they all walked out to the shop, the rope dangling from Chester's hand. The speaker slid open the left half of the shop's door, and the three of them walked inside. He found the light switch just inside the door and flipped it on. A ladder stood in the middle of the floor, directly under a crossbeam that was about twelve feet high. His knees buckled, but the silent one held him up.

"Now, Chester, I need you to put that noose around your neck for me and tighten it up real good. Understand, Chester?" He looked over the silent one. "I think he might need some help, partner."

Speaker came over to Chester, took the rope from his hand, and put the noose around his neck. Then he threw the other end of the rope over the beam above their heads.

"Okay, Chester, climb that ladder, just like you're gonna change a light bulb. Let's not make this too difficult."

Chester continued to sob, while Speaker took hold of the other end of the rope and pulled, causing Chester to stand straight, then on to the tips of his toes.

"Okay, Chester, take that first step up and it will be easier to breathe."

Chester's face was turning a deep red. He stepped on to the ladder. Silent One held him steady. Speaker again pulled on the rope and urged Chester to take the next step toward the end of his life. He did.

"That's good, Chester, you're doin' real good. Now just stand there. Don't move an inch."

Speaker then took the end of the rope and tied it off on the leg of the workbench, which must have weighed about a thousand pounds—it was made of solid oak. He cinched the rope tight.

"Okay, Chester, take one more step up the ladder, that's all. Do you see that warning label right in front of you? It's the one that says '*WARNING! DO NOT STAND ON TOP STEP*'. I'm not goin' to make you go up that high. I don't want you to hurt yourself. Just one more step, Chester."

He took the step with a little help from Silent One.

"That's good, Chester. You've been very cooperative. I really wish that it didn't have to be this way. You and your brother had a really good thing going, but I guess all good things must come to an end."

Speaker nodded to Silent One. He kicked the ladder hard enough that Chester lost his balance and fell backwards off the step that he was standing on. The rope tightened and Chester swung back and forth like the pendulum of a clock, his feet twenty-four inches off the cement floor of the shop. His eyes bulged. His body twitched in the final throes of death. His white hair had an Albert Einstein kind of look. The executioners watched until they knew Chester was dead.

Speaker felt a little sad. He thought to himself that he must be getting old and sentimental. Chester seemed like a nice guy. Of course, if he had really been a nice guy, he wouldn't have been messed up in the drug business, in which there were lots of bad people. It had never bothered Speaker before, this killing business. He shrugged. The melancholy passed.

"Let's go, we have a busy night ahead of us," Speaker said.

Silent One, still watching Chester, nodded in assent.

They walked out the sliding door of the shed, left the light on, and slid the door shut.

Chapter 65

Nicole had a hard time believing that anyone could talk her dad into anything, let alone taking a week off from work for a "family vacation." *Good luck with that,* she thought to herself. She couldn't remember the last vacation they had taken.

But it was true. She heard it herself, from her dad, when she called home at lunchtime. That was nine o'clock. He told her that mom was packing for her and that they would leave as soon as she got home from work. He didn't tell her where they were going, said it didn't matter.

It was a slow night on the chain and Nicole had plenty of time to think about everything. She wished it was busy, though, so she wouldn't have to think about it, especially Sherry. The only pleasant thoughts that she had all night was of the "date" she had been on earlier, but she doubted that Mike had the same thoughts. No guy had ever shown much interest in her before, and she thought it wouldn't be any different this time. She could only hope.

She looked at her watch, cracked crystal and all. It would be another two and a half hours of anxious waiting before the whistle blew. She had a queasy feeling in her stomach, afraid that something might go wrong. She tried to stop thinking about it, so she moved forward on the catwalk and gave a hand to the guy in front of her, pulling her own boards as well. He was new and appreciated the help. It made the time go by faster.

Lester the Molester, as the hit men called him, would be their next victim. They had something different in store for Lester than for his twin, but it would have the same deadly result. Speaker and Silent One had been doing this kind of thing for a while. They enjoyed their work and were paid well for it. Their employers appreciated their work as well.

Speaker and Silent One had no qualms about snuffing out a life since their clientele would not be receiving any "Citizen of the Month" awards. Most of them were druggies. The executioners figured that if people wanted to get into the drug business, well then, they knew that it could be dangerous.

They made the drive over to Lester's place out in Colton. He would be alone, too, just like Chester. There were no close neighbors, and even if someone did hear a gunshot, no one would think twice about it out here. Speaker checked his wristwatch. They wouldn't have much time with Lester if they were going to make it to their next appointment. *Too bad*, he thought, *I'd like to take my time with this one.*

They parked down the road an eighth of a mile from the driveway and walked the rest of the way. Earlier in the day, when Lester wasn't home, Speaker and Silent One went through the house looking for a handgun. They found one, checked to see if it was loaded—it was—and placed it back in the top left drawer of the oak, roll-top desk. Speaker hoped that Lester's routine would be the same tonight as most other nights.

Chapter 66

He was anxious for the night's events to get underway. He looked at the clock on the mantle of the rock fireplace—ten-thirty. Time wasn't passing fast enough, but there was nothing he could do about that. It was all set. The plan was in place. Waiting was all he could do. He sat in his favorite chair, an old, brown Naugahyde vinyl La-Z-Boy recliner. The twenty-seven inch Motorola was on, but he wasn't paying much attention to it. He reflected on how he and Chester had gotten into this business in the first place, and how it had turned into something bigger than either of them imagined. Now it was the family business, run by family.

Lester looked again at the clock. It was coming up on eleven thirty, and even so, he was not in the least bit sleepy. The TV was still on with some local sports guy giving the baseball scores. He sighed. Lester cocked his head to the left, toward the side of the house where the porch was. He thought he heard something, but there was a little breeze blowing. *It's probably just the wind*, he thought, and he went back to his reminiscing.

A few minutes later he heard it again, this time a little louder—footsteps—he was sure of it this time. He got up from his chair and walked as fast as he could to the den, and to the roll-top desk. Before he could get there, Speaker and Silent One crashed through the locked door, reaching him before he could get to his gun.

"Who the hell are you?" Lester screamed at the two men, but he sounded weak and frail. "What's the meaning of this? Get the hell out of my house!"

He tried to sound stern, but his voice, like Chester's, rose in pitch when he got excited, and it carried little authority.

"Are you done?" Speaker had an amused smirk on the right side of his face. "You seem a little more courageous than your twin brother. We were just over there and paid him a little visit, just like we are now, paying you a little visit. We don't have much time, though, because we have another appointment to get to. So we would really appreciate it if you would cooperate. That way, we can get on with the rest of tonight's business."

"Get the hell out of here!—Now!" Lester demanded, with no result.

"Well that just ain't gonna happen, Lester. But if you co-operate, it will be a lot easier for you, lots easier than it was for your brother. I really felt kinda sorry for him. You probably already figured out that this is the end. It's probably not the way you thought it would end, but then you never know, do you? But here's how it is, Lester. Word has it that both you and your brother were getting very depressed. The family business isn't going well, both of you lost your wives to cancer, and your health is deteriorating."

Lester just stared at Speaker, not knowing what to say.

"Cat got your tongue, Lester? Well, anyway, like Chester, you're gonna put an end to your miserable existence. Personally, I'd rather die like you're goin' to. Now Chester, well, he hung himself. But you? You're goin' to shoot yourself—much easier. It might be a little messier, but that won't be of any concern to you. So wuddaya say, Lester?—let's getter done."

Lester struggled, but it didn't matter. Silent One had him under total control.

"So, they say most suicides include a letter—your brother wrote one. But since we don't have the time to help you write one, you'll just have to be part of the small percentage of those who don't write one. You seem to be that type, anyway, at least to me."

To Silent One, Speaker said, "Why don't you sit him down at the table. He'll just do it there."

Silent One walked him over to the table and sat him down on the straight-backed chair. Speaker went through the arched entry of the kitchen and into the den.

"Lester, you got a gun in here, don't you? Is that where you were heading when we came in?" he yelled to Lester, sitting in the kitchen. He opened the drawer on the roll-top desk. "Ahh, here it is, Lester, loaded and everything."

Speaker walked back into the kitchen and Lester was crying, sounding very much like his twin. The bravado that he had exhibited before was no longer evident. He was falling apart, and understandably so. Then he started begging.

"C'mon, we can work this out. Listen, I'll give you more money than you're gettin' for this. Really! I'll make you guys rich. You won't have to do this anymore."

"But Lester, we like doing this. My pappy always told me that when you find something you like to do, well, you just keep doin' it. Pappy was pretty smart that way."

"Please, don't do it," Lester pleaded.

"Sorry, Lester, but you plain screwed everything up and well, this is the price you're gonna pay. But really, it will be over before you know it. Now, a little cooperation please—it will make it much easier."

Lester started struggling, but Silent One held him firmly in place.

"Now, Lester, take this here gun in your left hand. Yup, I know you and your brother are both left-handed—didn't matter much for Chester, though, danglin' from that rope, but this is different. You gotta kill yourself using the right hand—I mean your correct hand."

Speaker walked behind Lester and grabbed his hand by the wrist, but not hard enough to bruise. Lester had clenched his fist, but it wasn't hard to pry his fingers open. Then Speaker placed the gun in his hand and forced his fingers around it, still holding his wrist in a firm grip.

"All right now, Lester, let's do this right the first time, there's no time for messin' around. Now, open wide for daddy, Lester."

Speaker forced the barrel of the gun through Lester's lips, and then pried the teeth open. It was just a single shot, so he had to make sure it did more than just some minor damage. There was one final, feeble attempt from Lester before the shot went into his throat and out the back of his head—blood, bone, and brain smattering the wall behind him.

The executioners admired the new artwork on the wall behind Lester for a few moments, and then left for their next appointment.

Chapter 67

I spent the rest of the evening at home, going over several scenarios in my mind. Around nine o'clock, I called my old friend and partner, Dickey Cook. I filled him in on the case and began to pick his brain, just like we used to do. Dickey and I had a good conversation and he had some good thoughts and a few ideas to bounce off me. We always worked well together and I missed the camaraderie that we shared for so many years.

After I hung up, I downed a couple beers and watched TV for a while, but couldn't remember a single thing about the shows I watched. At eleven, the news came on. I watched for a while, but nothing much was happening. The Yankees beat the Mariners, but that wasn't too unusual, and the Portland Beavers, a Triple-A club, beat the Hawaii Islanders 3-2 in 10 innings. After the sports report was over, I got up and went to bed. It took me a long time to get to sleep, but finally, after counting about a thousand sheep, I drifted off in a restless sleep.

I woke with a start. I rolled over and looked at the oversized green numbers on the clock radio—12:33. I hadn't even been asleep an hour, and I wasn't sure why I woke up. Maybe it was a dream that I had already forgotten. I rolled over to go back to sleep, and then I heard something outside that sounded like breaking glass. I sat up, and at the same time, grabbed my Beretta off the nightstand.

I crept to the window of my bedroom, which gave me a view of the driveway on that side of the house. A distant street light gave some illumination, but I wasn't able to see very much. I crept to the other window and looked out back, but it was too dark to see anything. I put on my pants and a tee shirt, slipped on some sandals, and moved into the front room, the Beretta leading the way. With my back against the wall, I leaned slightly to my left and looked out that window.

The cruiser was in view, and it was obvious where the sound of breaking glass had come from. The wind shield on the driver's side had been smashed, the same with the side window. I didn't know if this was the work of someone who thought it would be cool to smash up a cop car, or whether this might be something else. This could be a ploy to get me to come outside. Maybe it had something to do with the case. Calling for backup seemed to be my best option. I dialed Mikey's number. He picked up on the first ring.

"Hello?" he answered, not sounding like he'd been asleep.

"Mikey, it's me. I need a hand over here at my place. I got a situation."

I gave him the details and told him to be careful, to shut off his lights when he got close, so as not to let anyone know of his approach. I hoped that we might be able to catch whoever it was. I waited in the dark living room.

Chapter 68

The whistle blew, and Nicole didn't wait around to pull the last boards off the chain like she did on most nights. She gathered up her leather apron, put her mitts inside the apron and rolled them up, grabbed her lunch bucket and thermos, and headed out. She didn't say anything to anyone about not being there the next day. She probably would lose her job, but that's better than telling the wrong person and end up losing her life. Tears welled up in her eyes as she thought about Sherry. She crossed the highway to the gravel parking lot and got in the Citation, locked the doors, and started the engine. She backed out of the space, spinning her tires in the loose gravel as she pulled onto the highway.

She crossed the railroad tracks past the old Dunton place, and turned at the Elbow Room toward Molalla. The anxiety she felt on the walk to the parking lot had subsided a little, but not much. In her rearview mirror, she could see a set of headlights quite a ways back. It was probably another coworker who wanted to get out of there fast like she did, though for entirely different reasons. She drove a little faster than the forty-five mile per hour speed limit, but she wasn't worried that she would get stopped, not at this time of night. She managed a smile, thinking she wouldn't mind getting stopped if Mike Benson was the one doing the stopping.

The smile quickly faded when she noticed that the headlights in her mirror were growing larger, getting closer. She increased her speed and kept looking at the headlights that were still gaining on her. It was only a mile to the city limits, and she figured that once she got there, she could find a safe place, even at this late hour. She passed the Baptist church, the one that Mike Benson went to, and came into town. A lone vehicle was coming toward her, making her feel that she wasn't alone on this particularly dark, summer night. The White Horse came to mind, and even though she wasn't twenty-one, she could go there for safety. She thought that maybe some of her fellow workers might show up, and they would help her if she needed it.

Mike drove out North Molalla Avenue, passing the police station on his way to Toliver Road, the one that the chief lived on. The streets in town were deserted, except for those cars that didn't have their own garage to stay in. Two sets of headlights were coming toward him. He looked at his wristwatch—it was a few minutes after one. It was probably some mill employees who had just finished their shift. The thought made him think of Nicole. Just before he turned onto Toliver, the small sedan passed him. It was her, and he felt a little twinge of what— excitement? She passed, and the twinge passed, too, as he thought of the situation at hand. A quarter-mile away from the chief's house, he turned off his headlights and slowed to a crawl. He found a place to park on the side of the road. He decided to go the last bit of the route on foot, armed with his .38 Special.

I waited in the darkness, moving from window to window, and then back again, but there was nothing that I could see. I figured that Mikey should be approaching by now, probably on foot. I continued to look out the windows, looking for Mikey, or the bad guys, if there were any out there.

Suddenly, glass broke. It was the window where I had just been, and then there was an instant inferno. A second window shattered. A Molotov cocktail exploded. From the back of the house a third window shattered, and I was surrounded by flames. It all happened in a matter of seconds, and that's all the time I had to make a decision.

The fire was spreading rapidly, as the accelerant, probably gas, made it imperative that I get out immediately, regardless of who was waiting outside. The second window that had broken looked to be the best route of escape. My pants caught on fire, and I didn't have any shoes on as I ran through the flames to the dark hole that I hoped was the window. Adrenaline coursed through my old veins. I didn't feel any pain, even as my legs burned. Shards of glass pierced my feet and the burning floor charred them. The house I lived in was far from being spacious, but the distance from where I was to the window seemed far, far away. When I got to the already broken out window, I launched my overweight body through the hole, which fortunately proved to be the window, flying through it head first. I must have looked like Dumbo on his maiden flight!

Mike walked across the tracks, still a thousand feet from the chief's driveway. He approached cautiously, and therefore, slowly. It was eerily quiet, no indication that this night was different than any other night in Molalla. He continued his cautious approach— three-hundred feet—*the length of a football field*, he thought. The darkness gave him good cover, and he proceeded with confidence that all would be well. He hoped it was just some punk kids earning themselves some bragging rights around their peers.

It was so quiet. And then it all changed, in an instant. Glass shattered, easily heard in the stillness of the night. Mike stood straight and looked toward the chief's house, but the Christmas trees out front obscured any view he might have had. He walked faster, though still being cautious.

Then he saw light, which he knew was caused by fire. Gunfire erupted, multiple shots, and he broke into a dead run. By now he could see the house, totally engulfed by flame. It had been just a few seconds. Silhouetted in the light of the burning fire, he could see two figures running from the house. He lost view of them, though, as they headed into the darkness and the empty field to the west of the house, which would soon be gone.

As he approached the house, he saw the chief lying prone, too close to the inferno. Mike got to him just as another blast rocked the night air, making it as light as day. The concussion from the explosion passed over the chief, but knocked Mike right off his feet and on to his butt. He got back up and continued to the chief's side. He was unconscious. Mike prayed that he wasn't dead.

When he reached the chief, he saw that there were at least three holes in his tee-shirt, which was now stained red from blood. He grabbed the chief under both arms and pulled him away from the intense heat.

Laying him on his back, he checked his airway, and then his breathing. The good news— he was still breathing, shallowly. No raspy, slurping sound came from the chief, and that was good news. He grabbed his right wrist, checking for a pulse, and was able to detect one, steady, but weak. Kneeling beside the chief, Mike applied pressure to the wounds, praying that the bleeding would stop and that the breathing would continue. He prayed, too, that the nearby neighbors were aware of the new 9-1-1 emergency number that had just been operating for a year, at least in the Molalla area.

It took twenty long minutes for the first emergency crews to arrive, but fortunately, one of the chief's close neighbors also happened to be the city of Molalla's most beloved doctor. When Mike saw the doc, a wave of relief spread throughout his body. This was the doctor who had brought Mike into the world, and he hoped that this same doctor would prevent the chief from going to the next one.

"Keep applying pressure, Michael," Doc Johnson said, and immediately took control of the situation. He shouted orders to his fellow neighbors, and then to Mike, he said, "Let's see if we can keep this one alive."

"I'd surely appreciate that, Doc," not knowing what else to say. "I'm sure the chief would feel the same way."

Chapter 69

Nicole walked inside and felt very strange doing it. All her life, she had seen the stallion on the outside of the building, but not being twenty-one, had never been through the doors. She saw the bartender and went directly to him, explaining her predicament to him. She told him that she wasn't of age, but he was very understanding and offered to let her stay until she felt safe.

She sat at a table in the corner and drank a Coke with nothing in it but ice. It was just a minute or two before the door opened, and Dennis, a guy she worked with, walked through the door. He looked around and saw Nicole sitting at the corner table and went over to talk to her.

"Thought you weren't twenty-one yet," he said with a crooked, but friendly, smile.

"I'm not, but I got freaked out driving into town, so I came in here. Were you right behind me?"

"Yeah, I got outta there as fast as I could—wanted to get my weekend started."

Nicole smiled, "Dennis, it's only Wednesday."

"Technically, it's Thursday. But still, you can't get started on the weekend too early."

Nicole laughed again. "You drive a pick-up?"

"Yeah, a Chevy."

"You got a lift on it?" she asked.

Nicole knew a few things about trucks and cars from her dad, whom she still believed had really wanted a son.

"Yup, six inch all the way around. Cherry red—I love that truck."

Nicole was relieved to hear that it was Dennis who had been following her and was driving fast, just so he could get a beer.

"Cool. You'll have to give me a ride sometime."

"No problem, I'd be happy to. So what were you freaked out about, anyway?"

"I don't know. Ever since my friend Sherry... well, I haven't been myself lately. The dark didn't use to bug me, but since the accident..." Her voice trailed off.

"I'm really sorry, Nicole. Hey, you want me to follow you home? I'd be happy to if you'd like."

"Thanks, Dennis, but I think I'll be okay now."

"Okay, but if you change your mind, let me know."

"Thanks, I really do appreciate it."

Dennis moved to another table, and Nicole walked over to the bartender.

"Hey, thanks for letting me hang out. I think I'll leave now."

"No problem. Come back when you can have a beer," he said, winking at her.

"I'll do that," she said, smiling back at him.

She walked out the door feeling much better. She heard sirens in the distance and thought there must have been an accident somewhere. She didn't notice the orange glow in the sky north-west of town. She walked to her car across the street. She was so ready to get out of this town. Thoughts of Sherry returned and tears again filled her eyes. She drove around the block and turned left on South Main. Nicole couldn't get home fast enough. She didn't notice the black Ford truck that was parked, with its lights off, at the Western Auto store. The truck pulled out behind her.

"Where is she? She should be here by now." Pete Parker paced back and forth in the living room.

"She'll be here. She will. Just give her time." Janice Parker, behaving out of character, was unusually calm.

They were packed and had loaded everything in the truck. They were just waiting for Nicole to get home from work. Janice had made a breakfast of hash browns, eggs and bacon for Nicole to eat on the road. Pete's mother was also waiting anxiously at her Canby home for the telephone to ring and her son to tell her that they were on their way.

"She'll be here," Janice said again, this time as if trying to convince herself.

The chief's house was pretty much gone by the time the first fire truck arrived. They quickly set up the hose and sent a stream of water into the heart of the flame, but it wasn't to save anything, just to put out the fire and maybe save some evidence to explain what happened.

While the salvage operation took place, two paramedics from the fire crew came and performed triage, waiting for the Life Flight helicopter to arrive. One of the paramedics took over for Mike, applying pressure to the wounds. He was grateful for the relief. He thanked God that Life Flight had been in service for several years now, thinking that the chief just might have a chance. A few minutes passed before they heard the distinctive sound of the helicopter, approaching from the north.

Mike stood behind the paramedics, keeping his eyes on the chief. He was unresponsive up to this point, and Mike prayed silently for any kind of sign that the chief would be okay. The light from the fire had diminished, but the lights from the chopper lit up the immediate area. As the medical crew moved him onto the stretcher, pressure still being applied to the wounds, Mike thought he saw the chief's eyelids twitch. He was sure he didn't imagine it, as he walked alongside him. Before they loaded him into the helicopter, his eyes suddenly flew open. His mouth moved but no sound came out.

"Wait!"

They stopped and looked at Mike.

"Look, his eyes are open. He's trying to say something." He leaned close to the chief's face. "What? What did you say?"

The chief turned his head to Mike. He rasped, "The girl..." and closed his eyes again.

They loaded him and were off into the dark summer night and the ten-minute flight to Oregon Health Sciences University, thirty miles away in the West Hills of Portland. The chopper was barely off the ground and Mike sprinted to his car a quarter mile away. He got in, pulled a U-turn, and for the second time in his life, he drove seventy-five in a twenty-five mile per hour zone, on the same road as the first time, but now it was to save a life.

Nicole drove as fast as she dared on the curvy, windy road up to her home. She thought to herself how dark it seemed tonight, unusually dark for mid-summer. There was no moon, and even the stars were hiding somewhere behind the darkness. Goosebumps tingled down her spine, but not because she was cold. In another couple of miles, she would be at the stretch of road where Sherry had crashed and, try as she might, Nicole couldn't help thinking about it.

She looked in her mirror and saw a set of headlights that appeared much too close. *Where did they come from*, she thought, *and why didn't I see them before?* There was still a good eight miles to go before she would reach home.

"It's bitchin' dark out here."

Even though Jeff Williams had driven this road at least a thousand times before, he was having a hard time negotiating the turns without his headlights turned on.

"Well then, turn on your damn lights. It don't matter none if she sees us. We got to nail her now, before she gets too much farther." Joe, Jeff's cousin was getting excited. The chase was the best part, at least that's what he thought up to now.

Jeff switched on the headlights and also the dual spotlights mounted on the top of the cab. He knew it would be more of a challenge this time because the girl was driving uphill. Shivers ran down his spine and he knew he was up for it.

Chapter 70

The truck was way too close and Nicole knew she was in serious trouble. She accelerated, spraying up gravel from the partially paved road, hoping to put some distance between her and her pursuer. There was no doubt in her mind that whoever was in the truck behind her was responsible for Sherry's death. She would kill them, she thought, as rage coursed through her veins, but didn't have a clue as to how she would accomplish it.

The truck was gaining on her even though she had the vehicle that should corner better. It was less than two car lengths behind her, and the rage was quickly turning into panic as she approached a sharp turn to the left. She hit the brakes as she rounded the corner and the rear end of the Chevy fishtailed, the right-rear tire going off the edge of the gravel shoulder. The other rear wheel caught pavement, though, and she was able to regain control. Nicole hoped that the truck wouldn't be able to negotiate the corner, but a check in the mirror told her that it did, although the distance between them had grown. *Not enough though*, she thought, as the truck again drew closer.

A series of turns—right, left, another left, another right—was coming up. Loose gravel was scattered all across the road. She would have to be careful not to let the car slide into the deep ditch on the right side of the road. It was still several miles before she would reach home, but she was determined. She convinced herself that she would make it.

The Chevy approached the turns and took the corners well. A quarter-mile of straight road was ahead of her. For a second, she thought that the truck didn't make it through the turns, but that hope was short-lived. The truck's headlights appeared, coming around the last of the three turns behind her. She didn't know what kind of engine that thing had in it, but it must have been huge with a lot of torque. In nothing flat, the headlights filled up her mirror.

The truck drew closer. She could hear the monster engine roaring behind her. The truck struck her bumper hard, but not hard enough to make her lose control. It rammed her again, this time even harder, and the straightaway was coming to an end. Another set of corners loomed ahead of her. She braked so she could make the turns, and the truck hit her on the left side of the bumper. There was loose gravel again on the road and the car went into a spin, nothing at all that Nicole could do. She prayed as the darkness spun around her, the headlights shining into the swirling dust. She came to a stop, still on the road.

Looking behind her, she saw the trucks tail lights and realized that she had turned a one-eighty, *more likely a five-forty*, she thought. She stomped on the gas pedal and sent gravel flying from the Chevy's tires. She hoped that she could get a good lead on the truck, figuring that it might have a hard time getting turned back toward town.

The curves that she had negotiated just seconds ago were approaching, and she started to think that she might get away. With her confidence back, the rage returned. She was determined to get revenge for Sherry and Sandi and whoever else these bastards killed.

She checked the mirror and saw no sign of the truck as she came out of the last turn. She accelerated—forty, fifty, sixty, up to seventy-five miles per hour before the next set of turns appeared ahead of her. There was still no sign of the truck, and she allowed herself a glimmer of hope of living through this nightmare. *If I could just get back to town,* she thought to herself as she came out of the last turn in that set of curves. The adrenaline was running high and she started shaking from it. She looked in the mirror—nothing but dark behind her, and that truck, somewhere, hidden in the darkness. Maybe they were giving up. She could only hope.

She focused her eyes on the road ahead as she again increased her speed, more confident with each passing minute. Another set of turns, not as sharp and not as many this time, came up in front of her. She slowed down and rounded the first corner, then the second

"NO! Dammit!" she screamed, slamming on her brakes to avoid the biggest buck she had ever seen, standing in the middle of the road. Hitting it would mean major damage to her car, not to mention the buck. She couldn't take the chance that her car would not be too damaged to drive.

She swerved to miss it. The tires had no traction on the loose gravel, and for the second time in the space of a few minutes, the Chevy went into a spin, but this time, it landed on its side in the deep ditch. The engine continued running, the headlights illuminating dry grass, and nothing more.

Nicole looked around and assessed her situation. She didn't think she was hurt, at least she didn't feel any pain. She touched her face, and it felt wet and sticky. She couldn't see anything, but she knew she was bleeding, but she couldn't tell how badly.

She had to get out of the car, and do it quickly. The truck and its occupant, or occupants— she really didn't know who or how many—would be here quickly, unless they really had given up. She didn't think that was the case.

She was able to unlatch the seat belt, which had probably saved her from a worse injury. She'd never complain about wearing a seat belt ever again! The front passenger side window was intact. Nicole hoped she would be able to roll down the window and crawl through it, up and out of the car.

When she first tried the window, she nearly panicked when the handle wouldn't budge, and then realized she was turning it the wrong way. She turned it the other way and it rolled down easily. She pulled herself up and out of the car and jumped down to the bottom of the ditch. She got her bearings, climbed out of the ditch, and headed into the forest, away from the road. They would be coming soon.

"Dammit, Jeff, git this rig turned around."

"Wuddaya think I'm doin', ya moron? The turn radius on this thing is worse than a semi!"

"Well, hurry, she'll be halfway back to Molalla the way you're goin'!"

"Well get out and tell me how far I can back up. Now!"

Joe opened the door and jumped to the ground, not bothering with the 'step up' to step down.

"Keep comin', a little more, a little more. Stop! Go forward now."

It took four turns forward and four turns back to get the truck pointed in the right direction, back towards town. Joe jumped back in the truck at the same time that Jeff floored it, before Joe could get the door shut. He almost fell out of the truck. He screamed obscenities at his cousin in a continuous flow. Five minutes down the road they saw a car in the ditch, the headlights still on. They had her.

"**I gotta go** find her. She should've been here fifteen minutes ago."

Pete Parker grabbed his already loaded 12-guage, grabbed another handful of shotgun shells and stuffed them in his coat pocket.

Janice Parker was crying, but not hysterically, "Find her, Pete. Please find her."

"I will," he said, and he was out the door.

Mike drove through the center of town, not even bothering to slow down at the four-way stop in the center of town. He prayed that there would be no one else at the intersection and, after going through it, thanked God that there wasn't. He drove like a madman, even though he didn't know if Nicole was in trouble or not. He hoped she had already made it to her house and that the Parkers were on their way down the hill, and away from Molalla.

Chapter 71

The big rig came to a stop, and Jeff and Joe jumped out of the truck simultaneously, making it look like they were in a synchronized Olympic event, although neither one of them would have a clue what that was. Jeff got there first.

"Shit! She ain't in here! Dammit!"

Joe came alongside and peered into the vehicle, "She can't be too far. Which way ya think she went?"

"Don't know. Hey, run back and get the flashlight on the seat."

Joe didn't argue, but was a little disgruntled that his cousin always told him what to do. He grabbed the flashlight and ran back to the car. Jeff shined the light on the car's interior. She was gone, but left something behind. It was a fair amount of blood on the side window. He shined it around the window that Nicole had climbed through, and again saw blood that wasn't even dry yet.

"Looks like she's bleedin' pretty good. Let's see if we can figure out which way she went."

Jeff shined the flashlight on the ground around the car. Drops of blood shone on the dry, blonde grass.

"I think she headed into the woods. My bet is she's going to try to get back to town, or at least to a house where she can get some help."

Joe tried to add to his cousin's deductions, but couldn't really think of anything to add except for, "Uh huh" or, "I think you're right, cuz." He knew that he was on the short end when God handed out the brains, and he resented God for it, even though he didn't believe there was one. More than that, he resented his cousin.

"Let's go," Jeff said, "We'll go parallel to the woods and see if we can't cut her off before she can get help. I think she'll slow down some losin' all that blood."

"Uh-huh. I think so too," Joe added.

"Let's get goin' then."

They hopped across the ditch, Jeff leading the way. He looked back at his truck on the side of the road and hoped that no one would come by. There wasn't much choice. They trotted across the pasture land and hoped that they were heading the right direction. Every little bit, they would stop and listen, and then parallel to the wooded hillside.

Chapter 72

Mike rounded the corner and slammed on his brakes. In the ditch on the right-hand side was a car, lying on its left side, facing him, its right headlight shining in his eyes. Another vehicle faced him on the opposite side of the road, a dark-colored truck—it looked black.

He got out of his car and ran and, although he couldn't tell the make and model of the vehicle, he knew in his gut that it was a Chevy Citation. Bile rose in his throat and he had to swallow hard to keep it down. He reached the Citation, looked in, dreading what he would see, but relief came when he saw that it was empty. The relief was short-lived, though, when he realized that she was most likely running for her life.

He walked across the road to look at the truck when another vehicle, from the opposite direction, rounded the corner. He drew his .38 Special with his right hand and shielded his eyes from the headlights with his left. A truck—it looked like an older Chevy—came to a stop, sliding on the loose gravel. A man got out, and when he stepped in front of the headlights, Mike could see a rifle cradled in his left arm, finger on the triggers of a double-barreled shotgun.

"Stop where you are. This is the police. Drop your weapon now!" Mike ordered, the adrenaline pumping out of the gland by the gallon, at least that's how it felt to Mike. "Stop," he ordered again, "Molalla police. Drop your weapon."

The man complied, laid down the shotgun by his feet and stood back up, hands in the air.

Mike thought that this was a friend rather than a foe. "Who are you? What's your name? What are you doing here?"

The man, who looked to be in his fifties, yelled back, "I'm Pete Parker. I'm looking for my daughter."

Relief spread through Mike's body, but the adrenaline was still having its effect as he spoke again to Nicole's father, "I'm Mike Benson. I came up here looking for Nicole, too. I was hoping that she was with you. I just got here myself. The car in the ditch—it's yours, but she's not in it. You have any idea whose truck this is?"

"I don't, but I don't think it's good, son. I don't think we should be standin' here wasting time with introductions. I'm here to find Nicole."

Mike heard the calm voice, but sensed the rage just below the surface.

"I'm with you. Pick up your weapon and let's go."

Mike went to his car and retrieved a flashlight that also served well as a club if need be. Pete Parker went back to his truck and grabbed a light as well. Mike walked over to the black truck and shined his light on the front left fender, which revealed a small dent and some missing paint. He rushed over to the car where Pete Parker was shining his light inside.

"There's blood in here, too much. I think she's running," said her determined father, intent on saving his daughter. "I know her. I think she went into the woods and is working her way back to town, maybe to get help at one of the neighbors around here."

They both shone their lights on the ground around the car. They saw the same drops of blood that Jeff and Joe had seen ten minutes earlier.

"Let's go then," and they started out on the same route the cousins had taken.

Chapter 73

Nicole stayed close to the edge of the forest, but far enough in to conceal her movement from anyone on the outside. She felt safer going this way, but it was also a lot slower. She made her way through the undergrowth of tangled vines and roots that broke the surface. She was not feeling as strong as when she started out, and she knew that the bleeding was worse than she had thought at first. Her legs were getting heavier and she was getting light-headed. The thought went through her head, *this is not good, definitely not good.* The toe of her work boot caught on a root, and she fell face-forward. Her stomach landed on a rock, knocking the wind from her lungs. She lay there unable to move, unable to breathe, and she started to cry.

"Suck it up, Nicole. Get a grip," she said out loud to herself.

She lay on the dry mixture of leaves and fir needles that covered the forest floor, waiting until she could catch her breath. She untangled her feet and got back up, pushing forward through the cover of the forest.

"Did you hear that?" Joe was the first to speak, "I heard somethin' coming from over that way." He pointed in the direction toward the woods, but wasn't sure if the noise came from ahead of them, or behind them.

They stopped and listened. Their breathing was the only sound they heard in the still, dark night. Standing still for a good minute, they heard nothing—no animal, not even the sound of a gentle breeze moving through the trees.

"I know I heard somethin'," Joe insisted.

"Well, whatever it was, it's quiet now. Let's keep going."

The two continued walking as quietly as possible so they could hear better, but at the same time, tried to keep up the pace. They went another ten minutes and came to a stop. They waited for their heavy breathing to subside—and listened.

Nicole continued her trek through the dark forest, all still except for the soft crunching underneath her feet. Try as she might, it was impossible to completely deaden the sound. Every time a twig snapped, she cringed and stood still for a few seconds before proceeding. As far as she could tell, the bleeding from her head had stopped, but she was feeling weaker, and the dizziness was getting worse. *Keep going—don't stop*, she urged herself forward.

It was so dark. She thought it was because of the moonless and starless night and the thick canopy of evergreens above her, but she also thought that she might be losing it. She concentrated on putting one foot ahead of the other. She had no idea how much time had elapsed since she started walking. Was it two thirty—three o'clock? She couldn't tell.

She took another step, and suddenly there was nothing under her to support her. She tumbled headlong into a dried up creek bed that was two or three feet lower than the ground she had been walking on. She let out a loud "Hmph" when she hit the hard ground. She prayed that her grandma's God would help her, and that whoever was after her hadn't heard anything. How could she know? She got up once again and trudged on through the thick darkness, each boot feeling like a block of cement attached to the end of her legs.

"**There! I heard** it again, over there!" Joe whispered.

"I heard it too. It has to be her."

The sound came from their left, directly across from where they were currently standing.

Jeff continued in a low voice, "Let's get ahead of her and go into the woods. She'll come right to us."

"That's just what I was thinkin'," Joe said.

They moved faster now, Jeff making sure that his flashlight was angled away from the girl. They went ahead another two hundred yards and then angled toward the woods, listening intently as they went. They reached the edge of the trees and walked into the thicker darkness another fifty yards. Jeff motioned for Joe to stop and wait, and then realized that it was too dark to see anything.

"Joe," Jeff said in a whisper that he hoped Joe could hear. "Stay here. I'm going over there a ways. We'll wait. She's coming right for us." Jeff hoped he understood.

Joe nodded in the darkness, but Jeff couldn't see it. He went deeper into the forest, and then, leaning up against a large fir tree, waited in anticipation. Five minutes later, Jeff heard footsteps—slow and deliberate, but impossible to be totally silent. The girl was walking right to him. He picked up a stick, part of an old tree limb and waited.

Slowly, ever so slowly, Nicole stepped across the too-brittle ground. She hoped that it wasn't as loud as it sounded, but to her, it sounded like it could be heard a mile away. Putting one foot ahead of the other, she didn't know how much longer she could go. She could have been walking in circles, for all she knew. She'd heard about that—people who were lost in the forest, and they keep walking in circles. She thought about stopping and waiting for help to come, but she knew that there was no one to help.

Her right foot came down on a small, dried up branch that snapped loudly underneath her foot. Another snap, one that she didn't cause, hit her ears, and then suddenly, everything turned a brilliant white. Nicole fell forward, unconscious, as Jeff stood over her, stick in hand.

Joe heard the commotion and talked, too loudly, "Jeff, is that you?—you gitter?"

"Shut up!" Jeff said, too loudly also. Then, more quietly, he hissed, "Joe, get your skinny little ass over here."

Jeff and Joe stood above her as Nicole lay there silently, her head bleeding again.

"This little bitch sure has caused us a lot of trouble," Jeff said, a crooked smile spreading across his face. "I think we ought to make her pay a little before we waste her. Wuddaya say, Cuz?"

Joe was smiling himself now, thinking lustily about the next hour or two. It was his lucky day, he thought. Joe was never one to hit it off with the ladies, so he thought it was about time that something good happened to him.

"I'm up for it, Cuz," giggling at his little joke.

Jeff's flashlight revealed the dark-haired girl that lay before them.

"Just to show you what a great guy I am, I'll let you go first, but let's wake her up first. It's a lot more fun that way."

"That's what I was thinking, too."

Someone was slapping her in the face, but she couldn't quite understand what was happening. Her body couldn't respond.

"Wake up, bitch. C'mon, wake up."

Was this some kind of bad dream? What was happening to her? Slowly she started to remember—driving home, the truck, the deer running in front of her, causing the car to land in the ditch— then running through the forest, trying to get to help, but she slowly realized that it was over. They had found her.

"Look, her eyes are movin'. She's comin' to."

Joe could hardly contain his excitement as he saw his prey lying before him. Jeff continued to slap her face, not hard enough to draw blood, but hard enough to bring her out of unconsciousness.

"Gitter her boots off, Joe. We're gonna teach this bitch a lesson."

"You got it, Cuz." He giggled with delight and anticipation.

Chapter 74

Nicole slowly realized what was happening, what they were going to do to her. She knew she was going to die, but what these freaks were going to do to her was worse than death. She kept her eyes closed, trying to buy time before they began the filthy, perverted plans that they had for her. She thought of what she could do, and remembered her Leatherman Tool in her front left pocket. If she could just get to it, and then get the blade open, she'd have a surprise for them.

She was weak and felt sick, but she still had a fierce determination to survive, even when she knew her chances were slim to none. The second freak, the shorter one, worked feverishly to untie her double knotted boots, and Freak 1 continued to pummel her face with one fist, shining the light in her face with the other.

She moved her left arm ever so slowly so she could retrieve the Leatherman from her pocket. *Slow, keep the eyes closed; slow, no resistance*, she repeated the thoughts in her mind. Her left hand was now in her pocket where she could feel the smooth, cool metal that was her only hope, maybe not to survive, but to at least inflict some pain on Freak 2.

It was in her hand. Slowly, she pulled it out of her pocket.

The trick would be to open the blade without Freak 1 or Freak 2 noticing. Freak 1 continued to beat her face, and she continued to feign semi-consciousness, and indeed, she did feel that she might pass out again. Her head ached. Her lower lip was split and bleeding, swelling to twice its normal size. She couldn't open her left eye, even if she tried. Nicole fought to remain conscious, concentrating on the weapon, now firmly held in her hand.

Freak 2 removed her boots and attempted to unbutton her jeans. Freak 1, all the while, inflicted more pain. It was all she could do not to struggle, not to give any indication that she knew what was happening. *It's now or never,* she thought. She raised her arms, slowly, to get the Leatherman open, and then to extract the three-inch steel blade—*almost there.* Her jeans were nearly off.

"Do it, Joe. Do what you wanna do," Freak 1 said through clenched teeth, still slapping and punching her face repeatedly.

Freak 2 was giddy with delight and started singing...

> *Little Red Riding Hood,*
> *I don't think little big girls should*
> *Go walking in these spooky old woods alone.*
> *Owoooooooo!*

He pulled down his pants and climbed on top of her, giggling, with slobber running down the stubble on his face. She squinted through swollen, bleeding eyes, and saw the face of a mad man, crazed by lust for sex and blood. *Now! It has to be now.* Nicole gripped the Leatherman, now in her right hand and took aim at the freak's neck. She screamed as she plunged the blade into his neck. She pulled it out and struck again. She felt the blood spurting from the wounds on the freak's neck. Over and over again, she kept stabbing—his neck, his eyes—his blood spilling onto Nicole and onto the ground around them.

Freak 1 realized what was happening. His face contorted in rage as he saw his cousin's life-blood draining from him. The freak's body lay prone on top of her, dead weight pinning her to the ground. She watched, through swollen eyes, as the live one raised his fist to send it through her skull.

Mike and Pete Parker had heard the scream and raced toward the source, just thirty yards away. When Pete saw one man prone on top of his daughter, and the other man about to crush her skull, he raised his twelve-gauge and pulled the two triggers at once, firing both barrels.

And then his face was no more—it was gone in an instant, red mist filling the place where his face had been. An explosion occurred simultaneously as Freak 1's face disintegrated. That was the last image in Nicole's mind as she slipped into unconsciousness.

Chapter 75

Thursday, July 19

Mike sat in a chair next to the chief's hospital bed in the Intensive Care Unit. Chief Thomas was going to be okay, at least that's what the doctor had told him. The chief had immediately gone into surgery upon his arrival at the hospital. Amazingly, none of the rounds had hit any major organs—all of the bullets had passed safely through his body.

Mike looked at the chief, sleeping now, and wondered how he had survived the brutal attack, just six hours ago. But Mike did know—deep down, he knew. He knew that God had saved the chief from what should have been a sudden and violent death. He prayed silently, thanking God.

His thoughts drifted back to the scene and events that morning out on Wildcat Road...

Mr. Parker had carried his daughter out of the woods, cradling her in his arms. When they reached the road, Mike ran two miles to where his car was parked, while Mr. Parker stayed with Nicole, who was drifting in and out of consciousness.

By the time Mike got back to them, a Clackamas County Police car was parked on the side of the road. The chief had stayed conscious long enough to get help and send it on its way.

Mike got out and introduced himself to the two officers—Peters and Hayward.

"We have an ambulance coming. She's going to be okay," Deputy Peters said.

Mike recalled the relief he felt when he heard those words. He saw that they had wrapped Nicole in blankets, and her father continued to cradle his daughter.

Mike said to the officers, "We need to make some arrests."

They looked at him, waiting for him to continue.

"Those two stiffs in the woods," he pointed in that general direction, "they may have been responsible for Sandi Riggs' murder, and I'm sure they're the ones that ran Sherry Johnson off the road. The truck parked up the road a couple of miles—it's theirs."

"You don't say—well, it just so happens that Sheriff Graham is getting a judge out of bed, as we speak, to get a warrant out," Peters said.

"How does he know who gets the warrants?"

"That chief you have, he's a tough old coot. He refused to pass out until he told everything to the paramedics who were working to keep him alive. He told one of 'em to stop messin' with him and to start writing. He's a tough one—don't think they make 'em like that anymore."

Mike smiled at that, "Yeah, you're right about that."

His thoughts returned to the present when the chief moved his hand on his covers. Mike saw his eyelids flutter a few seconds, and then they opened. The chief was looking right at him.

312

"Hey Mikey, you look like you've been through the ringer," he said in a raspy voice.

Mike laughed with relief, "You should take a look at yourself, Chief."

Later that morning, Mike drove out to the Williams' place where a county crew had gathered to tear up a driveway, one that had just been poured the winter before. Two state troopers were on hand, as well as a couple of Clackamas County deputies. A state medical examiner was there, too, just in case a body was, in fact, found under the concrete. They stood in a circle off to the side of the driveway, talking about the events of the previous night while the backhoe operator did his job.

Paul and Connie Williams were in custody. Their little girl—Kayleen—was in state protective custody and would soon be taken to a foster home. At the same time that her parents were arrested, officers had been sent to the residences of Lester and Chester Williams to take them into custody as well. It turned out, though, that they had both taken their own lives—one with a rope, the other with his gun. That was the initial report, and it would probably be confirmed by further investigation. Even so, Mike had his doubts as to the suicide theory.

Paul's brother, Tim, was at his place out in Colton when he was arrested. He wasn't aware yet that his son, Jeff, was already dead from a double-barreled shotgun blast to the face, and that his nephew on his wife's side of the family was dead too.

More arrests of the Williams family would be forthcoming. As it turned out, the whole family was involved, most of it anyway, and it was a large extended family. The "family business" was started by the twins. The community of Molalla would be stunned when the news broke that Lester and Chester, the sweet old men that everyone loved, ran a drug operation that covered a large portion of northwest Oregon and southwest Washington. Details of the business, that included some unsolved murders, would be discovered in the next several months.

The officers stood together listening to Mike tell his account of the story. The veterans surrounding him paid rapt attention as he described the scene at Chief Thomas' place, and then the chase through the woods with Pete Parker. Mike didn't add that he himself had a particular interest in the girl.

It was only twenty minutes into the dig when the backhoe operator lifted the scoop and shut the machine off. A crewmember had yelled and motioned for him to stop the machine. He had seen something.

"Hey, we got something. Come over and take a look," the operator called out.

The officers walked over to the site.

"Got a big piece of black plastic right here. Looks like there's something wrapped up in it," he said.

The officers gathered around and they were all very happy that the medical examiner was there—George was his name. None of the officers, Mike included, wanted to unwrap the black plastic that all assumed would contain the badly decomposed body of Sandi Riggs. George stepped into the shallow grave.

"Hey, could a couple of you give me a hand here? I need to get this out of the hole so I can take a look." No one moved. "Sometime today would be good."

Finally, a couple of the county workers—none of the cops— helped him pull the body bag out of the hole. Pulling on the corners of the plastic, they wrestled the bag and its contents out of the hole and onto the ground next to it.

George used a knife that had come from his ME kit and

started to work on the plastic. The body was wrapped multiple times, and no one in the Williams family imagined that it would ever be seen again. George made long, careful cuts through the plastic, pulling each layer back as he cut it. He didn't want to damage the contents, which struck Mike as being kind of funny when he thought about it.

At last, the final layer of plastic was cut. George pulled it back, revealing the contents. It was a corpse, which wasn't a surprise to anyone there. The first glimpse revealed the legs about mid-calf, and not unexpectedly, was still covered with clothing. He unwrapped the *package* while the onlookers watched, somewhat impatiently. They were anxious to see the whole corpse, but, at the same time, didn't want to see the gore.

The chest was seen next, revealing a plaid, button-down shirt. George seemed to enjoy the drama that he was in control of, a slight smile on his face, as the officers looked on with wide eyes. If George were to yell, "Boo!" they would probably all jump, just like at a scary scene in a horror movie.

He continued even more slowly, adding to the suspense. The plastic that covered the skull was removed. This was the first glimpse of the corpse's skin. Having been wrapped in plastic, buried under concrete and not exposed to air, the body was still intact to a large degree. When the face was at last revealed, a gasp escaped from all who were there, all except George.

Nearly thirty-six hours had passed since Mike Benson had gotten any sleep. He wasn't sleepy though—tired, but not sleepy. The ME loaded the corpse into his vehicle and then was taken to the lab where an autopsy would be performed.

Mike drove back to town and, all of a sudden, was very hungry. Seeing the dead body didn't affect his appetite. He went to

Big Burger and had a cheeseburger and fries drenched in ketchup, and one of their large, thick, chocolate milkshakes.

After lunch, he drove to the station. It seemed like forever since he'd been there, but really, it was only about twenty-four hours. So much had happened in that amount of time. He thought about the chief at OHSU. He would drive up to see him in a while. He parked in the usual spot at the back of the station and was unlocking the door when someone came up behind him. Normally, it would have startled him, but the adrenaline had worn off, and exhaustion was replacing it.

"Mike Benson."

Mike turned to see a familiar face, but that did not take away the surprise. It was Steve Carlson.

"I need to talk to you. Got a few minutes?"

Epilogue

Mikey walked into my hospital room. I was out of ICU and had my own private room. I woke up when he came in.

"Hey Mikey, how ya doin'?"

"I'm fine, Chief. Doc says that you're a living miracle. No way you should still be here, let alone talking to me like this."

"So I've been told."

"He said that if you felt up to it, I could fill you in on what happened last night after you were shot. So, are you feelin' up to it?" he asked, "Because I have a story for you."

"Let me hear it."

For the next hour, Mikey gave me the whole story in *living color*, as old Walt Disney would say—every detail. I almost felt like I was there, but of course I wasn't. He told me of Doc Johnson and other neighbors that helped out. He told me about the seventy-five in a twenty-five with a grin on his face. He spoke with great animation about the chase through the woods with Pete Parker, and the valiant rescue of Nicole Parker.

The assumed suicides of Lester and Chester Williams took me by surprise. We both speculated that there was more to it than that. He told me of the arrest of various members of the Williams family. Even Judge Maurer, who was married to one of Lester's nieces, was implicated. Deputy District Attorney Eric Holton was a cousin of the deceased, Joe and Jeff Williams. I was amazed that so much had happened in the nearly twenty-four hours since being in the hospital.

"Well, that's quite a story. I'm sorry I missed out on all the excitement. You did good, Mikey. Congratulations."

"Thanks, Chief, but you're the real hero here. It was your plan, and it worked. You're the real hero, especially in my book."

I felt a sense of pride, kind of like Mikey was my own son. I was getting sleepy, and I assumed that the story was finished, but I was wrong.

"There's more, Chief."

"Really?—Don't tell me you figured out who killed Sandi Riggs, too!"

"Well, not exactly—there's someone that came up here with me that I'll let finish the story and fill in all the middle parts."

"Steve Carlson? Is that who you're talking about? How'd you find him?" I asked, realizing that I was starting to sound like Mikey, with the "three question" thing.

Mikey grinned and walked to the door, opening it partially.

"Steve, come on in."

Steve Carlson entered the room and came over to shake my hand.

"Evenin', Chief. I'm sure glad to hear you're okay."

"Thanks. I am too."

"Are you feeling up to hearing more of this story?" he asked.

"Darn tootin'. Let me have it, with both barrels," I winked—at least I tried to.

"I think its best that I ask someone else to come in, if it's all right with you. Mike thought you'd say okay."

"If Mikey says it's good, then it's good with me."

My curiosity was kicking into overdrive. Steve stayed by my bed, and Mikey walked over to the door. He spoke to someone outside, and then, Steve's mother, Jennie Carlson, entered the room. It was a nice surprise to see her again, but I couldn't figure out why she was here. Then another person entered right behind her.

"What the...holy shit, Mikey! Pardon my French." I was looking at a ghost, but she looked awfully good for a ghost. I thought that the meds were making me hallucinate. "Mikey, you should've warned me! You could've given me a heart attack!"

She walked to my bedside and extended her hand, "Hi, Chief Thomas, I'm Sandi Riggs. I don't believe we've met."

I lifted my arm to shake her hand. I was weak, but determined, and ready for the "rest of the story", thank you very much, Paul Harvey. I, for once in my life, was speechless.

She hesitated a few moments before saying anything. She cleared her throat, opened her mouth, but no sound would come. She tried again. This time she spoke, so softly I could barely hear her.

Sandi told me that she was an addict. It started with pot, and then she added pills into the mix. Things went downhill from there—cocaine, heroin—snortin' it at first, and then she started using needles, something that she swore she would never do. She delivered drugs for the Williams family so she could support her habit.

"There are so many things I regret. One night last January—I don't know why I did it—I stole from them, from the family."

"How much did you steal?" I asked.

She squirmed. "It was a lot. I don't know why I thought I could get away with it."

I asked again, "How much?"

"Fifty."

"Thousand?"

"Yes. They found out. I knew they would, but you don't think right when you're high or when you need a hit, and that's most of the time. I tried to make it look like I didn't know anything, but they knew; they knew I was the one. I was scared to death, literally. They would kill me, not just for the money, but to teach a lesson to anyone else who might try to mess them over. I went to the only person I knew who would, or could, help me."

Steve came over and put his arm around her as she continued.

"Steve came up with a plan. I think it would have worked, but it was too late. I should have gone to him sooner. I was driving the activity bus that night, and the plan was for me to disappear as soon as the route was over. Steve's buddy would pick me up that night at the bus garage. He would be waiting for me. I would leave my car there, and just disappear."

"And who was Steve's buddy?" I asked her.

She looked at Steve.

He nodded, "Go ahead."

"Wes Strohmeier—he's the mechanic and maintenance guy for the bus company. He left the garage earlier that day. He parked his truck about a mile away where no one would see it, then doubled back on foot, and waited for me to get done with the route. He was waiting outside behind the garage so no one would see him. The plan was for us to walk back to his truck and leave."

"I finished the activity run around six and pulled the bus up to the big garage door. I got out and went through the side door, which was open. I thought that Wes had left it open accidentally. I walked inside and opened the garage door, then got back in the bus and pulled it inside. I got out and shut the door. After that, I don't remember what happened."

Steve stood by her, still with his arm around her shoulders.

He said, "I can tell you what happened after that. Wes was out behind the shop earlier, waiting for Sandi to get back. About a half-hour before she got to the garage, a car pulled up along the curb in front of the school, and a guy got out. He leaned back in and said something to the driver, then turned and started walking toward the garage. The car pulled away."

"Wes had to make a decision. If this guy was heading toward the garage, he, most likely, wasn't a good guy. Wes decided to get to the side door and let himself in before the other guy got there. It was a good thing that it was a cold, dark, and wet night, because the other guy didn't see him. Wes shut the door, but didn't lock it. He was in too much of a hurry to find a hiding place in the garage."

"He waited only a half-minute or so when he heard footsteps approaching on the gravel outside. He saw the door open, and saw the silhouette of the man. He had one of those big flashlights, about a foot and a half long. The guy shined it inside, found a suitable hiding place for himself, and then they both waited. Wes tried to think what would be best, and waiting seemed to be the best option."

"Wes carried a gun on him, but didn't know if the bad guy did or not. He wondered how it would play out—there was no way to know. About twenty minutes later, Wes heard the bus pull in the driveway and up to the door. The other guy hadn't moved at all as far as Wes could tell."

"Wes saw Sandi's silhouette in the doorway. She came in, switched on the light, and opened the big door. She walked back to the bus and drove it inside. She shut the bus down, and then got out to shut the big door. Then, Wes saw the intruder stand up from his hiding place and move toward Sandi. He raised that big ol' flashlight and was about to crush her skull, when Wes fired his gun. He's a good shot—won a few competitions—and this time, he found his mark.

"Sandi still got knocked out from the flashlight and didn't

come around until later. Wes checked for a pulse and found one for Sandi, but not the other guy. He was dead, and was making quite a mess on the floor. He gathered up Sandi and headed back to his truck, carried her all the way. It wasn't until he got her in the truck that she started coming around."

"Wes left the dead guy in the garage for someone else to find. He figured that the guy must have been a professional that the family hired. When he didn't report that the job was done, someone must have come and checked it out, probably the guy who dropped him off. That's when they moved the body and buried it later that night."

The drugs I was on made it difficult for me to remember everything Sandi and Steve told me. But I did have some questions that were floating around in the fog of my mind.

"Why didn't you come to me, or if you didn't trust the local police, go to the county or state police?'

She shook her head, "I was scared. They had people everywhere, even a judge."

"So you just let them frame Steve for your murder?" I asked.

"That was their plan all along. When they found out I wasn't dead, but everyone else figured I was, they decided to set up Steve to take the fall. And I know they were still trying to find me, to kill me. This operation they have, it's a big deal. Wes said it was best to hide where they wouldn't find me. If Steve would have been convicted, I would have been raised from the dead, so to speak."

Another question, "Where have you been all this time?"

She looked again at Steve and again he nodded.

"A lot closer than you ever dreamed of. Then again, you thought I was dead, along with everyone else. Wes's family has some property on the river about a mile above my place. You can't get to it on the county side. You have to go around on the Weyerhaeuser side, on the logging road. Wes had an old Winnebago that he kept up there. It needed a little TLC, but really, it wasn't bad. It was pretty comfortable."

"And you've been up there all this time?"

"Yessir."

"Who knew you were up there?"

"Just Wes and my mom."

"You're mom knew?"

"She did, but not 'til after your visit to her. She didn't know it when you were there. That's all. No one else knew."

"You know you put people through hell by not coming forward, Steve included. Another girl, Sherry Johnson, was killed. I was nearly killed!"

Tears welled up in Sandi's eyes. "I'm sorry—I'm so sorry." She buried her head in Steve's chest and sobbed.

Steve spoke up. "She didn't have much choice at that point. I knew something had really gone wrong. Wes wasn't able to get me the news that she was still alive until Friday night, after work. Sandi and I were going to take off together, but I got arrested Saturday morning, framed for the murder. You know what happened after that. She and Wes had no idea that someone else had information, and that the family would kill because of it."

I was fading fast, but there was one question that I wanted to ask. I just couldn't remember what it was. And then I drifted off to sleep...

Mike, Sandi, Steve, and his mother all filed out of the room after the chief fell asleep. They walked down the corridor, still talking about the whole affair. When they got to the bank of elevators, Mike told the others that there was someone else he needed to see. He waited there until the elevator doors opened and the three got in. They said their goodbyes as the doors closed.

Then he went down the corridor to room 321. The door was partially open, so he knocked lightly. There was no answer, so he knocked a little louder and opened the door a little more. She was lying on the bed looking at the TV, not really watching it.

"Hey, Nicole, how ya' doin'?" he asked quietly, not wanting to frighten her.

She turned to see Mike standing at the doorway. She attempted a smile, Mike thought, but it failed to break out on her swollen face. Even so, he took that as an invitation to enter the room.

"Nod doo 'ad...how a'oud you?" she answered through cut and swollen lips, and a badly bruised jaw. Both eyes were black, and her left eye was swollen shut.

"I'm fine. I'm just glad that you're okay. You look great!" He felt his face turning crimson and wished he hadn't made the comment, even if he did really mean it. "Well, I just wanted to come and say 'hi'."

"I' glad you did. Can you s'ay a 'ew 'inudes? I could use the co'any."

"Sure. I'd love to."

...and then I woke up. I remembered the question. *Where's the money?*

"Hey! Where's the money?"

CPSIA information can be obtained at www.ICGtesting.com
Printed in the USA
BVOW03s0922270514

354408BV00001B/1/P